Paper Wings

Also by Marly Swick

The Summer Before the Summer of Love

Monogamy

Paper Wings

Marly Swick

HarperCollins*Publishers*

HarperCollins books may be purchased for educational, business, or sales promotional use. For information please write: Special Markets Department, HarperCollins Publishers, Inc., 10 East 53rd Street, New York, NY 10022.

FIRST EDITION

Designed by Nancy Singer

ISBN 0–06–017434-X

96 97 98 99 00 ❖/HC 10 9 8 7 6 5 4 3 2 1

To my sister, Patricia

TROJANS

Our efforts are those of men prone to disaster,
our efforts are like those of the Trojans.
We just begin to get somewhere,
begin to gather a little strength,
grow almost bold and hopeful,

when something always comes up to stop us:
Achilles leaps out of the trench in front of us
and terrifies us with his violent shouting.

Our efforts are like those of the Trojans.
We think we'll change our luck
by being resolute and brave,
so we move outside ready to fight.

But when the great crisis comes,
our boldness and resolution vanish;
our spirit falters, collapses,
and we scurry around the walls
trying to save ourselves by running away.

Yet we're sure to fail. Up there,
high on the walls, the dirge has already begun.
They're mourning the memory, the aura of
    our days.
Priam and Hecuba mourn for us bitterly.

—*C. P. Cavafy*

PROLOGUE

Lee Harvey Oswald might as well have shot my mother through the heart. Sometimes in my confused memories of those days, when I try to reconstruct my mother's erratic behavior after the assassination, I see Jackie's face—disbelieving and devastated behind her black veil—instead of my mother's Scandinavian paleness and crumpled Kleenexes. I was only twelve at the time and there is no clear division in my memory between the public and the private world; to me, the public world was part of our household, a sort of light show emanating from our Magnavox console sitting in the corner of the family room, a backdrop to our daily lives. As far as I was concerned, our family might just as well have been riding through Dallas in that black open-air limousine, the bright sun shining, surrounded by useless Secret Service agents. My own version, if you will, of the single bullet theory.

Over the years, standing in line at various supermarkets, I would read those *National Enquirer* stories claiming that Kennedy was still alive. A vegetable in a wheelchair on a Greek island. Or a prisoner of Castro's in Cuba. And I would imagine, for an instant, my parents still married, celebrating what would have been their fortieth, their fiftieth wedding anniversary, having successfully weathered one crisis after another side by side—instead of what really happened. I recognized in those tabloid headlines my own inextinguishable desire to rewrite history. To imagine, at least, some weak flicker of that one brief shining spot having endured in the darkness of obscurity. We were, after all, a generation raised on happy endings. War was Bob Hope entertaining the troops. Marriage was Lucy and Ricky. Old age was Jimmy Durante—"Goodnight, Mrs. Calabash, wherever you are." Disease, death, disaster happened on the news to foreigners in foreign clothes speaking foreign languages.

The day that Kennedy was shot they sent us home from school early. I was standing in the girls' locker room, having just changed into my blue gym suit, when the principal's voice crackled over the intercom, solemnly informing us that the President was dead. The locker room smelled of sweat and wet towels and sickly-sweet deodorants. I felt sick to my stomach and scared as I put my camel-hair coat on without bothering to change back into my school clothes. The usual shrill bouquet of girls' voices had withered. A couple of girls spoke in hushed tones, but most of us just stood there silently, too shocked to open our mouths.

When I walked outside, the cold blast of November air felt good after the steamy, overheated locker room. The yellow school buses were lined up by the curb waiting for us. As I stood in line I took a couple of deep breaths and the nausea passed. There was snow on the ground melting into my white sneakers with my last name, "KELLER," printed in Magic Marker on the rubber heels. My legs were bare except for white popcorn anklets. I started to shiver. The bus driver opened the doors, and we filed onto the bus. The boys didn't push and shove and call out insults the way they usually did. I could see that Mrs. Sparks, the bus driver, had been crying. Usually she barked orders at us; today she just stared out the windshield as if we weren't even there. I remembered that during the campaign she had worn a Nixon-Lodge button on her plaid lumber jacket, but she seemed sad anyway. The bus was almost full. An eighth-grade girl I didn't know sat down in the empty seat next to me and whispered something to her friend in the seat in front of her. Usually I sat with Kim, but she had stayed home with a cold that day. I clutched my skirt and sweater and tights into a warm ball in my lap and felt lonely. As the bus pulled away from the curb, my English teacher, Mrs. Ritchie, smiled and waved at me and I waved back. She had a clump of pink Kleenex clutched in her hand. When I turned my head around a second later, she was sobbing and the handsome new shop teacher, Mr. McDuffy, had his arm around her shoulders. In class that morning, right before gym, I had given a book report on *The Story of My Life* by Helen Keller, and as the disquietingly quiet bus pulled away from the curb, I recited to myself the sentences of the report I had learned by heart and my cheeks burned as I remembered how the boys in the class had laughed when I read aloud the first letter Helen had ever written to her mother, which I thought was very touching: "Helen will write mother letter paper did give helen medicine mildred will sit in swing mildred did kiss helen teacher did give helen peach george is sick in bed george arm is hurt anna did give helen lemonade dog did stand up." My mother's married name happened to be Helen Keller, so I had always felt a special personal connection to her, as if we were distantly related.

The bus wheezed and groaned along Nokomis Road. As we got closer to our neighborhood, I wondered if my mother had heard the news yet. She didn't usually listen to the news until Walter Cronkite. She might not know. I didn't want to be the one to tell her. My mother loved Kennedy. I hoped my sister would get home first.

"You're Bonnie Keller's sister, right?" the eighth-grader asked, suddenly turning her attention to me.

I nodded. My sister was a senior, a cheerleader, and I could tell that this girl, overweight with mousey hair, thought of Bonnie as distant royalty.

"Is she still going with Roger Branstead?"

"Yeah."

The girl let out a dreamy peasant girl's sigh.

I shrugged. Behind his back my father and I referred to him as Roger Braindead.

The girl leaned forward and whispered something to her friend, who whispered something back. They seemed to have forgotten all about the President. I glanced across the aisle at Keith Matsumi. His eyes were closed and he was clutching his black violin case against his rib cage, a serious but serene expression on his face, as if he were lis-

tening to some sad, majestic music composed by someone long dead. He opened his eyes and I looked away.
Two years earlier, in fifth grade, his mother had come to
our class and taught us how to make origami Christmas
tree ornaments: red and green paper birds. Most kids
acted bored and embarrassed when their parents came to
school—especially their mothers—but Keith had looked
proud and respectful. The bus turned onto Mountain
Laurel Drive and wheezed to a halt at the corner. I said
"Excuse me" and crawled over the girl and clambered off
the bus along with Denise DiNardo, Kevin Crawford,
Keith Matsumi, and the Dinsmore twins, Ricky and
Robby. The boys walked off together. I took Denise's
hand—she had just started second grade and I baby-sat
for her sometimes. She looked confused and frightened,
as if she realized that something bad had happened but
didn't know what.

"The President died," I told her as we walked toward
her house, which was just on the other side of the
Quaves' house. "He was shot," I explained, as if trying
to explain it to myself. It still didn't seem real. Her mittened hand grabbed mine tighter and she started to cry.

"Is my daddy hurt?" she asked.

"No," I said, "your father's perfectly okay. There's
nothing to worry about. This is just something far away.
In Washington, D.C."

Mrs. DiNardo saw us coming and opened the front
door holding Denise's four-year-old sister, Dianne, in her
arms. Denise ran up the neatly shoveled walkway and
grabbed her mother around the waist, crying, even though
she didn't know what about. I turned around and headed
across the street to my house. It looked just as it had that

morning when I'd left for school. You couldn't tell that anything had changed. At the front door I cupped my hands and peered in through the glass. It didn't look as if my sister was home yet. Her coat wasn't hanging on its hook in the hallway. I couldn't see my mother, but I could hear the TV. I opened the door, hung my coat up, set my books and clothes down on the hall table, and followed the sound of the television into the family room. My mother was sitting on the floor in front of our TV set, crying into a bath towel. Her hair was wet and soapy. She was wearing a white brassiere and black slacks. Apparently she had been washing her hair in the kitchen sink, something she did twice a week, when Kim's mother knocked on the back door with the news. It was chilly in the family room—I could see goose bumps on my mother's arms—but she seemed oblivious to the fact that she was half naked and trickles of water were running off her neck and onto the carpet. When she looked up and saw me standing there, she caught her breath and bit her lip until she stopped crying. Then she took a deep, deep breath and said, "This is the worst thing that has ever happened."

I took a couple of steps closer to her and patted her awkwardly on the shoulder, trying to think of something to say. On the television screen Vice President Johnson was taking the oath of office. Jackie's nylons were splattered with blood and her hand rested on the coffin next to her. I walked over and changed the channel. As if maybe it was just a sad movie. A real tearjerker. "What are you doing?" my mother asked. I didn't answer her. Back then we only got three channels. It was the same picture on all three stations. That's how I knew it was real.

PART ONE

The summer that JFK won the Democratic nomination we moved into our new house on the east side of Madison in a subdivision called Timberlake Trails. Back then, 1960, the neighborhood was brand new and all the families were young. In my memory even the pets were young: puppies and kittens. Model families in model houses. There was no lake and all the streets were named after trees—Mountain Laurel Drive, Blue Spruce Lane, Weeping Willow Court— even though there were no trees on the square bare lots except for the few spindly saplings our mothers lugged home from the nursery in the trunks of their station wagons. Our fathers would dig the holes and we kids would pat peat moss around the scrawny trunks, no bigger than our own thighs, while our mothers in their pedal pushers and gardening gloves planted neat, bright rows of marigolds and pansies, like icing on a birthday cake. Now, three decades later, the spindly saplings, grown tall and matronly, shade the streets and offer privacy, but back then we had a clear view of each other's yards. Nothing was secret or hidden. The development was laid out as flat and color-coordinated as a board game: Candy Land or Chutes and Ladders. Fun for the whole family.

The Quaves were already there when we moved into our new house. There were seven houses on the cul-de-sac and the other five were still being built, so for that first summer we were each other's only neighbors. The Quaves had two girls: Marjorie, fifteen, who was one year older than my sister, Bonnie, and Kim, who immediately became my best friend. We were both going into fourth grade in the fall. On sunny days we drew lopsided hopscotch boards with colored chalk on the sidewalk or skipped rope. On rainy days we played house in her bedroom or mine. "The Bobbsey Twins," our mothers called us, pleased that it had worked out so conveniently.

At supper time the construction workers packed up and went home. The thunder of their hammers and the whine of their buzz saws was replaced by the clatter of dishes and the mutter of the evening news through the screen windows. Walter Cronkite. Huntley and Brinkley. Meat loaf. Tuna casserole. After the supper dishes were washed, our parents drank Tom Collinses in their adjacent backyards, careful not to scuff their brand-new grass with the metal lawn-chair legs. As the dusk gathered and we took our baths and changed into our baby doll pajamas, we could hear the buzz of our parents' voices, their laughter, and the *tink-tink* of swizzle sticks shaped like miniature golf clubs. Looking down into the backyard from my bedroom window, I could see the citronella candles burning and the nervous blink of my mother's Lucky Strike, like a firefly flitting here and there as she talked and gestured. In the deepening twilight the wooden skeletons of the houses going up all around us encircled them like a row of covered wagons on the open prairie. We were pioneers. It was, as Kennedy had just proclaimed, the New Frontier.

It was my mother's dream house. Before that we had lived in an older duplex in the older section of town, nearer to the university. My mother loved meeting with the builder and picking out her own color schemes. Everything fresh and modern. All that spring while our house was being built I accompanied her to various shops while she pored over big, thick books of wallpaper samples with a rapt, ferocious concentration, as if our family's future health and happiness depended upon her making the correct choice. And there were so many patterns to choose from! "What about this for the upstairs bathroom?" she would ask me. "Or do you like the foil better?" I would frown and consider and then point to whichever one I suspected she was leaning toward and then she would smile and pat me on the cheek, buoyed up by a brief moment of certainty before she would sigh and flip back through the book and begin to lose faith. "Maybe the poppies would look too busy in such a small room? We might get less tired of the seashells, do you think?"

And it would be the same at the carpet store, with rainbow after rainbow of shag and pile, wool and acrylic. Not to mention ceramic tile and linoleum. Light fixtures, kitchen cupboards, appliances, faucets. When we got home from an afternoon of shopping, my mother would kick off her shoes and collapse on the couch, her eyes closed, as if to shut out the endless array of options. "Suzanne, honey, would you bring me a Coke and two Bufferin?" she would ask me. She seemed simultaneously exhausted and excited. At night she couldn't sleep. I would wake up to go to the bathroom and find her kneeling on the living-room floor with bright patches of carpet and drapery samples laid out in front of her like a tarot deck.

Like most men, my father was no help. He was virtually color-blind. Whenever he got dressed up, he would come out of his bedroom dangling a fistful of ties like a gaudy silk octopus—and ask for our opinion. Usually my mother and sister would disagree and he would turn to me "to break the tie, no pun intended." Usually I would side with my mother, but he would wear my sister's choice because she was his favorite. When my mother would confront him with wallpaper and carpet samples he'd just shrug and say, "As long as it's not pink, it's fine with me," giving my sister and me a little homophobic wink. This was his sitcom dad self, benign and befuddled.

At other times he seemed more like a biblical patri-arch—stern, rigid, and exacting. He was an optometrist, and he liked for things to be tidy and clear. He washed and waxed his car every weekend until it shone like a Christmas ornament. The garage, his domain, was as neat and clean as an operating room. Frequently at mealtime he would frown down at his place setting, pointedly scraping away at some dried speck of food on a fork or plate until my mother would bring him a new fork or plate from the cupboard. One of their biggest arguments was after a New Year's Eve party where my father had politely requested that the hostess remove her glasses for a moment while he straightened the earpieces and polished the lenses with his cocktail napkin dipped in champagne. It was in his genes, my mother said. She liked to tell everyone how his mother wore white cotton gloves to read library books.

Shortly before we moved to the new house my mother decided to take the framed black-and-white wedding photograph hanging on the wall of their bedroom into a photography shop and have it colorized. I think she thought it looked too drab and old-fashioned for her vision of the new house. I stood beside her while she told the clerk what color everything should be. In the picture she was wearing a rose-colored suit with tiny pearl buttons. Black high heels. Blonde hair. Magenta lipstick. My father's suit was navy blue. His tie was maroon with navy stripes. Sandy-brown hair. My mother's bouquet, she told the clerk, consisted of pale pink roses and white baby's breath. When the clerk asked about eye color, my mother hesitated for a moment and then said, "Blue." She squeezed my hand as I started to protest, "But your eyes are hazel!" The clerk said the photograph would be ready in ten days. As we walked out to the car my mother said, "I always wanted blue eyes. Your father will never notice the difference." And, of course, he didn't. But it always bothered me. Whenever I looked at the photograph, my mother's fake blue eyes seemed flat and glassy, like a doll's, and her lipsticked smile seemed fake, too, as if the moment you looked away it would disappear.

The day before the movers were scheduled to move us, after nearly a month of delays while my parents argued with delinquent painters and wallpaper hangers, my mother and I had a picnic in the empty house. My sister refused our mother's coaxing to come along, saying she'd already promised to go swimming with her best friend, Janet, even though this surprise picnic clearly meant a lot to my mother. So I tried twice as hard to be entertaining as we sat on a sheet on the newly laid beige wall-to-wall carpeting eating our tuna sandwiches and Fritos. The smell of plaster and paint and carpet glue was so strong that I couldn't really taste anything, but I complimented her on the sandwiches anyway. "This is great tuna salad," I said. "Did you put something special in it?"

"Pickle relish." My mother smiled and tucked a stray strand of hair back behind my ear. My sister had inherited my mother's thick, naturally wavy hair, but mine was thin and wispy. Baby's hair.

After we ate, we walked dreamily through the empty rooms. First downstairs, then upstairs. The drapes had not yet been hung and my mother seemed almost dazed by the sunlight flooding through the large, bare windows, awed by the bright, pristine spaciousness of it all— for the moment, at least, content with all the choices she had made.

In the absence of furniture, the wallpaper seemed almost alive. In the kitchen, tea kettles whistled and ivy twined itself through the copper handles. In the powder room, pink sea horses cavorted in aqua waves. In my sister's room, daisies seemed to sprout from the pale-green walls. And in my room, ballerinas tied their toe shoes and pirouetted. The harried wallpaper hanger had done my room last, in a rush to meet the deadline, and I noticed that the seams were crooked. In a couple of spots it looked as if the ballerinas' legs and arms had been ampu-tated, but I didn't say anything. My mother looked so happy. Until we walked into the master bedroom, and then her face fell.

"Oh, no," she gasped, "it's pink! It was supposed to be warm beige. Remember?"

I nodded. The walls were a soft pink with silvery-green bamboo trees. It had been my mother's favorite pattern, the one she'd loved at first sight, and the only one she hadn't changed her mind about.

"They must have made a mistake," she said, rummag-ing through her purse for a swatch of wallpaper samples that she finally located. She walked over to the window and riffled through the samples until she found the bam-boo pattern. "See, here. It's beige." She held the patch against the wall and squinted at it. It matched the wallpa-per exactly. "What do you think?" she asked me.

"I don't know," I said reluctantly. "They look sort of the same, I guess. It's hard to tell."

"Oh, god," she groaned. "You know how your father feels about pink." She lowered the window shades. "See, now it looks beigeier. It's all this sunlight, makes it look pinkish."

I nodded again, anxious to agree. "Dad's mostly home at night. Anyway, you know how bad he is at colors."

"That's true." She stuffed the samples back into her purse. "If we don't say anything, he'll never know the difference." She seemed calmer, but the instant of perfect confidence was gone.

The day we moved into the new house, the Quaves walked over and invited us to dinner. "Nothing fancy," Betty Quave said. "We're just going to grill some hamburgers, but I figure you'll be too tired to cook." The families had become acquainted from all the times we'd been over while the house was still being built, but this was different. We were neighbors now.

At six o'clock we walked next door. My father and sister had taken the time to shower and put on fresh clothes, but my mother and I were still dusty and sweaty from unpacking. It was a hot, humid night, the first of August, and the sprinkler was on in the Quaves' front yard. Impulsively, my mother grabbed my hand and charged into the spray, tugging me along behind her. The water felt cool and refreshing. My mother was laughing, dodging the spray as it undulated back and forth. I was clapping and shrieking, egging her on. It seemed as if along with the new house I was getting a brand-new mother, younger and happier than my old mother, who got migraines and begged us to be quiet.

"For godsakes, Helen," my father said. "We barely know these people. What are they going to think?"

Mrs. Quave opened the front door and waved. When she saw my mother standing there soaking wet, she laughed.

"Geez, Mom." My sister rolled her eyes and hurried toward the house, as if to disassociate herself from such retarded behavior.

My mother's plaid blouse and red pedal pushers were clinging to her body and frizzy strands of blondè hair had worked loose from her hasty attempt at a French twist. I thought she looked beautiful, like Marilyn Monroe in *Niagara*.

At the door my mother kicked off her wet sneakers before we went inside. I was already barefoot. Their house was the mirror image of ours, so it felt familiar but strange at the same time. Whereas our furniture was Danish modern, Mr. Quave had inherited a lot of antiques, dark wood and Oriental rugs. He had also inherited two factories that made artificial fruit and flowers. Everbloom Inc. Everywhere you looked there were vases of plastic flowers or bowls of wax fruit. I knew my mother would be thinking, Too much clutter. She hated clutter. "Just more to clean," she always said.

In the backyard Mr. Quave, Charlie, was standing in a cloud of smoke by the barbecue grill. He waved his spatula and said, "Howdy, neighbor." My father gravitated over to talk man talk. Kim was shucking corn at the picnic table. I sat down next to her on the bench and she handed me an ear of corn.

"I like your ring." She pointed to the garnet ring my parents had given me for my last birthday. "Is it your birthstone?"

I nodded.

"Mine's a topaz," she said. "I hate that. When's your birthday?"

"January twentieth," I said.

"Mine's November twenty-sixth. Sometimes it's on Thanksgiving," she told me.

"My sister's is in November."

"Really? What day?"

We talked nonstop while her mother mixed up a pitcher of Tom Collinses and passed them around to the adults. I followed Kim inside and got a Coke. My mother and Kim's mother were in the kitchen chatting while Mrs. Quave sliced some onions for the hamburgers. They seemed to hit it off. My mother didn't seem to have many friends in our old neighborhood. Mostly she just sat around the house and read library books when she wasn't doing the laundry or cleaning. They were talking about Kennedy. My mother was crazy about John Kennedy. Her eyes lit up whenever she talked about him. Or Jackie. Back in April he had covered nearly every inch of the state, campaigning for the Wisconsin primary, along with Hubert Humphrey, and my mother had shaken his hand. After which she'd had an argument with my father over pasting a Kennedy bumper sticker to the fender of our car. My father scraped it off. He said he still hoped Adlai Stevenson would get into the race, but more important, we knew, he didn't want anything ruining the looks of his new Bonneville. The night that Kennedy won the nomination at the Democratic convention, my mother was glued to the TV. She was so excited she opened the bottle of champagne the builder had given them when they signed the papers for the new house. "I thought we were saving that until we moved in," my father said. "I want to drink a toast," she'd exclaimed. "To our new president and our new house!" As she clinked her glass against my father's, some champagne sloshed over the rim onto my father's slacks. He frowned and muttered to himself as he dashed to the kitchen for the sponge. My mother, entranced by Kennedy's acceptance speech, didn't even seem to notice that he was gone.

"Well, of course we're Catholic," Mrs. Quave was saying, "so naturally we—" Kim and I let the screen door bang shut on our way out.

My father was holding out a platter while Mr. Quave speared hamburgers and piled them on. Everyone seemed to be having a good time except for my sister, who didn't seem to know what to do with herself. Marjorie was lying in a chaise longue in the far corner of the backyard reading a book. She had barely acknowledged our presence when her mother pointed out that they had company. Bonnie was sitting a few feet away from Marjorie, throwing a stick for the Quaves' Beagle puppy, Pickle. Kim had told me they named him that because he'd once eaten a whole dish of unattended baby gherkins.

Our mothers pushed open the screen door bearing aloft a pot of steaming corn on the cob and a bowl of potato salad just as Mr. Quave speared the last hamburger on the grill. We all sat down at the picnic table and attacked the platters of food, except for Marjorie, who had to be coaxed to the table and then ordered to set her book aside for dinner. As we ate, our parents shared horror stories about incompetent workmen, the joys and tribulations of building a new house. Even though she was exhausted, my mother's face was flushed a becoming pink and she talked and joked easily, unlike on other social occasions when she seemed to sit back and let my father do the talking. She even stuck her tongue out at my father when he suggested that maybe she didn't need another Tom Collins.

"Your mother's really fun," Kim said as she led me up to her room to show me her new dollhouse.

"She didn't used to be," I said. "I guess it's the new house and all. Or maybe it's Kennedy." I remembered my father grumbling that she was like a teenage girl with a crush. "They should never have given women the vote," he half joked. My mother ignored him. In fact, she did seem to take more care with her appearance these days. She always put on fresh lipstick to watch the evening news. But I knew my father wasn't really jealous. He said to me once, "It's nice to see your mother feeling more peppy." Both my father and sister had a lot of pep.

It was after dark when we said our good-nights and walked next door to spend our first night in our new house. It felt a little spooky. The bare downstairs windows looked like giant blackboards. There were still big cartons and crumpled newspaper scattered around. The walls were blank, our pictures stacked up, waiting to be hung. Especially after the homey clutter of the Quaves' house, our house seemed cold and impersonal. It felt better upstairs. My mother had already managed to hang frilly curtains in my sister's and my rooms. In our old duplex, Bonnie and I had shared a bedroom. For months I had been excited about the prospect of having my own room, but now, as my mother kissed me good night and turned off the light, I felt lonely and a little scared. In the moonlight the ballerinas looked like aliens staring at me from outer space. I could hear my mother and father speaking softly in their room across the hall as they got ready for bed. My father hadn't said anything about the pink wallpaper. I could hear the Quaves' puppy barking next door and then Kim's mother calling him inside for the night. It was much quieter than our old neighborhood. No traffic. You could hear the crickets. When I closed my eyes I saw the old house as it had looked with our furniture gone. Empty and shabby. Nail holes in the plaster walls and faint stains in the carpeting. It looked so small and dingy, compared to the new house, that I felt sorry for the family moving in.

In the morning while our father was helping our

mother hang the new drapes in the master bedroom, my sister bustled in to complain that the movers had cracked the glass top to her vanity table. She squinted in the bright glare of morning light. Our mother, standing on a chair, was snapping the drapery hooks over the curtain rod while our father held the excess yardage aloft. The drapes were a beautiful moss-green raw silk, an extravagance that my mother had worried herself sick over, canceling the order and then reinstating it when my father told her to go ahead and get what she wanted. My father wasn't a spendthrift, but he believed in quality. My sister yawned and stretched and then suddenly seemed to take note of her surroundings. "Pink." She wrinkled up her nose. "I thought Daddy didn't like pink."

My mother turned and glared at her. "It's called warm beige. It's not really pink. Is it, Suzy?"

I shook my head. "It's just in a certain light," I said. "It's sort of an optical illusion." My father had taught me all about optical illusions with a book he had in his office full of pictures that looked one way at first and then another after you stared at them long enough.

"That's right." My mother smiled gratefully in my direction. "Wait till these drapes are up."

But it was already too late. My father was frowning at the walls. "It certainly looks pink to me," he grumbled. "Whoever heard of a pink master bedroom?"

"Well, if you were so concerned, you should have looked at the samples when I asked for your opinion."

"I told you anything was fine as long as it wasn't pink. That's all I asked."

"You couldn't even tell it was pink until Bonnie opened her big mouth!" my mother snapped.

"I thought you said it was beige," he said.

"It is beige!"

He shrugged and held up the palms of his hands in mock surrender. "Whatever you say, dear."

Bonnie snorted and rolled her eyes. I grabbed her arm and yanked her out of the room just as our mother burst into tears. Our father patted her hand and told her it was all right. But whenever guests came over, he always referred to it as "the Jayne Mansfield suite."

By the following week the cartons were all unpacked and the pictures hung. We had stopped wandering around asking each other if anyone had seen the scissors or the dictionary. We had established our old routine in our new house. Except that three mornings a week my mother and Betty Quave volunteered at the Kennedy campaign headquarters downtown while Marjorie supposedly kept an eye on us. Mrs. Quave and my mother each paid her fifty cents a morning to baby-sit, but all she did was sit and read. She had skipped a grade and was supposed to have a genius IQ. My sister, who had given up on Marjorie, rode her bike over to the public pool where she and her friend Janet slathered themselves with Coppertone and flirted with boys. Kim and I had the run of the house. We could have drunk a quart of liquor and set the house on fire without Marjorie ever taking her nose out of her book.

But we were doing some reading of our own. I had found my mother's copy of *Peyton Place* hidden behind a row of paperbacks in the headboard bookshelf of my parents' bed. We took turns reading it aloud. I didn't really understand most of it, but I knew it was a dirty book because I had seen my sister and Janet whispering and smirking over it in our old house. Pretty soon we had memorized the page numbers of the best passages. Our favorite was the one where Rodney Harrington and a bad girl named Helen are sitting in the parking lot of a drive-in restaurant sort of like Dairy Queen, we figured, and Helen suddenly unbuttons her blouse.

"'"Look at that," she said, cupping the breast with her hand, "no bra. I've got the hardest breasts you ever played with,"'" Kim read aloud, giggling, and acting it out as best she could without any breasts.

Then it was my turn. "'Rodney raced the car motor violently in his eagerness to be gone from the drive-in's parking lot. Helen did not rebutton her blouse, but leaned back in the seat, leaving her breast exposed. Every few seconds, she inhaled and sat up a little, running her hand sen-sensu-ously—'" I stumbled over the unfamiliar word—"'over her bare skin, flicking her nipple—'" I would collapse in giggles, unable to continue, and Kim would grab the book and pick up where I left off "'with a snap of a fingernail.'" She hiked up her white undershirt and flicked her nipple until I grabbed the book back.

"'"Let me," he said,'" I read, "'reaching for her as he sped along the highway toward Concord.'"

At the end of the scene, although we were never quite sure, it seemed as if Rodney crashed the car into an oncoming trailer truck and they both died, since there was no further mention of Rodney or Helen in the rest of the book.

I could tell that my mother looked forward to the mornings she volunteered at the campaign headquarters.

She washed and set her hair on brush rollers the night before. And the next morning she would hum to herself as she put on makeup, including foundation and mascara, which she usually didn't bother with at home. She always wore a skirt and heels. Since it was too hot for a jacket, she had pinned a Kennedy-Johnson campaign button on the strap of her purse. Mrs. Quave always drove because my mother didn't drive. The story was that when she was sixteen and her uncle George was teaching her to drive, she had backed the car over her little cousin's doll carriage. When she got a good look at the squashed baby doll trapped inside the mangled carriage, she just lost the stomach for it and never did get her driver's license. But now, living in the suburbs, she was talking about maybe giving it another try.

At the campaign office, a cramped storefront not far from where we used to live, my mother answered the phones and occasionally typed letters. Before she married my father she had worked as a secretary, and even though she hadn't been near a typewriter in over a decade, she said it all came back in a flash, as if she'd only taken a long weekend off. Sixty-five words per minute. Mrs. Quave, who was more of an extrovert than my mother, agreed to call long lists of registered Democrats and hit them up for contributions. It was mostly married women and college students who had the time to volunteer. The college boys liked to flirt and joke with the married women since they knew it was safe—no one would take them seriously—and the couple of times I visited the headquarters, it felt like a party was going on. There were coffee and doughnuts and the phones were always ringing off the hook. Once my mother answered the phone when Bobby Kennedy called to speak to the office manager. At dinner that night she told us all about it, how he'd thanked her for being so dedicated and said Jack— Jack!—really appreciated their efforts. She was dishing spaghetti onto my father's plate and she got so carried away, the spaghetti slid off the plate onto the linoleum floor, and then there wasn't enough left for the four of us, but she said she wasn't hungry anyway. She just ate salad and bread. I offered her some of mine, even though spaghetti was my favorite thing, but she just smiled and said, "No thank you, dear, I'm fine." And as soon as the dishes were washed, she went upstairs and wrote in the brand-new journal she had bought to record this period of her life because, she said, some day it would be history.

Even though the house was messy, and dinners, on the days my mother volunteered, tended to be cold cuts and store-bought potato salad, my father didn't complain. He was busy with his new office and he seemed glad that my mother had become so energetic and outgoing. She seemed to be emerging from some long period of hazy exhaustion punctuated by difficult pregnancies, two miscarriages, Nana's death, and frequent debilitating migraines. I overhead her telling Mrs. Quave that she felt as if she had been living underwater for the past ten years and had finally broken through to the surface. Bonnie and I were both in school all day, her strength and spirits had finally returned following the miscarriages, and she felt as if she had entered a whole new era of her life. Mrs. Quave squeezed her hand and said how glad she was that they were neighbors.

On the mornings that they didn't volunteer, my

mother and Kim's mother would usually get together for coffee after the men had left for work. I loved to listen to them talk and would skulk around, trying to eavesdrop, hoping they would forget I was there. I liked to listen to their stories. Especially my mother's. Listening to her tell Mrs. Quave the story of how she met my father or how he proposed to her, I felt as if I were hearing about some movie in which my mother and father played the leading roles, dressed in the costumes I remembered from old photo albums, black-and-white pictures with wavy edges. It didn't seem real. I had a hard time believing in my parents' lives before I was born, as if I had given birth to them and not the other way around.

Especially my mother. She rarely spoke about her childhood. When I asked questions she said she really didn't remember very much. And she had no pictures of herself before she graduated from high school. They had all been ruined, she said, in a flash flood the summer she moved to Chicago and stored some boxes in her aunt and uncle's basement in Kansas City. All I knew was that she'd grown up in a small town named Troy, Nebraska. (My father liked to introduce her at parties as "my wife, Helen of Troy." He found the Helen Keller jokes less amusing.) A town so small it only had one traffic light. She was an only child and then an orphan when her parents were killed in an accident when she was sixteen. And then she lived with her Aunt Eva and Uncle George and their three kids in Kansas City for a year before she took a job as a secretary in Chicago and married my father two years after that. Her father had been personnel manager at the Maidenform factory that manufactured brassieres and girdles, a fact that caused my mother agonies of embarrassment as a young girl whenever anyone asked her what her father did for a living.

I had never met any of my mother's relatives or been to Nebraska. Her past seemed sad and foreign, unlike my father's, who had grown up in New Glaurus, an hour away. We would spend every holiday at the old white farmhouse where he'd grown up with Nana and Gramps and his two brothers. Until Gramps died of a heart attack when I was a baby, and Nana bought the duplex and moved into half and gave my parents the other half so that they could take care of her. My mother told Mrs. Quave how Nana had congestive heart failure and diabetes and how, for nearly three years, while Bonnie was a toddler and I was just a baby, my mother had to shop and cook and clean for her. Eventually she lost most of her sight. My mother and father would take turns reading to her—mystery novels. Nana couldn't sleep without the radio on and it used to drive my mother crazy hearing it through the wall all night. Nana died when I was four. All I remember clearly was her false teeth in a glass by the bed and the smell of butter rum Life Savers, her one vice. My mother told Mrs. Quave that she sometimes dreamed that Nana was still alive in the old house, starving to death with the radio drowning out her cries for help. My mother cried and said she felt guilty because she had been so relieved when Nana died. Mrs. Quave patted my mother's hand and said it was perfectly understandable that she'd felt that way, who wouldn't? And then she told a story about how she and her mother-in-law didn't speak for nearly a year after a Thanksgiving altercation concerning canned cranberry sauce. "It was the best year of my life," Mrs. Quave said and my mother laughed. She always seemed to know just what to say to make my mother feel better.

But sometimes the things they said to one another made me uneasy and I would lie in bed at night thinking about them until I fell asleep. Like the time I overheard them talking about how my mother had been so depressed after I was born that the doctor had to pre-scribe pills just so she could get out of bed in the morn-ing. Then she caught sight of me lurking outside the door and changed the subject. Or the time I heard them laugh as she was telling Mrs. Quave about this dog she'd had named Queenie that used to howl along on key whenever she practiced the piano as a little girl. Only I knew that it was my father who had the singing dog. I'd been hearing the same anecdote for years at family gath-erings at the farm, which his brother Howard inherited, and had even seen a snapshot of my father, about my age, sitting at their old upright piano with the legendary Queenie, a black-and-white mongrel, howling at his feet. One of the few facts my mother had volunteered about her childhood was that she never had any pets growing up because her mother believed they carried germs. I wanted to ask her why she had lied, but I didn't want to admit that I'd been eavesdropping.

In September we started at our new schools. Luckily, Kim and I had the same teacher, Mrs. Brach, the most beautiful teacher in the school. She had been Miss Wisconsin in 1955. On her desk, next to a picture of her husband and little girl, she kept a framed newspaper pho-tograph of herself in a white evening gown wearing a satin banner across her chest, holding the silver flute she had played in the talent competition. In the first month of school, all the fourth graders had to choose an instrument to study. Kim and I both chose the flute. We both adored Mrs. Brach, who looked like an angel with her blonde flip and pastel angora sweater sets. She had a sweet voice and always smelled flowery. We knew she kept a small bottle of Shalimar in her top desk drawer; we had witnessed her dabbing it behind her ears and onto her wrists during the lunch break. For Christmas that year, both Kim and I gave our mothers Shalimar dusting powder.

My sister had started her first year of high school and spent most of her time practicing for cheerleader with her new gang of girlfriends. Tryouts were in the spring. In the evenings, after supper, she would talk on the phone until our father ordered her to hang up and do her homework. He acted exasperated, but we knew he was glad that she was so popular and outgoing. He liked to talk about how in his day he had been vice president of his class and the star of the track team. Our mother, on the other hand, never talked about her own high school days, and when pressed, said she really didn't remember much. The phone in the upstairs hall had a cord just long enough for my sister to carry it into her bedroom, shut the door, sit on the floor, and lean her back against the door as she whispered and giggled to her friends. Sometimes I'd press my ear to her door and eavesdrop, but her conversations, at least what I could hear of them, struck me as less interesting than my mother's conversations with Mrs. Quave. They were mostly about people I didn't know.

When she wasn't gossiping on the phone, my sister

studied fashion magazines. *Seventeen*, *Mademoiselle*, *Glamour*, *Vogue*, and *Harper's Bazaar*, which she bought with her baby-sitting money. She wanted to be a fashion designer. When we moved into the new house, she had retrieved Nana's old black sewing machine in its wood and iron cabinet from the basement and painted it white to match her room. Then she began haunting fabric stores, looking through big books of patterns for simple skirts and jumpers she could sew. I went with her a couple of times and watched as she flipped through the *McCall's* and *Simplicity* pattern books. It reminded me of my mother poring over all those wallpaper sample books except for the fact that my sister seemed to know precisely what she wanted the moment she saw it; she never seemed to agonize or suffer a moment of self-doubt. Then, pattern in hand, she would choose the fabric: navy wide-wale corduroy, khaki gabardine, pink-and-white-striped seersucker. She would go home, eager to get started, and lay out the tissue pattern pieces on the fabric, moving them this way and that like puzzle pieces until she got it right. Then she would pin the pieces flat and cut them out with pinking shears. My mother had no interest in sewing, but Mrs. Quave did, and in the beginning, when my sister had a question, she would run next door. Pretty soon she was turning out professional-looking skirts, jumpers, and blouses all on her own, as if, my father joked, she'd been born with a silver thimble in her mouth. Even Mrs. Quave said she had never seen anyone learn so fast. And the home ec teacher chose Bonnie to be in charge of the annual fashion show, where all the girls modeled the clothes they had made in sewing class that term. Everyone marveled at her prowess as if she were some kind of idiot savant. She wanted a deluxe Singer zigzag machine for her birthday, which was November fifth. It cost over a hundred dollars, but I figured my father would probably get it for her anyway. He seemed to approve of her "industriousness"; he didn't even seem too disappointed when she brought home all Bs and a C plus in geometry on her report card that fall.

On Labor Day my mother had finally agreed to quit smoking, and she was tense and irritable around the house that September. My father didn't like smoking—he thought it was a filthy habit—and had always made a big show of emptying my mother's ashtrays whenever he came across one with so much as a single butt in it. He said it set a bad example for us girls. And as soon as we moved into the new house, he began to work on my mother. He didn't want the new house to reek of smoke. He argued that once the smoke permeated the fresh new carpeting and draperies, that was it—they'd never get it out again. The time to quit was now.

My mother wavered. She had smoked two packs of Lucky Strikes a day since she was eighteen and she couldn't imagine being without them. In fact, I couldn't imagine my mother without her cigarettes either. Even though I didn't like the smoke or the way she smelled when she kissed me, I was a little nervous about the prospect of her quitting. She had turned over a new leaf in so many other ways, it seemed, that maybe this was pushing it. She had even allowed Mrs. Quave to talk her into learning how to drive: "If you can't drive, you'll be stuck at home. You don't want to be dependent on other people, do you?" On the mornings they didn't volunteer at the

campaign office, they had begun driving lessons. My
father approved. He thanked Betty and told her he had
been offering to teach my mother for years. He was looking forward to not having to chauffeur my mother and us
around anymore. As an incentive to quit smoking, he said
he would buy her a car—her own car—if she quit for six
months. Mrs. Quave told her she was nuts if she didn't
take him up on it before he changed his mind.

I don't think any of us realized what we were asking,
how hard it would be for her. To us it seemed simple,
you just stopped. But to my mother it was like amputat-
ing a limb. "It's like cutting off my right hand," she complained to me once during the first week of not smoking
when she dropped a glass and broke it as she was putting
it away in the cupboard. "I feel all off balance. My natural rhythm is broken." She bent down to pick up the
shattered glass and immediately cut her finger. I ran to
the bathroom for a Band-Aid. When I got back to the
kitchen she was running the cut under cold water at the
sink and crying. I handed her the Band-Aid.

She said "Thanks," turned off the faucet, dried her
hands on a dish towel, and held out her finger while I
bandaged it, the way she used to do for me when I was
little. Except I didn't kiss it.

She fished a pack of Wrigley's Spearmint out of her
apron pocket, unfolded the silver wrapper, and popped
the stick of gum into her mouth. "Want one?" She held
the pack out toward me.

"Sure."

"Promise me you'll never start smoking," she said to
me, still teary-eyed. "Then you'll never have to go
through this."

"Okay," I said. It didn't seem like much to promise at the time.

She glanced at her gold Bulova wristwatch and said, "It's almost show time."

I snagged a Coke from the refrigerator and followed her into the family room, where my father was reading the paper in his favorite chair. On TV, in the shows I watched, the fathers always seemed to have their favorite chair. I wondered why the mothers never did. My mother walked over and turned on the television set. It was the night of the first presidential debate and my mother had given me special permission to stay up late. The Crawfords, who had just moved into the house on the other side of us, had invited us over to eat dessert and watch the debate, but my mother had made up some excuse because she didn't want to listen to Hank Crawford going on about how Kennedy was just a rich playboy who was going to land us all in the poorhouse. He had a Nixon bumper sticker on his red Impala convertible.

My mother adjusted the picture, frowning as she fidgeted with the Contrast control, as if she couldn't get it sharp enough, until my father told her to leave it alone. She hollered upstairs to my sister, "The debate's starting!" My sister shouted "Okay!" but didn't bother to come down. She wasn't much interested in current events.

The debate had pre-empted the *The Andy Griffith Show*. Instead of Andy and Barney, we saw Kennedy and Nixon standing there at their podiums. As my father folded up the newspaper, my mother glared at him and told him "Shhh!" He rolled his eyes and winked at me.

My mother dragged her chair closer to the TV set. Her hands were clenched into fists in her lap and when Kennedy started to answer the moderator's question, she closed her eyes and mumbled a little prayer, just the way she had at Bonnie's ballet recital earlier that year: "Please God, don't let her fall." One of my sister's pink satin toe shoes had come untied partway through her solo and she'd had to stop and retie it, but she still got a standing ovation. Only after she had curtsied and left the stage did my mother seem to start breathing again. When she unclenched her fingers, there were red half-moons in the palms of her hands where the nails had bitten into the flesh.

Fortunately, Kennedy's performance went more smoothly than my sister's. As he spoke, my mother nodded her head vigorously in support and occasionally clapped soundlessly when he scored a particularly good point or witticism. When Nixon spoke, she shook her head and wrinkled her nose as if she smelled something rotten. Once she reached toward the coffee table where she had always kept her pack of cigarettes and sighed when she remembered she'd quit. She jammed her thumb into her mouth and started to gnaw on it. Since she'd stopped smoking, her thumbs looked like ground meat.

"Helen, get your thumb out of your mouth," my father said. He hated this new habit of hers almost as much as smoking.

She ignored him. I tried to hand her a stick of gum, but she batted my arm away. Miffed, I scooted over, onto my father's lap. He always smelled clean and spicy. My mother didn't even seem to notice.

I must have fallen asleep and he must have carried me up to my bed because the next thing I knew it was morning and my mother was shaking me gently, saying, "Rise and shine, Sleeping Beauty." When I opened my eyes, she was smiling.

"Who won?" I asked.

"Kennedy, of course," she said. "Nixon looked like something the cat dragged in."

I got up and headed for the bathroom. A minute later I could hear her in the kitchen, whistling. After I was dressed, I ran downstairs for breakfast. She'd made pancakes. Usually I just had frosted flakes or a powdered doughnut if I was lucky.

"How many do you think you can eat?" she asked me.

"Three," I said, reaching for the Aunt Jemima syrup as she flipped them jauntily onto my plate.

My sister walked in wearing one of her new outfits and sat down at the table and took a sip of orange juice. "Wow, pancakes," she said, impressed despite herself.

My mother smiled. It was the calmest and sunniest I had seen her since she quit smoking.

On the bus going to school that morning, Kevin Crawford sat behind us, and when he heard Kim and me talking about the debate, he butted in and said, "Kennedy was wearing makeup. He flew in his own Hollywood makeup guy."

"How do you know?" Kim demanded.

"My father said so." When he saw that we weren't convinced, he added, "He read it in the newspaper."

"I don't believe you," I said.

"It's true," he protested.

"Shut up!" Kim looked like she was going to take a

swing at him with her lunch box. He shrugged and slumped back in his seat.

"His father's a Republican," I whispered in Kim's ear. I knew that she took any remark against Kennedy personally since she was Catholic, too. Sometimes she worried about my soul because we didn't go to church except once in awhile on holidays.

In October they tested our eyes at school and sent home a note for my parents saying that I needed glasses. My father took it personally, as if it were an insult that someone else should have to tell him, an optometrist, that his own daughter needed "vision correction," as the note phrased it.

"Why didn't you tell me you were having trouble seeing?" he asked.

"I didn't know," I said. "Maybe it's a mistake."

The next day was a Saturday, and he took me down to his new office, which was in a little shopping center between a beauty salon and a jewelry store. For the first couple of weeks my father had complained about the smell of permanent-wave solution from the beauty salon, which had rented the space next to his office after he'd already signed the lease, but now he didn't seem to notice it anymore. Lorraine, the owner, cut our hair for free, and in return my father gave her and her husband a big discount on prescription sunglasses. My father's office was closed on the weekends, and I liked being in there when it was empty. I was intrigued by the rows and rows of eyeglass frames—men's, women's, children's. I already had the frames I wanted all picked out—the tops were light blue with silver speckles. My father and sister both wore glasses, and I thought they were neat even though my sister hated hers. At the movies she would wait until the lights dimmed to put them on and then slide them off as soon as the credits began to roll at the end. In school, she just went around squinting.

My father took me into the examination room and told me to sit in the leather chair. Then he walked over to a little sink and washed his hands. Over the sink he had hung a framed poster labeled "CROSS SECTION OF THE EYE." It was so gross—all these hairy blood vessels like a bloody spiderweb—that I had to shut my eyes and breathe deeply so I wouldn't throw up.

"You okay, Suzy Q?"

I nodded. He pressed a pedal on the floor and raised the chair, then moved some big black binocular-type contraption in front of my face.

"What's that?" I asked suspiciously.

"It's called a photoropter. I'm going to do what's called a retinoscopy."

"Does it hurt?"

"No, of course not. Now lean forward," he said. "Rest your forehead against here." On the far wall was a lighted square with rows of printed letters. "Now, what's the smallest line you can read?" he asked me. I read the letters off slowly, hesitantly, one at a time—"E, D, F, C, Z, P"—and he began flipping different lenses up and down in front of my eyes. "Okay," he said. "Which is better? This?" Flip. "Or this?"

I couldn't see any difference.

"What do you mean, better?" I asked, stalling for time.

"Which is clearer, less blurry." He flipped back and forth again. And then again. I still couldn't really tell, but

I could feel him getting impatient so I said, "The second one, I guess."

"Okay. Now how about these? This one." Flip. "Or this one?"

"Could I see them again?"

He sighed and flipped them back and forth again.

"The second one," I said, even though I wasn't sure. I felt like my mother sweating over the wallpaper samples. The exam seemed to take forever. In the end my father decided I was borderline and just gave me some eye exercises to do for a couple of months. He said those tests at school were primitive—all they used was a big eye chart—and not very accurate. I went home disappointed. The only consolation was that my sister seemed jealous that I didn't need glasses after all.

A couple of weeks later my mother went to Lorraine's to get her hair trimmed and came back wearing a flowered silk scarf that she didn't remove until she was safely inside the house. I gasped. Her hair, usually a soft, golden blonde, was bright platinum, like Marilyn Monroe's. My mother frowned at herself in the hall mirror and groaned.

"She said she was just going to brighten it a little," my mother said. "Bring out the natural highlights."

I didn't know what to say. She looked sort of glamorous but unreal. She didn't look like my mother. She didn't look like *a* mother. "It looks nice," I said tentatively.

"I hate it," my mother declared. "I should never have let her talk me into it. I mean, look at *her* hair. It looks like a maroon bird's nest."

"Will it wash out?" I asked.

My mother shook her head and muttered, "Christ, I wish I had a cigarette." She walked over to the kitchen cupboard and took out a bottle of Bufferin and shook two into her palm. As she was filling a glass of water, she looked over at me and said, "Suzy, honey, would you do me a favor?"

I nodded.

"Would you run across the street and ask Mrs. Gusdorf for a cigarette? Just one," she added when she saw the expression on my face.

"What about your new car?" I balked. I was looking forward to us being able to go wherever we wanted without my father.

"We don't have to tell him," she coaxed. "I'll smoke it outside. It can be our little secret, can't it?"

"I guess so."

She smiled and swallowed the two aspirin. I put my coat and gloves on. It was freezing cold out. The Gusdorfs lived next to the DiNardos, on the other side of the street. There was only one empty house left on our cul-de-sac and it had been sold to a family who was supposedly moving in just in time for Thanksgiving. I pressed the Gusdorfs' doorbell and jumped up and down on the stoop as I waited, trying to keep warm. Mrs. Gusdorf opened the door, holding her baby girl on her hip. The baby was crying, and Mrs. Gusdorf looked messy and tired. She was a large woman anyway and had been struggling to lose the extra weight she had put on when she was pregnant. She was always on some new diet and chain-smoked to keep from eating. My father referred to her as Frau Metrecal.

I asked if my mother could please borrow a cigarette.

Mrs. Gusdorf laughed and said, "Of course, come in."
She set the baby down on a blanket in the middle of the
living-room carpet while she went to the kitchen. I knelt
down and held out my finger for the baby to grab in her
fist. I loved babies and wished my mother could have one
even though she'd explained to me that she couldn't
because of the miscarriages. Jackie Kennedy was expecting a baby in November, a couple of weeks after the election, and I was looking forward to having a baby in the
White House. I hoped it would be another girl, like
Caroline.

"Here you go." Mrs. Gusdorf bustled back in, holding
three cigarettes out to me.

"She only wants one," I said.

"Take them all," Mrs. Gusdorf insisted.

I tugged my finger out of the baby's tiny pink fist—
she had a surprisingly strong grip—and took the cigarettes and said thank you.

On the way back to my house I stopped at the curb
and dropped two of the cigarettes into the sewer. Then I
ran inside and presented my mother with Mrs. Gusdorf's
Viceroy.

My mother patted my cheek and said, "I don't know
what I'd do without you." She already had her car coat
on and her lighter in hand. She opened the back door,
stepped out into the yard, and lit the cigarette. "You keep
watch!" she hollered to me. "Tell me if anyone's coming."

"Okay," I hollered back. I sat down at the table and
flipped through the new issue of *Time* magazine. There
was a full-page color picture of Helen Keller in a blue
print dress and a pearl necklace, with her fingertips skim-

ming a big book written in braille. She looked like a kindly, beautiful grandmother with snowy-white hair. The caption said, "How easy it is to fly on paper wings— Helen Keller." I always felt weird when I saw or heard her name because it was my mother's name. Her married name. Her maiden name was Helen Hansen. "She almost didn't marry me because of my name," my father liked to tell people, "but I was irresistible. And I wouldn't take no for an answer."

I glanced out the window. My mother was bent over, burying her cigarette butt in the snow. Her new hair was practically as white as Helen Keller's.

When my sister burst in from cheerleading practice, she did a double take and squealed, "It's a wig, right?"

I glared at her and signaled for her to shut up, but she just giggled and said, "I thought Halloween was last week."

At supper time my father managed a more diplomatic response, but as he ate his Hungarian goulash, he kept glancing at my mother surreptitiously, as if he couldn't quite believe his eyes.

The next day Mrs. Quave took my mother to her hairdresser, an older woman named Verna who had turned her basement into a little beauty parlor with only one sink and one hair dryer. My mother said that when she removed her scarf Verna had shaken her head and clucked like a mother hen. "Don't you worry," she'd said. "We'll fix it." And she did. My mother returned home bareheaded and smiling, her hair magically restored to its usual color.

My sister's fourteenth birthday was three days before the election, and she was put out by the fact that no one seemed to be paying any attention to this fact. My mother was too busy typing letters to every registered Democrat in the Second District and talking on the phone to her fellow volunteers who, like my mother, seemed to have whipped themselves up into a frenzy of anxiety and anticipation. Mrs. Quave had a long list of the names and addresses of people with no transportation who she was supposed to chauffeur to various polling places. She had urged my mother to take her driver's test so that she, too, could help with transportation on Election Day, but my mother said she was too nervous to deal with it until after November eighth.

Our father was attending an optometry seminar on contact lenses in Chicago the weekend of Bonnie's birthday. Even though she had planned a slumber party with four girlfriends that Saturday night and didn't need him around, she acted as if she were deeply wounded. I knew she was just trying to make him feel guilty so that he'd spring for the fancy new sewing machine. I also knew that my parents had already decided to buy it for her, so all her theatrics were for nothing. I was worried that my gift wouldn't arrive in time. Every day when I got home from school, I checked the mail first thing. I had sent away for some customized garment labels I'd seen advertised in the entertainment section of the Sunday newspaper. They were white satin with gold embroidery that would read "Fashions by Bonnie."

Our family celebrated my sister's birthday on Friday evening, so that my father could be there. Since my mother wasn't much for baking and was too busy typing, Kim and I baked a chocolate cake with marshmallow frosting from a mix. It came out lopsided, but we managed to disguise the caved-in side with globs of frosting. On his way home from the office my father picked up a pizza, my sister's favorite food, from Angelo's, as well as the new sewing machine from Sears. The garment labels arrived that afternoon, just in the nick of time.

Everyone was in a good mood. My sister was thrilled with the Singer zigzag. She complimented me on the cake and said the garment labels were really cool. She wolfed down her cake and ice cream and then ran upstairs to try out the new machine. Mrs. Quave had given her a new pattern and four yards of blue velveteen. My parents and I sat around the kitchen table for a few minutes having seconds on dessert while my sister's new sewing machine rumbled overhead. I had burned the roof of my mouth on my first bite of pizza and I could feel a blister forming. My father was telling us about how Mrs. Crawford had brought in Kevin's little sister, Lisa, who was only three. She had amblyopia, lazy eye, and my father had put an adhesive patch over her good eye in order to strengthen the weak eye. He figured she would probably have to wear the patch about a month, or maybe two. My mother nodded, but I could tell she wasn't really listening. She was anxious to wash the dishes and get back to her typing. This was the final round of letters before the election. They had to be in the mail by the next day or they might not reach potential voters in time. According to the polls, the race was too close to call, so every vote could make a difference.

My father went to bed early, the same time as me, since he had to be in Chicago by eight A.M., but my mother stayed up half the night, typing as if her life depended on it. I fell asleep to the *peck-peck-peck* of the

Smith-Corona that my father had bought for my sister as a graduation gift from junior high. When I woke up the next morning, my father was already gone and my mother was sound asleep on the living-room sofa with one of Nana's crocheted afghans wrapped around her. On the card table, her makeshift desk, were stacks and stacks of letters all addressed and ready to go.

My sister's slumber party was that night. Bonnie spent most of the day making a plaid flannel nightgown on her new machine. Brian, one of the college boys from the campaign office, stopped by to pick up the letters and take them to the central post office before it closed at noon. He was handsome, with wavy, dark hair and a nice smile. My mother offered him a cup of coffee and a slice of birthday cake. They sat in the kitchen joking around for over an hour. My mother was tired—I overheard her saying she'd gone to bed at three-thirty—but she was animated and talkative. I could tell they liked each other. He waited until the last minute—twenty of twelve— seemingly reluctant to leave. He kept complimenting my mother on the coffee even though it was just Folgers instant. On his way out he told my mother that he had asked some of the other volunteers over to his apartment to eat chili and watch the election returns on Tuesday evening, and invited my mother to join them. She said she'd think about it—she seemed flattered by the invitation—and then told him he'd better hurry or the post office would be closed by the time he got there and she didn't want to think she'd missed her beauty sleep for nothing. He said she didn't look like she'd missed any beauty sleep to him. My mother just laughed and gave him a playful shove out the door. As soon as she heard his engine start up, she turned and looked in the hall mirror and fluffed her hair, still blushing.

At seven o'clock my sister's friends arrived: Janet, Melanie, Tina, and Laurie. They spread their sleeping bags out in the family room in front of the TV. From upstairs my mother and I could hear them shrieking and giggling as the Jiffy Pop kernels exploded like distant gunfire inside the aluminum foil bonnet and the frozen pizzas burned in the oven. Even though we could smell the pizzas burning, we didn't say anything. Bonnie had given us strict orders to stay upstairs, out of sight. My mother and I were sitting on her bed playing canasta. The house felt different with my father away. As if we were all playing hooky from something. My mother and I had skipped dinner and were snacking on Cheese Whiz, Ritz crackers, Vienna sausages, apples, and Hershey's kisses, which we'd carried up to the master bedroom

"This reminds me of the camping trips your father and I used to take before you kids were born," my mother said, fishing the last Vienna sausage out of the can. "We couldn't afford hotels, so we had this little pup tent and we'd drive to some national park for a night or two just to get out of the city."

"Why don't we ever go camping?" I asked. "It sounds neat."

My mother shrugged, finished shuffling the cards, and started to deal us another hand. "It's just something you do when you're young and romantic. And you don't need a good night's sleep." She yawned and covered her mouth with her hand. "Look at me. It's eight-thirty and I can hardly keep my eyes open."

"Tell me about how you met Dad," I begged. I loved

to hear stories about my mother and father before we were born.

My mother yawned again and said, "You've heard it a million times." She discarded an eight of clubs. Down below I could hear "Lonely Boy" by Paul Anka cranked up loud on my parents' hi-fi.

"Tell me again," I insisted.

"Okay." She sighed. "It was June. I was standing at the bus stop on Michigan Avenue, waiting for the bus after work." She unwrapped a Hershey's kiss and popped it in her mouth. "You really want to hear this?"

I nodded.

"It's your turn to discard," she pointed out. "And it was windy—you know they call it the Windy City—and this speck of grit or something suddenly blew into my eye. I pulled a Kleenex out of my purse and tried to get it out. My eye was tearing and it hurt like crazy, and I knew the bus was going to arrive any second. Then this man— your father—walks over and says, 'Excuse me, Miss, but maybe I could be of assistance. I'm an optometrist.'"

I giggled. My mother mimicked my father's tone of voice perfectly.

"So I was startled and embarrassed, but in too much pain to protest and I said, 'All right.' He told me to tilt my head back and he lifted my eyelid slightly and did something or other and—presto!—the damn thing came right out and I thanked him. And then the bus pulled up and we both got on."

"But it wasn't really his bus," I butted in.

"Right, but I didn't know that till later. I figured he was waiting for the same bus. And when he asked if he could sit next to me—the bus was almost full anyway—I said okay. He had on a nice suit and was very polite. In those days there weren't so many crazies running around. You didn't have to be as careful as you do now. I mean, you know, I've told you, you should never, never talk to strangers, right?"

"Right." I squirmed impatiently. "I know."

"Okay, well, so we talked and one thing led to another, and when I got to my stop, he got off with me and walked me the two blocks down Halsted to my apartment building, and asked if I'd like to have dinner some evening and I said yes."

"And then you found out he'd only been in optometry school for a month and he didn't even take that bus. He'd gone way out of his way just to meet you."

My mother laughed and sighed. "He brought roses. No one had ever brought me roses before. Plus, the war was on, and there were hardly any men around between the ages of eighteen and thirty. My girlfriends at work were all green with jealousy. They acted as if I'd hit the jackpot."

Downstairs, "Lonely Boy" ended and was immediately replaced by Bobby Darin's "Dream Lover."

"Of course, your father was very sensitive about not being in the army. He'd wanted to enlist, but they wouldn't take him because of his bad eye. He was very touchy about it. He thought no woman could fall in love with a man who hadn't fought for his country."

"But you did," I said, "didn't you?"

My mother patted my hand and smiled. "I don't think I can finish this hand"—she yawned again—"I'm so tired I can't even see straight."

"That's okay." I picked up the cards and put them back in the carrying case. "I'm sort of tired, too."

Without even bothering to change into her nightgown, my mother slid under the covers and I kissed her
good night and tiptoed out of the room. It was too early
for bed, so I sat on the stairs spying on my sister's slumber party. "Put Your Head on My Shoulder" was playing,
slow and romantic. Two "couples,"—Bonnie and
Melanie, and Tina and Laurie—were slow-dancing cheek
to cheek with their eyes closed. Janet was sitting on the
sofa looking left out. Janet Andretti was my sister's oldest
friend, who went to a different school and didn't really
know my sister's new friends. The girls all had poofy
blonde flips except for Janet, who had straight, thick
black hair to her waist and dark brown eyes with beautiful
long lashes. Her father was Italian. He owned an auto-
body shop that specialized in fancy foreign cars. He had
been trained as an opera singer, and would frequently
burst into some booming aria from *La Traviata* or *Don
Giovanni* as he mowed the lawn or waxed his Alfa-
Romeo, which he had purchased half totaled and had
lovingly rebuilt. His mother, who didn't speak much
English, lived with them and seemed to spend most of
her time either at church or in the kitchen making delicious ravioli from scratch. After a couple of minutes,
Janet caught sight of me sitting there on the stairs and
motioned to me. She had known me ever since I was a
baby. She held out her arms and we slow-danced at the
foot of the stairs, with me stepping all over her
stockinged feet. I closed my eyes and let Paul Anka's
voice vibrate deep inside me. I thought about my father
bringing red roses for my mother, only they weren't my
father and mother yet. They were just two people going
out on a date. My father with his bad eye from a fire-

cracker accident when he was only four years old. The reason he had decided to become an eye doctor. The reason he had not gone off to war and never met my mother.

The day of the election it was gray and overcast, with sleet falling off and on. In the morning as she sent us off to school, my mother seemed nervous and distracted. The TV was on in the family room. She didn't even notice that my sister had skipped breakfast. And when I opened my lunch at school, I discovered that she had forgotten to put any lunch meat in my sandwich—all I had was two pieces of Wonder bread with a layer of mustard, cut neatly in half. My father was going to go home at noon, and they were going to eat lunch out and then cast their votes at the polling place, an Episcopal church not far from our house. Mrs. Quave was going to be busy all day driving people to and from the polls. My father knew how much the election meant to my mother and I could see that he was doing his best to buttress her spirits. He was privately convinced that Nixon was going to win and worried about what a defeat would do to my mother's rejuvenated joie de vivre. We all knew that my mother had a natural tendency toward gloominess. All summer we had basked in the glow of her sudden radiance, as if the gray clouds hovering over her head had finally drifted apart and allowed the sunlight to shine in. But I think we all sensed that this new buoyancy was as fragile as a bubble.

To keep herself occupied my mother baked a double batch of Toll House cookies like some mother on one of my favorite shows—Donna Reed or June Lockhart.

When I opened the front door, the house smelled sweet and warm. My mother was in the kitchen scraping the last batch of cookies off the cookie sheet with a spatula. They were slightly charred on the bottoms. I poured myself a glass of milk and ate a couple of cookies with the chocolate chips still soft and melty, the way I liked them.

"These are great," I said.

My mother was licking the cookie dough out of the mixing bowl with her index finger. An almost empty bottle of Gallo Rhine wine was on the kitchen table next to a half-full glass. My mother's eyes looked a little glassy and her cheeks were flushed, which could have been from bending over the hot oven. It was only three-thirty. I knew that my father didn't approve of cocktails before five.

"What are you doing?" I asked as she picked up the glass of wine and took a sip.

"A little something to relax my nerves," she said. "Since smoking is verboten."

The phone rang and she floated over to answer it, reaching a bit unsteadily for the receiver hanging on the wall. "Brian!" she exclaimed. "How's it going?"

She listened for a minute as he must have filled her in on what was going on down at the campaign office and then she said, "Well, I'd love to come, but I really can't." I figured he was asking her if she were coming over for his election returns party. "It's sweet of you to think of me, but I've got a hungry family to feed." She laughed, but I could tell she wished she could go. "I'll be right here. Call me if there's any news." She hung up and took another sip of wine.

"You could go," I said. "Bonnie and I could make dinner."

"That's sweet." She patted my cheek. "But I think your father would feel a little abandoned. Anyway, the Quaves are coming over for coffee and cookies. Poor Betty's been running herself ragged all day, driving all over town in this miserable weather."

"Who's ahead?" I asked.

"It's too early to tell. Besides, the Democrats don't vote until after six, when they get off work." She took a package of hamburger out of the refrigerator and set it on the counter next to a bag of hamburger buns. "I thought we'd have sloppy joes. You better do your homework if you want to watch TV later."

I snitched another cookie and went up to my room. I just had a couple of pages in my math workbook to do. Then I figured I'd go over to Kim's for a while. I was working on the last math problem—we were learning about fractions and most of the problems had to do with cutting up pies—when Bonnie thundered upstairs and paused by my doorway.

"Boy, Mom's really looped," she giggled. "She dumped a can of chicken noodle soup on top of the hamburger instead of the sloppy joe sauce."

I giggled, too, and then felt guilty.

"She better drink a gallon of coffee before Dad comes home," she said. "Either that or a cold shower." Then she disappeared into her room with the telephone and closed the door. A minute later I heard her snickering to a friend.

I walked downstairs into the kitchen where my mother was drinking a cup of instant coffee and fishing noodles out of the sloppy joe sauce. The wine bottle was corked and put away.

"I'm going over to Kim's for a while," I told her. "I'll be back by five-thirty."

"Okay." She reached into the cupboard for the Bufferin bottle and shook two into her hand. "What a day," she sighed. "I wish you could just wake me up when it's all over. It's all this waiting I can't take."

"I hope he wins, but it won't be the end of the world if he doesn't," I said, echoing what my father had told her as he left for work that morning.

She just looked at me, disappointed, and said, "You sound just like your father." She downed the two aspirin in one swallow. "What would he know about the end of the world?"

All evening long we sat in front of the television watching the returns tallied up in dribs and drabs, waiting for the polls to close in California. The commentators kept showing a shaded map of the United States, predicting who would get the winning combination of electoral votes with which states. The lead kept seesawing back and forth. My mother chewed on her thumbs, groaning and cheering as Kennedy's fortunes rose and fell. Around ten o'clock, when it was announced that Wisconsin had gone for Nixon, she burst into tears. My father tried awkwardly to console her, sitting next to her on the sofa with his arm around her, but she would not stop crying until Mrs. Quave said, "That does it! We're putting the house up for sale tomorrow and moving to Illinois." Kennedy had won big in Chicago. My mother smiled and dried her eyes with a napkin, which was clenched in her fist.

Mr. Quave yawned and said he'd better hit the hay, tomorrow was a workday. After the Quaves left my father turned to me and said, "And you've got school tomorrow, young lady." My sister had already lost interest and gone to bed without even being told to.

"Oh, let her be," my mother said. "This is history."

"It could be hours yet," my father protested.

My mother shrugged. "When she's sleepy, she'll fall asleep. Right?"

"Right," I agreed. I could tell she didn't want to be alone. On weeknights my father always went to bed at ten-thirty, read for half an hour, then turned off the light.

He stood up and stretched. My mother looked at him and frowned. "How can you go to sleep not knowing?"

"The outcome's going to be the same whether I sleep or not."

My mother shook her head. I could tell she felt it was her duty to stay up, that maybe it would make a difference. Some sort of sympathetic magic. My father went upstairs and came back down with two pillows and two blankets. We thanked him as he kissed us good night and Walter Cronkite announced that Nixon had taken Ohio.

I don't know when I fell asleep, but I dreamed that Kennedy lost the election and they moved into the empty house at the end of our cul-de-sac. Caroline was riding a pony in the backyard and all us neighborhood kids were lined up, holding tickets, waiting for our turn.

By the time we left for school the next morning, we still didn't know. My mother handed me my lunch money and said to keep my fingers crossed. She seemed pretty optimistic even though her eyes were shadowed with dark circles.

On the bus, Kevin Crawford told us his father had said that when all the votes from California were counted up, Nixon would be the winner, too bad for the Pope. Kim yelled at him to shut up.

I forgot all about the election during science and art. The art teacher, Mr. Savas, made the rounds of a number of different schools and only came to our school on Wednesdays. This Wednesday he showed us how to make collages with wax paper. After art class, we had early lunch period. I stood in the cafeteria line while Kim, who had brought her lunch, saved me a place at our usual table. I was glad my mother had been too tired to make my lunch because Wednesday was spaghetti day. I carried my tray over to the table and sat down between Kim and Mary Jo Martinson. When Mary Jo saw my butterscotch pudding she offered to trade me her cupcake and I said okay. The cafeteria was noisy, as always, and it took a couple of seconds for the static of the intercom to cut through the hubbub and capture our attention. The principal, Mr. Stapleton, announced that John F. Kennedy was the new president of the United States. I still remember it clearly: the smell of peanut butter and spaghetti sauce, the waxy little milk carton with its straw poking up, the white squiggle on my Hostess cupcake, the bedlam of shrill whooping and booing, the scrape of our chairs against the worn linoleum, and the scratchy softness of my mohair sweater as I placed my hand over my heart to recite the pledge of allegiance. I didn't know who I was happier for—Kennedy or my mother.

Fueled by the flush of victory, my mother went down to the Department of Motor Vehicles bright and early the next morning and took her driver's test. She got 100 percent on the written exam and just barely passed the driving part, she was so nervous, but she got her license. Or at least a pink temporary license that would be followed by the real thing in six weeks. To celebrate, my father took us out to dinner at China Palace. We were in high spirits. My mother and father were drinking Chinese beers with red dragons on the labels. My sister made us laugh by reading funny-sounding dishes off the menu: Sautéed Happy Family, Ants Climbing Trees, Hot and Spicy Bean Turd (a misprint that had been crossed out and corrected in blue ink to read "Curd," whatever that was). At my insistence my mother drove us home from the restaurant, which was only a mile or so from our house, while my father and sister ducked and braced themselves in mock terror even though she drove about twenty miles under the speed limit. When her permanent driver's license arrived in the mail six weeks later, she was smiling, with her eyes closed, in the picture. My father joked that if she ever got stopped by a cop, he'd think she was the real Helen Keller.

For Thankgiving that year we drove out, as always, to the farm. My father's brothers, Uncle Howard and Uncle Carl, were very close. Carl lived just down the road from Howard—he had bought the old Guterson place with the money Nana left him. My father had used his share to open his office in the mall. Uncle Carl was a hog feed salesman, and his wife ran a kennel. My father, the youngest, was the only one who had gone to college and moved away. Even though Madison was less than an hour from New Glarus, it might as well have been New

York. Howard and Carl each had five kids, three boys and
two girls, in the same exact order—"What were the statis-
tical odds?" my father would marvel, as if there had to
have been some sort of collusion at work—and the
cousins were as close as brothers and sisters. My sister
and I hated holidays at the farm. And I don't think our
parents liked them much better than we did. Oddly
enough, it was our mother who always insisted that we
go. "Family is family," she'd say. "Blood is thicker than
water." We figured she felt this way because she was an
orphan. Because even though she knocked herself out to
be charming and helpful, the aunts always managed to
hurt her feelings. They were both overweight and wore
sensible shoes. I think without Aunt Lucille (Howard's
wife), my mother and Aunt Ruth might have been
friends. My mother loved animals and liked to talk with
Ruth about her kennel. She would have liked to get a
dog, but my father said he'd grown up with animals and
didn't want some damn dog digging up the lawn and
tracking mud through the house. When my mother
argued that the dog could stay outside, my father just
snorted and said, "Who do you think you're kidding?"—
he knew that would last about five minutes. But Ruth,
who was sweet and timid and not too bright, didn't dare
do anything to rub Lucille the wrong way.

Aunt Lucille always made sure to ask my mother to
bring the pies every Thanksgiving because she knew my
mother didn't have a white thumb. For years my mother
slaved away, rolling out uncooperative piecrusts that
either disintegrated into floury crumbs or stuck in a gluey
mass to the rolling pin as she cursed under her breath.
Finally she gave up and bought the pies at Mettler's

Bakery. But this year my sister had baked pumpkin pies in home ec. And the home ec teacher, Mrs. Buehler, had even insisted that they make the pie filling from real pumpkins. My mother had protested that that was ridiculous. "Canned is perfectly good," she'd said. "Life is too short to make your own pumpkin-pie filling." But now she bragged to Aunt Lucille on my sister's behalf. "And she made that outfit she's wearing, too," my mother told her. "She's got a regular booming business going. Her friends pay her to make them clothes."

Lucille nodded in approval even though she didn't approve of Bonnie's wearing lipstick and mascara. Any more than she approved of contact lenses, which my father was just beginning to sell on a regular basis. She thought they represented the pinnacle of vanity, and that the fools who wore them deserved to go blind. My father, who considered them the greatest invention since the wheel, simmered silently, knowing that there was no use arguing with Lucille.

This particular Thanksgiving was even more tense than usual, because the rest of the family were die-hard Republicans. We sat down at the table. Uncle Carl said grace. As the last "amen" was still echoing in our ears and Uncle Howard had started in on the turkey with his carving knife, they started in on Kennedy. My mother nervously fingered her water glass, no doubt wishing it were wine. Aunt Lucille, a teetotaler, refused to serve alcohol at her table although the men drank beer, and lots of it, from Carl's private stash in the big new freezer in the new garage he'd financed with his share of Nana's money. I could see that my mother was suffering and I thought maybe if they knew, they'd let up on it, so I said,

"My mother volunteered for his campaign. She worked really hard."

"That figures," Aunt Lucille muttered, reaching for the gravy boat. "I guess a lot of fools out there are just susceptible to a pretty face."

"Now, Lucille," Uncle Howard broke in, trying to head off unpleasantness.

"These sweet potatoes are just wonderful." Aunt Ruth nudged her way into the conversation. "Did you do something different this year?"

You could see Aunt Lucille wavering for a moment, trying to decide whether to give in graciously for the sake of family harmony, and then she turned to Ruth and smiled. "Why, thank you. I added orange marmalade and pecans. I saw the recipe in *Family Circle* while I was waiting in Dr. Hoffmayer's office."

Everyone breathed a sigh of relief. Uncle Carl commented on how the weather sure was odd for this time of year. My father patted my mother's hand on the tablecloth, as if calming an agitated dog, and that seemed to be what did it. She jerked her hand away, threw down her napkin, and marched outside. We all sat there, stunned, for a few minutes, waiting to see if she would reappear. Aunt Lucille sniffed and mumbled something about some people being so "touchy." The cousins kept shoveling in the food, seemingly oblivious to the crisis. Finally, after what seemed like too long, my father got up and walked out into the yard. The conversation lagged while he was gone although Aunt Ruth and Uncle Carl did their doomed best to keep it going. After maybe five minutes my father came back and said, "She's sitting in the car." His tone of voice sounded apologetic. "She doesn't want to come back inside."

Aunt Lucille said, "Well, how childish."

Abruptly my father turned to her and said, "You're the big bully! You think you're the only one in the world with an opinion worth having and you always have one, even though you're usually dead wrong. You wouldn't know—"

"Now wait a minute, Glen," Uncle Howard interrupted, holding up his hand in a gesture of peace. "It's Thanksgiving, after all. I'm sure we can all just calm down here and start over on the right foot."

But my father was already striding into the hallway and grabbing our coats from the coat tree. Thrilled, I jumped up and ran over to him and wriggled into my jacket. I was proud of him for standing up for my mother. He held my sister's new fur-trimmed parka, waiting impatiently for her to join us. My sister shrugged, popped a Brussels sprout into her mouth, and scraped her chair back from the table. My father yanked open the door and then slammed it behind us without even bothering to say good-bye.

Our car was parked a ways off, near the barn. It was snowing lightly—a soft, pretty, blanket of white. My mother had the radio on, and was listening to some beautiful classical music. Violins and flutes. Her head, with her eyes closed, was resting against the seat. When we all climbed in, she opened her eyes and laughed.

"I don't see what's so funny," my father said as he tore down the long driveway, flinging gravel, unconcerned for once about the Bonneville's paint job. "Those assholes," he mumbled under his breath.

My sister and I looked at each other in shocked delight; our father never used that kind of language. We didn't know he had it in him. My mother turned her head around and winked at us in the backseat.

When we got home, my mother made us ham-and-cheese sandwiches. My sister took hers up to her room to talk on the phone. My mother and father were drinking beer. My father drank two in a row, hardly touching his sandwich. "Some Thanksgiving," he said. He looked as if he were on the verge of tears, which scared me because my father never cried. "They always hated me. I was the baby of the family and after the accident, which was their fault—who gives a four-year-old kid a lit firecracker?—Mom always treated me special. I didn't have to do as many chores. I guess she was afraid I'd injure the other eye somehow. They ganged up on me. They used to torture me when she wasn't around. And my father didn't do anything. He thought I was just a mama's boy."

My father's voice sounded high and thin. For the first time I could imagine him as a little boy being bullied by his big brothers. My mother got up, and I thought she was going to give him a hug, but she just opened the refrigerator and handed him another beer. "Let it go," she said. "That was then, this is now."

My father looked up, stung by her tone. She was staring out the window into the darkness. "I've always loved snow," she said dreamily. "Ever since I was a little girl."

The next day was Kim's tenth birthday, and Jackie Kennedy gave birth to a new baby. A boy, unfortunately. I gave Kim a nurse's outfit with a blue cape, white cap, and black bag containing a stethoscope, thermometer, and vial of candy pills. We took turns being the patient. When it was my turn to be the nurse, I told Kim that she was Mrs. Dionne giving birth to quintuplets. I lined up five of my dolls and kept pulling them, one by one, out from underneath the blanket and exclaiming, "Oh my, oh lord, another one! I don't believe it!"

As soon as Thanksgiving was over, the Christmas season officially began. Since the neighborhood was brand-new, it was everyone's first Christmas in their new house. Our fathers nailed up strands of colored lights while our mothers—the artistic directors—stood by the snowy curb frowning and gesturing: higher, lower, more to the right, the left. The Dinsmores spelled out "N-O-E-L" with huge tinselly letters across their picture window. The DiNardos set up a life-size nativity scene on their front lawn, with my sister's old Betsy Wetsy lying in the baby Jesus's cradle. The Matsumis, the last family to move into our cul-de-sac, strung thousands of delicate white lights around all their newly landscaped shrubs. At night it looked like a huge crystal spider web, and we all agreed that they had done the most artistic job, except for Hank Crawford, who said, "I'll be damned. I didn't know Buddhists went in for Christmas." Mr. Crawford's brother had been killed at Pearl Harbor and he wasn't too thrilled about some Japanese family living right next door even though they were third-generation Americans and Dr. Matsumi was a professor at the university. The Gusdorfs set up Santa's sleigh and four reindeer on their roof.

We all had big fir trees that had to be sawed off at the top in order not to scrape the ceiling. If our parents dared to suggest we buy a smaller tree, we sulked until they gave in. Our fathers stood around the tree lots, bored, clouds of steamy breath escaping from their mouths as they made small talk with the guys who worked there while our mothers examined each tree, searching for the one with the best shape, no bald spots or curving trunks. Usually, despite my mother's vigilant scrutiny, our tree would have one bad side, which we would turn to the wall and try to disguise with gobs of tinsel. That year, though, my mother managed to find a perfect tree, a tree so full and symmetrical it was hard to believe it wasn't artificial.

Almost every weekend there was a party. Christmas Eve, New Year's Eve, New Year's Day. Everyone wanted to give a party to inaugurate their new houses. Or to recip- rocate everyone else's hospitality. Since baby-sitters were hard to come by and we all lived so close together, our parents would usually take us kids along to play upstairs until we fell asleep. The youngest kids would wear paja- mas under their coats. And when the party was over, our fathers and mothers would carry us, half asleep, home and slide us into our own beds.

Even now, I can close my eyes and picture, one by one, our mothers' cocktail dresses. Mrs. Quave's emerald brocade that contrasted festively with her red hair. Mrs. Gusdorf's dignified navy blue taffeta. Mrs. Crawford's slightly too low-cut purple chiffon. Mrs. DiNardo's red velvet in which she resembled my sister's tomato pincush- ion. Mrs. Matsumi's embroidered Suzy Wong dress. Mrs. Dinsmore's coffee lace. My mother's black crepe de chine with the satin bows perched like butterflies on the shoul- ders. Before and after the parties, the dresses hung in plastic bags in the backs of their closets like patient, glam- orous ghosts, faintly redolent of Emeraude or Shalimar or Evening in Paris.

Since they couldn't afford new dresses for each party,

our mothers haunted the department stores for new and dramatic accessories. Rhinestone belts, silk roses, sequined cummerbunds, costume jewelry. My sister, who had a genius for breathing new life into old dresses, was in constant demand during the holiday season, adding ruffles, removing sleeves, scalloping hems, scooping necklines. She made so much money at her sewing machine that she gave up baby-sitting. She already knew the intimate secrets of their houses, having prowled through drawers and cupboards after their kids were asleep, and now she learned the intimate secrets of their bodies as well. Mrs. DiNardo's Cesarean scars, Mrs. Gusdorf's inverted nipple, Mrs. Dinsmore's falsies, Mrs. Crawford's suspicious bruises. Only Mrs. Quave, who did her own alterations, and Mrs. Matsumi, who seemed to have a whole treasure trove of stunning silk dresses for every occasion, were exempt from my sister's revelations. And our mother, who seemed to feel it would be violating some vague incest taboo. In those days, none of us ever saw our parents' naked bodies.

Caught up in the holiday spirit, my mother decided to give a New Year's Eve party. She had never, to my knowledge, given a party before—except birthday parties for my sister and me, after which she would usually go to bed with a headache. My father was all for it. He was pleased to see my mother throwing herself into the social whirl. "Coming into her own," as he called it. I could see he felt that they were finally living the life he had imagined they would live when he asked her to marry him. He had been drawn to her because she had seemed so sad and fragile—a delicate, tightly curled bud—and he saw himself providing her with the physical and emotional nutrients she needed to blossom forth. And now, at long last, after he had just about lost hope, here she was: his late bloomer.

My mother threw herself into the party preparations as if it were the inaugural ball. I went with her to the Hallmark shop where she dithered over which invitations to buy, and finally, uninspired by the selection, decided to be daring and make her own. She spent two entire evenings making the invitations out of construction paper and glitter and painstakingly writing them out with a new red rapidograph. When they were ready to go, I walked from house to house, nestling them in the mailboxes.

Next came the menu. My mother checked out half a dozen books on canapés and hors d'oeuvres from the public library and took notes in a new spiral-bound note-book like a college girl studying for a final exam. In the lavish color photographs, the canapés looked as if they belonged in a jewelry store, under glass.

During the week between Christmas and New Year's, my mother used us as guinea pigs for various canapés and hors d'oeuvres, trying to finalize her selections. Rumaki, stuffed mushrooms, crab puffs, dolmades, curried meat-balls. My sister and I hated most of them. Since I could see that my mother had worked herself up into a state of major anxiety, I managed to choke mine down or surrep-titiously wrap it up in my napkin, but Bonnie would take a suspicious nibble—as if my mother were trying to poi-son her—and shout "Barf!" and pretend to gag. "Why don't you try something *normal*, like onion dip and potato chips?" she'd complain, undermining my mother's shaky confidence. For once, though, my father didn't take Bonnie's side. "Don't listen to her," he told my mother. "She has plebian tastes."

When she wasn't fretting over sample canapés, my mother was engrossed in reading *To Kill a Mockingbird*. When she finished it the first time, she read it a second time more slowly. Some sections brought tears to her eyes. She said it was the best novel she'd ever read. She tried to get my sister to read it, but Bonnie wasn't interested. I said *I* wanted to read it, but my mother said I was too young. "Wait a couple of years," she said, "when you're a little older." I tried to read it anyway, but I didn't really understand a lot of it. My mother was reading it for her book club, which Mrs. Matsumi had started. They met once a month, on Sunday evenings. My mother had been reluctant to join since the group included faculty wives, most of whom had graduated from college, and my mother worried that she would seem uneducated, having only completed high school and a year of secretarial school. But Mrs. Matsumi knew that my mother read a lot and wouldn't let my mother say no. "Just try it once," she coaxed. "If you don't enjoy it, you don't need to come back." So my mother went to the first meeting. There were six other women. They drank wine, nibbled on finger food, and discussed some alarming book about the exploding world population. She came home all aglow, fired up, and bent our ears on the subject the next night at dinner. She couldn't wait for the next book club meeting.

One evening during Christmas vacation my sister's old friend Janet spent the night. Bonnie and Janet had been drifting apart ever since we'd moved out of the old neighborhood and into a different school district. For years Janet had been like part of our family, and we were all happy to see her again. Since her last name was Andretti, my father always teased her by calling her Janet Spaghetti. He thought she was a dead ringer for Natalie Wood. She was our favorite of my sister's friends. Her new friends all seemed silllier and snobbier and more boy-crazy. When Janet saw my mother reading *To Kill a Mockingbird*, her dark eyes lit up and she said, "We just read that in school. Isn't it great?"

"You read this in school?" My mother sounded surprised.

Janet said she had a new English teacher from New York who had a beard and published poetry. Some of the parents weren't too keen on him, but the students loved him. My mother and Janet talked animatedly about the book, referring to Scout and Atticus as if they lived just down the street, until my sister huffed in and shot Janet a dirty look and said, "Come on, let's go back upstairs."

"It was nice talking to you, Mrs. Keller," Janet said apologetically as my sister dragged her away.

"It was nice talking to you, too, Janet," my mother replied. "We miss you, you know."

After they tromped upstairs, my mother sighed. I had the feeling she was wishing that my sister were more like Janet. I couldn't imagine my mother and sister ever having a regular conversation. Like two people who liked each other.

The morning of the party I heard my mother rattling downstairs in the kitchen at six A.M. I know what time it was because I looked at my new Cinderella watch with the pale-blue wristband, a Christmas present from my parents. It had come in a glass slipper. Time seemed to move more slowly since I'd started wearing a watch. I was always glancing at it, surprised by how little time had passed since the last time I'd looked. And I was always asking my mother and father what time they had, worried that because mine was a kid's watch it was designed to tick faster so that I'd have to go to bed earlier.

Even though it was still dark out, I got up and went downstairs. My mother was standing in the dining room in her faded peach bathrobe, her hair still set in brush rollers, surveying the table. She had ironed Nana's damask tablecloth and set out the new silver candelabra and chafing dish. I had gone with her to the S & H redemption center the week before, where she had turned in forty-seven books of green stamps for the candelabra and the chafing dish. We'd had to wait around for several minutes while the busy clerks hustled into the back room and eventually staggered back out with the cardboard boxes containing our merchandise. My mother had cut out an S & H green stamps ad from *Time* or *Life* that she and Mrs. Quave thought was hilarious. It showed a picture of a housewife, and underneath it said: "She works 58 hours a week. Walks 9 miles a day. Serves over 4,000 individual meals a year—more nutritious meals than your mother cooked." It was taped to our refrigerator.

At breakfast, like a general planning a military campaign, she gave us our marching orders, a neatly printed list of duties. My father was to shovel the walk and buy the champagne, whiskey, gin, and vodka at the liquor store. My sister was to tidy up the bathrooms and dust the living room. I was to vacuum the carpets and make the beds. Meanwhile, my mother raced around the kitchen—chopping, grating, mincing, mixing, slicing—like a woman possessed. At one point in the afternoon my mother sent me next door to borrow a couple of silver trays from Mrs. Quave. She asked me how things were going and I said I'd always thought parties were for fun, but they seemed like an awful lot of work, and she laughed as if I'd made a joke. Kim asked me if I wanted to play Clue—one of her Christmas gifts—but I said I had to go back and help my mother. You can help if you want, I told her, and she said okay. The three of us formed an assembly line. I spread cream cheese on small round slices of cocktail bread, Kim added a paper-thin slice of cucumber, and my mother aimed a dollop of red caviar in the center. Then we moved on to the crab puffs and crudités.

After all the elaborate preparations, I was afraid my mother would be too frazzled and exhausted to enjoy herself, but at five-thirty, while my father ran out to get submarine sandwiches for our dinner, my mother went upstairs and soaked in a hot bubble bath. She brought the radio into the bathroom and listened to soft, relaxing music. While my father and sister and I ate our subs, she remained upstairs, saying she wasn't hungry. I cleared the table while my father examined the champagne glasses and whiskey tumblers, holding each one up to the light and polishing away any cloudy spots. My sister turned on all the Christmas lights and set little crystal dishes of nuts and candies in strategic locations. We walked around straightening this or that, too restless to sit. The house felt strange, like a stage set before the curtain rises.

At seven-fifteen my father went upstairs to shower and

change into his suit. My mother came back down to the kitchen to complete the last-minute preparations. She was all ready except for her dress, with her old robe over her black slip and fuzzy pink slippers over her nylons. Made-up, perfumed, bejeweled. Her dangly rhinestone earrings twinkled in the overhead light as she ladled curried meatballs into the silver chafing dish. She looked refreshed and almost relaxed, humming some song she had been listening to on the radio.

At a quarter to eight I hung around outside my parents' bedroom watching as my mother straightened my father's new tie (a Christmas gift from Bonnie), and my father cautiously tugged at the zipper of my mother's black dress, inching it up slowly as she held her breath. She had gained five pounds over the holidays and had already made a New Year's resolution to lose them before Valentine's Day. My father stood behind my mother, resting his hands lightly on her nearly bare shoulders, and they smiled at each other's reflections in the mirror for a moment.

"I better get the ice bucket ready," my father said, and my mother nodded, leaning toward the mirror and smoothing her eyebrows with a wet fingertip.

"You look beautiful," I told her. The rhinestone necklace and earrings glittered in the mirror and lit up her face. But she didn't seem to hear me. She seemed to be frozen in some state of suspended animation. Then the doorbell rang and we could hear my father opening the front door and welcoming the first guests, who were stamping snow off their shoes. A second later my father ran up with a couple of coats that he handed to me to put on my bed, my room having been designated as the coat room. I recognized Mrs. DiNardo's gray Persian-lamb jacket. There were snowflakes melting on the fur. I could hear Denise and Dianne asking where I was. My parents had set up snacks for us kids in the family room. Kim and I were supposed to keep all the littler kids from running wild. My sister was spending the night at a friend's house and Marjorie, Kim's sister, was baby-sitting for the Gusdorfs because their baby was too young to bring along. I followed my mother down the stairs. She held onto the bannister to steady herself in her black high heels with the rhinestone clip-on bows. According to my Cinderella watch, it was 8:07.

By eight-thirty our house seemed to pulse with voices, laughter, smoke, perfume, music, and the tinkle of ice cubes in glasses. My father mixed drinks while my mother floated from one conversation to the next, reaping compliments on the food, the table, the house. Looking at her now, like a queen with her buoyant blonde hair and sparkling diamonds, it was as if she were someone completely different from the worried woman in the ratty chenille bathrobe and hair curlers who had started out the day. I could see my father beaming as the other husbands paid her court.

In addition to our neighbors, my mother had invited a few of the campaign volunteers and the members of her book club. With the ex-volunteers, she talked about the coming inauguration, the cabinet choices that were being announced or rumored, and rehashed the election returns. With the book club ladies, she chatted about various books and the new bookstore that had just opened not far from us. With the neighbors, she chatted about children, schools, and home improvements. I was struck by how full her life had become since we'd moved to our new house. It was as if she'd left her old self behind in the old house. I wondered if the people who'd moved into the duplex after us ever felt the ghostly presence of a slightly depressed, solitary woman reading piles of library books. Or lying in her room with the shades pulled, a wet washcloth draped on her forehead, suffering from a migraine. Since we'd moved into our new house, my mother's migraines had been less frequent and less severe. Her doctor had put her on a new medication that seemed to be more effective, but she hardly ever even had to take it.

In between spying on the adults, I had my hands full keeping the kids in line. Lisa Crawford wet her pants and burst into tears. She was still wearing the adhesive eye patch my father had prescribed for her weak eye, and it was creepy seeing her cry out of only one eye. Robby Dinsmore spilled Hawaiian Punch on my father's favorite chair. Denise and Dianne DiNardo got into a punching match over who was crowding whom on the sofa, just like my sister and I used to do. There was a four-year age difference between them, just like Bonnie and me, and my mother gave Mrs. DiNardo all of our hand-me-down toys and clothes. Dianne was wearing my old flannel pajamas with the rubber feet, which made me feel especially protective of her, and I let her sit on my lap, where Denise couldn't torture her.

Usually the parties broke up before midnight—we were an early-to-bed, early-to-rise sort of neighborhood—but since it was New Year's Eve, no one could leave before 1961 was ceremoniously ushered in. My father planned to uncork the champagne at the stroke of midnight. In the family room, everyone but Kim, Denise, Kevin, and I had fallen asleep. Dianne, sound asleep in my lap, was sucking her thumb and dreaming. I could see her little eyelids fluttering. In the living room I could hear the adults listening to Johnny Carson as the count- down began in Times Square. The Matsumis had brought over their portable TV. I was struggling to keep my eyes open, since normally I never got to stay up this late. Kim and I rolled our eyes and smothered giggles as Mr. Crawford crashed into the hall table, knocking the phone to the floor with a jingly crash, on his way to the powder room.

My mother paused at the door to the family room, holding an empty silver tray, and asked how we were doing. She looked a little dazed, but happy. Before we could answer, the phone rang. At first I thought it was just Mr. Crawford knocking the phone off the table again, but it continued to ring until my mother hurried into the kitchen to answer it. I heard her gasp and say, "Oh, my god." I thought maybe something had happened to my sister. A car accident. I pushed Dianne off my lap and fol- lowed my mother into the living room. She whispered something to my father and hurried over to the Gusdorfs, who were chatting with the Quaves. Mr. Gusdorf reached out and caught his wife's glass as she let it slip from her hand. They all set their drinks down and flew out the front door without bothering to get their coats. Mrs. Gusdorf's glass teetered on the edge of the mantle and then toppled off, splashing dark liquid onto the beige carpet.

I went back into the kitchen, where my father was reeling off directions to the Gusdorfs' house into the phone. "Hurry," he shouted, "for godsakes, hurry!"

"Who was that?" I asked as soon as he slammed down the receiver.

He brushed past me, and hurried back into the living room, where a hush had fallen and everyone was huddled together, waiting. "The ambulance is on the way," he told them. "I'm sure everything's going to be fine." He looked white and shaky and didn't sound all that convincing. My mother had left with the others, and he kept looking anxiously out the window in the direction of the Gusdorfs' house as if he wanted to bolt after her but felt it was his duty as the host to stay put.

"What happened?" I asked Mrs. DiNardo. My heart was pounding.

"Marjorie says the baby's choking." She patted my hand distractedly as she stood up. "I think I'll check on Denise and Dianne."

She left me standing there alone. On the miniature television screen the ball in Times Square was descending and the lighted billboard was flashing 11:57. I looked at my Cinderella watch. It was two minutes slow. The champagne bottles were lined up on the dining-room table but no one made a move toward them. Mrs. Matsumi walked over and clicked off the TV. Everyone turned toward the front windows as we heard the wailing siren round the corner into our cul-de-sac. My father walked over and told me to go back to the family room and keep an eye on the kids. I protested that Kim and Mrs. DiNardo were in there already. I didn't want to leave. "Please." He held up his hand for silence. "Just do as I say."

It seemed like an hour, but it was only fifteen minutes later that my mother came back, breathless and shivering but smiling. "The baby's going to be fine," she announced. "Everything's under control."

Everyone let out a collective sigh of relief and started to talk at once, crowding around my mother, clamoring for details. It was as if the party had died and then, just in the nick of time, come back to life. My mother explained that, apparently, the baby had pulled a plastic grape from the bowl of artificial fruit on the kitchen table when Marjorie set her down for a moment to check her diaper. (I shut my eyes and pictured the baby's chubby fist. I felt the strength of its grip on my finger.) The baby must have slipped the grape into her mouth, and when Marjorie picked her up, she started choking and turning all red in the face and couldn't catch her breath. Marjorie had panicked and called here. By the time they all got to the Gusdorfs', the baby was purple. Fortunately, Betty Quave had taken a CPR course, and knew what to do; the plastic grape popped right out. The baby was breathing again by the time the paramedics arrived. They said she seemed fine, but they took her to the hospital just to be on the safe side.

My mother paused for a breath and Kim, who had been listening with wide, scared eyes, said, "Where are my parents?"

"They took your sister home," my mother told her. "Poor Marjorie's pretty shaken up. How 'bout you? You want to go home, honey?"

Kim nodded, and my father hoisted her up and gently smoothed her rumpled hair. "Come on, kiddo. I'll take you next door."

"Suzy, go get Kim's jacket," my mother said.

I ran upstairs and came back down with her pink parka

that matched mine. My mother draped it over Kim's shoulders and my father said, "Back in a minute. Don't anybody leave." We felt the blast of icy air as the door opened and shut behind him.

"Well," Mr. Crawford said, weaving toward the dining-room table. "All's well that ends well." He picked up a bottle of champagne, poured the first glass, and handed it to my mother. "Happy 1961!"

My mother's hand was still trembling as she raised the glass and took a sip. Mr. Crawford filled the glasses, sloshing half of it onto the tablecloth, and passed them around. The champagne sparkled and fizzed.

"A toast to our lovely hostess," Mr. Dinsmore said, holding his glass aloft.

"*L'chaim!*"

"What's that mean?" I said.

"To life," my mother answered soberly as she clinked her glass against the others', and I could see she was thinking about the baby. About how we would all be feeling at this moment if the baby had died. About how incredibly swiftly—in less time than it takes to uncork a bottle of champagne—you can fall from the heights to the depths.

I know that because that's what she told me—or words to that effect—when I got up in the middle of the night with a stomachache from all the candy and cheese puffs I'd consumed during the party. I saw the light on downstairs and found my mother at the kitchen table smoking butts from the ashtrays my father had made it a point to empty into the trash before going to bed. My mother was sitting there with three or four of the longest butts, different brands with various color lipstick rings, lined up in front of her. When she heard my footsteps, she crushed out her lit cigarette and hurriedly swept the other butts into the palm of her hand. She only had twenty-nine more days to go before the six months were up and my father gave her the new car he had promised.

"It's just me," I said.

"Thank god." She sat back down and relit the butt. "The house reeks of smoke anyway. I figured your father wouldn't notice."

"My stomach hurts," I complained.

She nodded, unconcerned, and said, "I keep thinking about the baby. What if she'd died? Everything would be different"—she snapped her fingers—"just like that. That's how it happens." She closed her eyes and exhaled a long, tremulous stream of smoke. "God knows how any of us can sleep at night."

She was scaring me. She hadn't bothered to remove her makeup and there were smudges of dark mascara ringing her eyes. She had tied a scarf around her hair to try to preserve the set for one more day, and she looked like some gypsy fortune-teller staring down at the glass ashtray as if it were a crystal ball.

"My stomach really hurts," I said, aggrieved that she seemed to care more about some baby that might have died but didn't than about her own daughter's health. "Maybe it's appendicitis."

She reached over and rested her palm flat against my forehead for a moment. "You'll be as good as new in the morning," she said. "Go back to bed."

I snatched up the rest of the butts and doused them under the faucet one at a time, then tossed them back into the trash. She just watched me. I thought she might be angry, but when I turned around to face her, she pulled me closer and gave me a kiss. Mollified, I trudged back upstairs to bed. And in the morning, just as she had predicted, I felt fine.

The next day, New Year's, the Quaves had invited us over to watch the Rose Bowl—or at least watch our fathers watching the Rose Bowl. Wisconsin was playing Washington. During the holidays the Quaves' house was a jungle of plastic poinsettias, holly swags, pinecone wreaths, and mistletoe hanging in every doorway. A huge cornucopia of wax fruit sat on the dining-room table. As I followed my mother into the kitchen, I saw the Golden Delicious apple that Mr. Crawford had tried to take a bite into on Christmas Eve after he'd drunk too much spiked eggnog. You could still see his toothmarks in the wax. Kim was upstairs practicing the flute. Her mother said she'd be down in ten minutes and offered me a cup of mulled cider. It turned out that Kim had real talent for the flute and had become Mrs. Brach's pet. I had already given it up. Fortunately, my flute was only rented. For Christmas, Kim's parents had given her her own flute in a black leather case lined with blue velvet.

"Where's Bonnie?" Mrs. Quave asked, setting a plate of homemade ginger snaps on the table.

"She wanted to stay home and sew," my mother answered. "As if she doesn't have enough clothes. How's Marjorie?"

Mrs. Quave shook her head. "She hasn't come out of her room. She doesn't want to talk about it. She feels so guilty, and she thinks everyone's talking about how it was all her fault."

My mother shook her head. "These things happen. No one blames Marjorie."

"Tell her that." Mrs. Quave sighed.

From the living room we could hear our fathers groaning and Mr. Quave cursing over something in the football game.

"And Charlie—" Mrs. Quave rolled her eyes and lowered her voice—"was up half the night worrying over being sued. Those were Everbloom grapes. He called his lawyer at eight A.M. this morning—tracked him down in Bermuda—and talked for twenty minutes. Then he called up the plant manager and told him to get the design department working on kid-proof grapes. Ones you can't pull off the stem."

Kim hollered for me to come up, so I ran upstairs to her room. We played Clue and then the Barbie game, which one of her aunts had sent her. Pickle got in trouble for chewing up the dagger and the revolver from the Clue game while we were busy playing Barbie. When it was dark out, my mother called upstairs and said that it was time to go home. Our fathers seemed down in the dumps. I could tell that Wisconsin had lost. "Forty-four to eight," my mother bent down and whispered into my ear.

On January twentieth, my tenth birthday, President Kennedy was inaugurated. It was the second time in my life that the inauguration had coincided with my birthday, but this was the first one that I was old enough to remember. It seemed like the whole nation was celebrating my birthday. At least all the Democrats.

My parents surprised me with a ginger kitten with white paws. I had been begging for a kitten ever since I could talk, and I couldn't believe it when I looked up from blowing out the candles on my birthday cake and my father flicked the lights back on and I saw my mother holding the kitten with a big red bow around its neck. My sister gave me a fancy yellow rhinestone cat collar.

I spent the rest of the evening playing with my kitten. He was a male and I decided to name him Jack, in honor of the new President. When I went to bed, my mother was lying on the sofa in her robe and fuzzy slippers, watching the festivities, the various inaugural balls, on TV. I carried Jack upstairs and settled him under the covers next to me. I fell asleep listening to him purr. But sometime later (11:32 according to my Cinderella watch), I woke up and felt the empty space beside me. I looked around my room and couldn't find him. I could hear the television still on in the family room, directly underneath my room. I ran downstairs and was about to ask my mother if she'd seen Jack when I saw him curled up, sound asleep, on her lap. I felt a stab of jealousy.

Jackie was on the television wearing a long white gown with long white gloves.

"Doesn't she look lovely?" my mother murmured, her eyes fixed on the screen.

The kitten mewed in protest as I scooped him up and scolded him for running away from me. "You're mine," I whispered into his fur. "You're supposed to love me best." He wriggled out of my arms and ran underneath the couch. I stood there examining the angry red scratch on my pale wrist, watching the tiny beads of blood rising to the surface. On the TV an orchestra was playing a waltz or something. Everyone was dancing, including the new President and First Lady. Suddenly my mother leapt up and pulled me toward her and waltzed me around the den, humming to herself with her eyes closed. I held back at first, stiff and self-conscious, but gradually I let the music carry me along, resting my cheek against the soft warmth of my mother's robe, and finding myself effortlessly following her lead. Waltzing or fox-trotting or whatever it was we were doing.

PART TWO

Two weeks after President Kennedy's funeral I came home from school and found my mother sitting at the kitchen table with her coat on, writing a note to my father. It was the first time since the assassination that I had seen her dressed. Her hair was washed and brushed, although not set. She had just pulled it into a stubby ponytail. When she saw me she folded the note in half and slipped it under the saltshaker so I couldn't see what she had written. There was a glass of milk and a couple of Fig Newtons on a napkin on the table.

"Have a snack," she said, sliding the cookies toward me, "and then we'll go." She glanced at her watch.

As if in reflex I glanced down at my own wrist. A small gold watch with a dainty black band that I had bought with my baby-sitting money to replace my old Cinderella watch. "Go where?" I mumbled, my mouth full of cookie.

"Nebraska," she said matter-of-factly, as if we went there every day.

At which point I noticed the two suitcases standing by the door leading into the garage. Her heavy white Samsonite and my red-plaid canvas overnight bag. I was astounded. For days on end my mother had dragged herself around the house in her bathrobe, barely speaking. Not bothering to cook or clean or even bathe. Not answering the telephone. A walking zombie. As far as I knew, she had not set foot outside the house since the afternoon of the assassination, when I was sent home from school early and found her crying. Sitting in front of the TV in her brassiere with her hair dripping wet. She hadn't washed her hair since then. Until today. And now here she was, dressed and packed, ready to travel over five hundred miles.

"What about your doctor's appointment?" I asked. I knew my father was planning to leave work at four o'clock and personally escort her to the doctor's office since she had ignored the last appointment he'd made for her. He understood what a blow the President's death had been to her, but he felt she should have snapped out of it by now. She was acting like a grieving widow, he said. She seemed more stricken than Jackie.

"I don't need a doctor," she said. "I'm not sick." She grabbed my empty milk glass, rinsed it out, and set it in the dish drainer. "Do you have to go to the bathroom before we leave?" she asked as if I were ten years old.

"This is crazy," I protested. "I've got school tomorrow. Why are we going to Nebraska? Did someone die or something?"

"I don't know why exactly, but I'm going." She stood

up and pulled on her leather gloves. "I can go alone. I just thought you might like to come with me."

I thought about running next door to ask Mrs. Quave's advice, but she was having a difficult pregnancy, confined to bed for the final six weeks until the baby was due, and I was afraid that by the time I got back, my mother would be gone. She had tried calling my mother, but my mother wouldn't answer the phone. They hadn't been as close lately anyway, ever since they'd had an argument over birth control. My mother knew that Mrs. Quave didn't really want another baby at her age. Marjorie was a sophomore at the university and Kim, like me, had just started junior high school that fall. My mother didn't have much use for religion.

"What about the cat?" I asked, looking at Jack's bowls of food and water sitting on the floor next to the suitcases.

"Your sister will take care of him. He'll be fine." My mother looked out the window and frowned. "I want to get a good start before dark. They're predicting snow." She picked up her heavy suitcase and opened the door.

"How long will we be gone?" I said, picking up my bag and following her out to the garage, still in shock. I couldn't believe she would really go. She had never driven more than ten miles outside Madison and was afraid to drive in snow. Even in good weather she still drove below the speed limit.

"A couple of days," she shrugged. "Maybe longer. Does it matter?"

Of course it matters, I thought, but just set my suitcase in the open trunk on top of hers. She slammed the trunk and climbed into the driver's seat.

My father had lived up to his promise and bought my

mother a new Nash Rambler. It was turquoise with white upholstery. She had seemed awed and intimidated by the shiny new car. She was used to driving Mrs. Quave's beat-up old Fairlane. The first week she would go out to the garage and just sit behind the wheel, listening to the radio, getting the feel of it. It was February—the weather was unpredictable and she was afraid of skidding on black ice. At night she studied the owner's manual from cover to cover, sometimes asking my father questions about second gear or high beams versus low beams. My father, who wasn't very mechanical compared to most fathers, enjoyed answering my mother's questions. The second week, on clear days, she ventured out to the grocery store and back. Then to the dry cleaner's or post office, cautiously expanding her driving radius. I always went with her, no matter how boring the errand, out of the sheer thrill of sitting there beside her, breathing in the brand-new car smell. Before each outing my mother would visualize her route, sometimes even consulting a map, and would not turn the key in the ignition until she knew precisely where she was going. It drove my sister crazy, and they had a big fight when my mother refused to drive Bonnie to a movie on State Street because the traffic was too dense and the streets were too confusing near the campus. Bonnie called her a wimp and said it was a waste of a perfectly good car. But by the spring, when the weather warmed up, my mother was cruising around town, slowly but surely. And on particularly nice afternoons, she even took to going on drives out in the country. Sometimes I'd go with her and sometimes she'd go alone. Still, after almost three years, the odometer read 6,895 miles the afternoon we backed out of the garage en route to Nebraska.

My mother had a map open on the seat between us, with her route highlighted in yellow Magic Marker. I picked it up and studied it. Just as I'd suspected, our destination was Troy, Nebraska, my mother's hometown, which none of us had ever been to. As far as I knew she had not set foot in the place since she had left it over twenty years ago. Or had any desire to. In fact, two summers earlier we'd taken a family vacation to the Grand Canyon, and on the long drive home along Route 80— mile after unscenic mile of flat cornfields—my father had suggested that we take a little detour to Troy. It was only twenty or thirty miles out of our way. "What do you gals say we have lunch in Troy?" my father had suggested. "Check out the place where your mother's face launched a thousand ships." He winked at us in the rearview mirror. Bonnie and I said "Okay," mildly interested in any diversion from the boring drive, and my father seemed all set to take the exit off 80 until he smiled over at my mother and saw the look on her face.

"What's the matter?" he asked, crestfallen. "You don't want to go?" I don't know what he'd expected. I guess that she'd be charmed by his interest in her hometown, his willingness "to lose time" when he was so notoriously hell-bent on "making good time" on long trips.

My mother shook her head grimly and said, "It's out of our way, and there's nothing there to see. It's just a dull little town like a million others. Anyway, it's too early for lunch. I'm not hungry."

It was true that we'd had a big breakfast in Ogallala, but it was, in fact, lunchtime. My stomach was growling. However, something about her tone of voice didn't invite discussion. My father shrugged and shook his head, as if to say there was no understanding women, and sailed past the exit. Twenty minutes later we stopped at a McDonald's in Lincoln. My mother, I noted, didn't have any trouble eating a cheeseburger and french fries.

My mother saw me studying the highlighted map and said, "I thought we could spend the night in Iowa City. It's supposed to be a pretty little town."

"Okay," I said. It would be dark before we got there and I knew my mother didn't like to drive in the dark. Plus, I remembered that she had asked my father to stop in Iowa City on that same drive back from the Grand Canyon, later in the same day that we had driven through Nebraska. "I've always been curious about the town," she'd said. My mother liked to check out various colleges and universities, using Bonnie and me as an excuse, even though my father said that it was a ridiculous waste of money to go to college somewhere else when we had one of the best universities in the country in our own backyard. Anyway, he'd looked at the little clock on the dashboard—he had traded in his Bonneville for a Buick LeSabre—and said he didn't want to take the time, even though it was dinnertime, and we had to stop somewhere to eat. I figured he was just getting back at her for having rebuffed his earlier suggestion to eat lunch in Troy.

I turned on the radio and fiddled with the tuner until I got a song I liked. "It's My Party" by Lesley Gore. I had read an interview in *Teen* magazine and knew that she went to Sarah Lawrence College, a girls' school in New York. There was a photograph of her in front of a beautiful old building, surrounded by girlfriends, and I'd decided that that was where I wanted to go to college.

When I mentioned it that night at dinner, my father said, "Good luck. I hope you can get a scholarship."

"Oh, Glen," my mother sighed. "You don't need to be so negative. It doesn't hurt to have goals."

"Do you know how much those schools cost?" he protested. "Twenty-five-hundred dollars a year! They're for rich girls."

My mother had shot me a look that said "Don't mind him" and had changed the subject. She had wanted my sister to go to Vassar, where Jacqueline Bouvier had gone, but the guidance counselor had told her that Bonnie's grades weren't high enough. Besides which, Bonnie didn't want to go any place where there were no boys. She had a thin stack of college admission applications she had to fill out by January fifteenth. She had already taken the SATs twice. I couldn't really believe that my sister would be going away next year, even if it was just to a dorm across town. I couldn't imagine the house without her, even though she was hardly ever home anymore, and when she was, she was usually in her room with the door closed.

As we drove past the outskirts of Madison, the commercial areas thinned out and then disappeared as we cruised along the highway into farm country. The sky was bleak and gray, the ground frozen a stubbly brown with skimpy patches of stubborn snow here and there, like shaving cream. My mother gripped the steering wheel tightly in both black-gloved hands, her shoulders hunched forward, her eyes focused on the road. She didn't seem to be in a vacation spirit. Usually when we went on trips, she brought along a generous stash of Life Savers, candy bars, and gum, which she would dole out to us like party favors. I had become almost accustomed to my mother's depressed silence during the past couple of weeks. I had a lot of questions, but I didn't feel like asking them. My mother's heavy silence seemed like some contagious virus that had spread to my own vocal cords. After Lesley Gore there was a commercial for Tab and then "I Will Follow Him" by Little Peggy March, another of my favorite songs. As the dusk settled and deepened, I thought about my father coming home from work and finding the note. I didn't know what it said, but I knew it wasn't very long. Two, three sentences at the most.

At five o'clock the news came on the radio. Frank Sinatra Jr. had been found alive after having been kidnapped three days earlier, blindfolded and drugged. His father paid $240,000 in ransom money. The city of New York had renamed Idlewild Airport. From now on it would be known as the JFK International Airport. I turned the dial until I found some music. My mother hadn't listened to the news much since the funeral. Lyndon Johnson's Texas drawl affected her like fingernails on a blackboard. She thought that Lady Bird was an idiotic name for a grown woman. Let alone the First Lady.

The weekend of the assassination had seemed like some grim, surreal camping trip. My father closed his office and came home early. He built a fire in the fireplace. Outside it was gray and frigid, the neighborhood deserted. My parents had been planning to go to a small dinner party at the Matsumis' to celebrate the publication of Dr. Matsumi's new book on Japanese internment camps during the war. But of course they didn't go out. And neither did the DiNardos, whom I was scheduled to baby-sit for that evening. Even my sister canceled her plans. It was the first Friday night since I could remember that the four of us were all home together. We ate whatever was in the house—sandwiches, Dinty Moore beef stew, Chef Boyardee ravioli, hot dogs and beans. We ate off star-spangled paper plates left over from a Fourth of July barbecue. Nobody bothered to clean up the kitchen. We were out of cat food, so Jack ate a can of undiluted clam chowder and then threw up. It seemed impossible to leave the house, as if we were all marooned in our own houses, miles from civilization. But instead of a campfire we huddled around the TV set. I don't think we turned it off once the whole three-day weekend. My mother never went to bed. She just dozed fitfully on the sofa. I was sitting right next to her on the sofa when Jack Ruby shot Lee Harvey Oswald on the TV—*live*—right in front of our eyes. My father gasped and shouted, "Did you see that? Did you see that? My god, what next?" But my mother just sat there, perfectly still and silent, seemingly unmoved, as if nothing could surprise her anymore.

It was a two-lane highway, dark and mostly empty. Every so often we would get stuck behind some farm vehicle going even farther below the speed limit than my mother. Outside Dubuque, the traffic thickened and I could see my mother grip the steering wheel tighter as she negotiated the tricky route through the congested center of town during rush hour. Once she missed a sign and we had to backtrack for a few blocks until she found where she should have turned. She seemed panicky, on the verge of tears. It was an old, run-down riverfront town. I saw two girls about my age walking out of a record shop. One of the girls had limp blonde hair like my own, whipping around in the damp wind, and I felt sorry for her having to live in such a dismal place, although maybe when the sun was shining it wasn't so bad.

Half an hour or so outside Dubuque, my mother stopped for gas in a little town called Cascade.

"You hungry?" she asked as the attendant, a teenage boy with a limp, filled the tank and cleaned the windshield.

"A little," I said. Actually I was starving, but I knew she wanted to wait and eat supper in Iowa City, which was still maybe a hundred miles away.

"You have to use the john?" she asked.

I shook my head.

"Well, I think I will." She got out of the car and walked into the rest room. I fiddled with the radio but couldn't get any good songs. It was cold in the car. My mother seemed to be taking a long time. I remembered that on our trip to the Grand Canyon, somewhere in Colorado, my mother had asked my father to pull off at a rest stop. My sister and I waited in the car while she went into the bathroom. My father got out and stretched his legs. We waited and waited, my father glancing impatiently at his watch. My sister was embroidering a white halter top she'd made. I was doodling around on my Etch-A-Sketch. Finally my father stuck his head in the backseat and said, "Why don't you girls go inside and see what's taking your mother so long?"

"I'm busy," Bonnie snapped. "Suzy can go."

"Why do I always have to do everything?" I fumed as I got out of the car and slammed the door shut and trudged around the side to the ladies' room.

My mother was standing at the sink in her pale-yellow Ban-Lon shell and white underpants, furiously washing her matching shorts in the sink.

"What's the matter?" I said.

"Oh, Suzy, thank goodness," she sighed. "Would you run out to the car and get me another pair of panties and shorts from my suitcase?"

I looked more closely and saw a rusty bloodstain on the back of her white underpants. I knew she must have unexpectedly started her period. My sister had started hers the year before and my mother had taken that opportunity to explain to me all about menstruation—or "the curse," as she and Mrs. Quave called it when they were speaking privately.

"What'll I tell Dad?" I asked, embarrassed.

"Tell him I had an accident. Just get the shorts, okay?"

A fat woman in a flowered muumuu and rubber thongs walked in with a chubby little boy in tow. He looked at my mother standing there in her underpants and said, "Why's that lady in her underwear?"

"None of your beeswax," his mother said, pushing him into an open stall.

I ran outside and told my father my mother'd had an accident and needed some clothes from her suitcase. He didn't ask any questions, just opened the trunk and then popped open her white Samsonite suitcase. I rummaged around and grabbed a pair of pink panties and black Bermudas and ran back to the ladies' room. My mother was chatting to the fat woman, who was washing her hands at the next sink. They were from Milwaukee, as it turned out. As my mother thanked me and ducked into a stall to change, the fat woman winked at me, as if including me in the vast sorority of bleeding women.

I shivered and turned the car heater up full blast.

Through the plate glass I could see my mother paying for the gas. A few sparse snowflakes were starting to fall like listless confetti. Across the street, in the darkness, a neon martini glass blinked on and off. My mother hurried back to the car, sat down in the driver's seat, and dumped a small pile of candy, Life Savers, and gum into my lap. "Trick or treat!" She seemed to be in a better mood. As I opened up a box of Junior Mints and she held out her hand for me to shake a couple into her open palm, I thought maybe the trip might turn out to be okay after all. Anything was possible. The events of the past month had proved that.

I closed my eyes, lulled by the steady rhythm of the road, and rested my head against the seat. It was too dark to see much anyway, even if there had been something worth looking at. Pretending to be blind, I groped for a Junior Mint, popped it into my mouth, and let its cool sweetness melt on my tongue. Ever since I'd seen *The Miracle Worker* a few months earlier, I'd been pretending to be blind whenever I had nothing better to do. In one of my mother's magazines I had read an article about how Patty Duke had prepared for the role of Helen Keller, walking around with a blindfold on for days on end. When I grew up I wanted to be a teacher like Annie Sullivan. Either that or an actress like Patty Duke.

Suddenly I smelled smoke and opened my eyes. There was a pack of Lucky Strikes lying on the dashboard. My mother took a long drag and then reached out and nonchalantly flicked her ash into the open ashtray.

"What are you doing?" I asked accusatorily.

"What does it look like?"

I cracked the window and fanned the air vigorously, barking out a forced cough.

"We all have our little weaknesses, Suzanne," my mother said. "Your father's, for instance, is being holier than thou." She looked at me pointedly.

I rolled the window back up. My mother smiled. For the first time in two weeks. Something inside her seemed to relax as she settled back in her seat, inhaling deeply and exhaling slowly, as if her lungs were reluctant to relinquish the smoke after such a long period of abstinence. Three years. As the smoke filled the car's interior, I floated in a haze of nostalgia. Back to a time when my mother bought Lucky Strikes by the carton and bought me candy cigarettes that I used to smoke along with her, imitating the way she would pick flecks of tobacco off her lip and cup her hand to catch the falling ashes.

By the time we entered Iowa City, the pack was almost empty, and the smoke was so thick my eyes were watering.

"Abstinence makes the lungs grow fonder," my mother quipped as she lit her second-to-last cigarette.

I knew she would never be able to successfully fumigate the car and that my father would feel betrayed when his keen nose detected the smoke. The only time I ever saw him seriously lose his temper with my sister, who could do no wrong, was when he caught a whiff of smoke from her clothing and demanded that she dump the contents of her purse onto the kitchen table. There was a half-empty pack of Salem Menthols, which he seized and crushed in his palm. Then he grounded her for two weeks. Although he relented and let her attend two football games to fulfill her sacred duties as a cheerleader.

A sign for the Hawkeye Motel glowed up ahead: VACANCY.

"We might as well check in here," my mother said. "Then we can go into town for dinner."

She drove into the nearly empty parking lot and pulled up in front of the office. I sat in the car with the motor running while she checked us in. When she climbed back into the driver's seat she handed me a big, square, gold key embossed with the number 217.

"He says it's on the other side of the pool," she said, squinting and craning her neck. It was hard to read the room numbers in the dark.

"There." I pointed to a room on the second floor near the end.

She pulled into a parking space and shut off the engine. We lugged our suitcases up the narrow stairway. As her suitcase clanged against the metal stairs, she said, "I asked for a second-floor room because I heard on the news it's safer for women traveling alone."

I handed her the key, and she unlocked the door and flicked on the overhead light. It was a nice enough room, with two double beds. Green shag carpeting and matching green print quilts.

"Which bed do you want?" my mother asked.

"Doesn't matter."

She hefted her suitcase onto the bed nearest the window, then inspected the bathroom. "Looks nice and clean," she reported back.

I'd had to pee for the last fifty miles. The instant she came back out I made a beeline for the bathroom. When I'd finished peeing, I unwrapped a tiny bar of soap and washed my hands. There was an extra bar of soap which I slipped into my bag. I liked to collect them as souvenirs.

My mother had turned on the TV and opened her

suitcase. "It's kind of chilly in here," she said, shrugging her arms into a beige cardigan. "I turned up the heat."

Walter Cronkite was on. The picture was fuzzy—he looked like a figure in one of those paperweights you shake to make the snow fall—and the volume was so low you couldn't hear him. Still, he was a familiar and comforting presence in a strange motel room. I had never been in a motel before without my father.

"Have you ever stayed in a motel without Daddy?" I asked.

My mother was standing in front of the mirror applying lipstick. Lipstick! I thought, she must be feeling better. She hadn't even used deodorant since the assassination. She touched up her lip line with the tip of her pinky finger and said, "When I first moved to Chicago, I rented a room in the YWCA for a week before I found an apartment to share."

"How old were you?"

She blotted her lips with a tissue and tossed it into the trash basket. "Nineteen. Well, almost nineteen."

It was hard to imagine. I remembered seeing an old photograph of her standing with a friend, a fellow secretary, on the shore of Lake Michigan. They were wearing light summer dresses, their full skirts ballooning in the breeze. With one hand my mother was modestly deflating her skirt, and with the other hand she was clamping down her straw hat, which seemed to be threatening to blow off across the water. The friend was laughing, but my mother's expression was serious. She looked beautiful but terrified, as if she were standing in the middle of a hurricane.

"It's almost seven," she said. "You must be starving."

I nodded. I was feeling a little sick from all the candy.

"Let's drive into town and find a nice restaurant." She snapped off the TV and yanked the drapes closed, then slipped the room key into her coat pocket.

"Aren't you going to call Dad?" I asked as she headed for the door.

"Not now," she said. "I'm hungry."

"He must be worried." I hesitated, staring at the black telephone on the night table between the two beds. But she was already out the door.

It had stopped snowing. We cruised straight into town and found the university on the banks of a river. The town was much smaller than Madison. The downtown was only two or three square blocks of shops and restaurants. We parked and walked to the sidewalk, where a couple of college girls were standing at a bus stop, chatting. They both wore big fluffy earmuffs, and as they spoke, their breath puffed in the cold air.

"Ask them if they know a good place to eat," my mother bent down and whispered in my ear.

"Why don't you?" I protested. I knew that both my father and sister would march right up to the girls without a second thought, but my mother and I were introverts. My father would shake his head when we balked over asking directions from strangers. "You're two of a kind," he'd say. "Shrinking violets."

"Never mind," she said, walking past them. "We'll find something."

And a minute later she stopped in front of a place called The Brown Bottle and read the menu posted on the window. "They've got spaghetti," she said. "How's that sound?"

I followed her into the dim interior of the restaurant. The hostess looked at us and said, "Only two?"

My mother nodded and we followed the hostess's clicking high heels to a booth in the corner.

"Is there a cigarette machine?" my mother asked. The hostess pointed around the corner. "Be right back," my mother said. I opened the large red menu. The smell of marinara sauce and the Italian music playing in the background reminded me of Janet Andretti's house, and I felt a little homesick for Madison.

My mother slid into the booth, unwrapped the fresh pack, and lit up. I slid the glass ashtray over toward her. "Thank you, honey." She opened her menu. "I feel like a glass of Chianti." She rubbed the back of her neck. "I'm a little stiff from all that driving."

"What are you going to eat?" I asked pointedly. I had not seen her eat a regular meal since the assassination. She must have lost at least five pounds.

"Fettuccini Alfredo," she said. "Does that meet with your approval?"

I nodded, encouraged, but still skeptical about how much of it she would actually eat.

The waitress came and took our orders. She looked a little like my sister, the same sleek blonde page boy and startling aquamarine eyes, like the ocean in a tourist postcard. I could tell she wore tinted contact lenses like Bonnie's. Our father's business had boomed in the last few years, with everyone trading in their glasses for contacts. My sister was constantly popping one out by accident and ordering everyone to freeze in place until it was found. I was usually the one who first spotted the tiny blue sphere lying on the floor or tablecloth. Once I even found it floating in Jack's water dish. My father joked that I should have business cards printed up—"Suzanne Keller: Private Eye"—and leave them on the counter in his office. My mother had even flirted with the idea of getting herself a pair of blue contacts, the color of her eyes in the wedding photograph she'd had colorized, but she couldn't stand the thought of a foreign object in her eye. We had all borne witness to my sister's un-stoic agony as she followed my father's schedule, increasing the number of hours she wore them each day until her eyes adjusted. A triumph of vanity over cowardice.

The waitress brought my mother's Chianti and my Coke along with a basket of bread. I buttered a thick slice of bread and wolfed it down as my mother sipped her wine. The few other customers were mostly older; it didn't seem to be much of a college hangout.

"I bet that's a writer," my mother whispered and gestured to a man with shaggy gray hair, a beard, and steel-rimmed glasses sitting alone and reading a book. "There's a famous school for writers here, you know."

I did know because my mother had mentioned this fact when she was trying to persuade my father to stop in Iowa City on our way home from the Grand Canyon. My sixth-grade English teacher, Mr. Ziller, had mentioned to my mother at a parent-teacher conference that he thought I had genuine writing talent and should be encouraged.

"Flannery O'Connor studied here," my mother said.

I nodded as if I knew who that was. The waitress brought our food and my mother asked for another glass of wine.

"Looks good," my mother said, twirling a forkful of fettuccini.

As I sprinkled parmesan over my spaghetti I wondered what my father and sister were doing for dinner.

"Mmmm," my mother murmured, "delicious."

The bearded man took a ten-dollar bill out of his wallet and left it on the table. As he walked by our booth I noticed that the book he was carrying had a long technical-sounding title, something about geophysics. "He's a scientist," I said. My mother shrugged.

By the time I had polished off most of my spaghetti, my mother's plate was still heaped with fettuccini. She had eaten, at most, maybe half a dozen bites.

"I thought you said it was delicious."

"It is." She took another small bite. "It's just very filling."

My mother smoked another cigarette while I ate a dish of lime sherbet. She yawned, covering her mouth, and said, "Excuse me. I assure you it's the hour, not the company."

I looked at my watch. "It's only eight-twenty."

"All that driving made me sleepy." She stifled another yawn. "I'm looking forward to getting into bed. How about you?"

Since the assassination she hadn't bothered going to bed. The days and nights blended together as she lived in her bathrobe and dozed on one of the sofas in the living room or family room.

"I'm sort of tired, too, I guess," I admitted.

She paid the bill and we left.

Back in our motel room with the door safely chain-bolted, we changed into our pajamas, turned on the TV, and got into bed. *The Fugitive*, with David Janssen, was on. We had missed the first few minutes, so the plot was difficult to follow, plus, I kept waiting for my mother to pick up the phone and call home. My mother's eyes kept drooping shut and I was afraid she would fall asleep. When the next commercial came on, I said, "Don't you think we should call Dad and tell him we're okay?"

My mother sighed and slid deeper under the covers. "You call him." She gave an exaggerated yawn. "I'm too tired. Tell him I'll call tomorrow." Then, as I was dialing, she added, "Don't tell him where we are."

"Why not?"

"Because he's liable to do something crazy like come get us or send the police or something."

"The police!" I said, shocked. "What for?"

"Who knows?" She got out of bed and went into the bathroom. I figured if anyone was going to do something crazy, it wasn't going to be my father.

The phone started to ring and my father picked it right up, as if he'd been standing next to it, waiting.

"Hi," I said, "it's me. Suzanne."

"Where are you?" He shouted to my sister, "It's them!"

"I don't know exactly. Some little town in Iowa, I think." It sounded lame and unconvincing.

"Let me talk to your mother."

"She's in the bathroom. Taking a bath," I lied. "She said she'd call you tomorrow."

"What's going on there? What's this all about? Are you okay?"

"I'm fine," I said. "She just wants to—"

"What's the number there?" he interrupted. "I'll call back in ten minutes. I want to speak to your mother."

"I've got to go," I said. "We're fine."

"Wait a min—"

I hung up the receiver and sat there, shaking. I don't know why I didn't just give him the number that was clearly printed on the dial. Part of me wanted to call him right back and tell him where we were. *"We're at the Hawkeye Motel in Iowa City! Come get us!"* But another part of me didn't want to let my mother down. After all, she could have left me behind, too.

When she emerged from the bathroom, she had set her hair in brush rollers and tied a chiffon scarf around her head. I took this as a positive sign. Maybe she knew what she was doing. Maybe it made perfect sense and would all become clear to me soon.

"What did he say?" She turned off the overhead light and crawled back under the covers.

"He wanted to know where we were and stuff. He sounded kind of upset."

"What did you tell him?"

"Nothing. I told him you'd call him tomorrow."

She stretched her arm out across the space between our two beds and gave my hand a little squeeze.

"I want to get an early start in the morning," she mumbled, half asleep.

Within ten minutes she was snoring very lightly, more like a purr, really, than a snore. I missed Jack purring on the pillow beside me, even though the minute I fell asleep he would go find my mother and curl up with her. I wondered what Kim would think when I wasn't at the bus stop in the morning. I watched the end of *The Fugitive* and then turned off the TV and got back into bed. I had left the bathroom light on like a night-light.

Outside on the highway I could hear traffic, trailer trucks grinding their gears as they passed slower trailer trucks. Earlier in the afternoon some of the truck drivers had tooted their horns and waved at my mother and me, as if we were two teenage girls out for a joyride. Tomorrow we would be in Nebraska. It was a straight shot down Interstate 80. No more two-lane highways, stuck behind poky tractors or horse trailers. Five or six hours at the most. We could be there by lunchtime. I figured my mother must have some sort of plan she just wasn't ready to talk about yet.

I fell asleep and in the middle of the night I woke up and was frightened by the sight of my mother's empty bed. I sensed her absence even before I turned on the lamp to confirm it. Panicked, I called out, "Mom?"

"In here!" she called back from the bathroom.

I leaped out of bed, afraid she was sick, and ran to the bathroom. She was sitting on a pillow on the floor, her back resting against the tub, reading a book, smoking a cigarette.

"What are you doing?" I grumbled, my heart still pounding. "I thought you were so sleepy."

"Well, I woke up," she shrugged, "and couldn't get back to sleep. I didn't want to disturb you."

By the number of butts floating in the toilet bowl, it looked as if she'd been up for some time. "I have to pee," I said.

Her knees cracked as she stood up and left the room to give me some privacy. She left the book open on the tile floor. It was Dr. Matsumi's book, *Prisoners of War: From Pearl Harbor to Manzanar*. He had presented my mother with an autographed copy, as he did everyone in our neighborhood, but my mother was probably the only one who would actually read it.

I flushed the toilet and got back into bed. In the room down below we could hear a TV blaring. My mother got up and headed back toward the bathroom. "You should try to sleep," I said. "It's three-fifteen."

"Who's the mother here?" she joked.

"Good question."

"I'm just a little nervous," she confided, tucking me in and kissing me on the forehead.

"About what?"

"Tomorrow." She turned off the light.

"What about tomorrow?"

"I don't know," she said. "That's the point." She stood by my bed for a moment as if she didn't know where to go.

It was a big double bed. I patted the empty side. "You can sleep here if you want."

"Thanks, honey, maybe I will." She slid in next to me, fluffed her pillow, and let out a sigh.

Within minutes she was asleep, while I lay there wide awake and restless, trying not to disturb her, until dawn.

The next morning we ate breakfast in the motel coffee shop. I was wearing the same plaid kilt and Shetland sweater from the day before because my mother had packed all the wrong clothes. Things I never even wore anymore, things that didn't match. When I complained about it, she said she would buy me some new clothes in Lincoln. She looked rested but seemed wound up and jittery. She lit the wrong end of her cigarette and had to stub it out, looking around, embarrassed, to see if anyone had noticed. A nice looking man in a booth across from ours smiled and winked at her. Flustered, she dropped a forkful of scrambled egg onto her slacks. She dipped her napkin in water and dabbed at the stain, a furious blush spreading from her cheeks to her throat and across the open V neck of her chest. She managed to choke down maybe a third of her eggs and a half slice of toast while I made short work of my blueberry pancakes. At the cash register on the way out, she tapped her fingernail against the glass candy display case and said, "You want anything?" I pointed to several kinds of candy, Life Savers, and gum, which the clerk piled in a heap on the counter. My mother seemed to be in a daze, not paying any attention until the cashier, an old biddy with a beehive, said, "My, someone has a sweet tooth."

Snapped out of her reverie, my mother looked at me and shook her head. "We're only going to Nebraska, not California."

Sheepishly, I handed two Baby Ruths, a 5th Avenue, and a Mars bar back to the clerk.

It was one of those hard, bright, diamondlike winter mornings with the sunlight reflecting off the sparse snow that covered the flat fields like a lace tablecloth. My mother was wearing her dark glasses. A cigarette dangled precariously between her lips as she gripped the steering wheel with both hands while a huge truck shuddered past us, blasting its horn.

"There should be separate highways for trucks," she said.

"Good idea." My feet were propped against the dashboard. I was already bored stiff and we had only been on the road for an hour. If my father were there he'd have yelled at me to get my feet off the dashboard, but my mother didn't care. I looked at my watch and realized that I'd be in social studies right at this moment if I were back home. I didn't much like the teacher, Mr. Svoboda. Spit gathered in the corners of his mouth when he talked, and everything he said was taken right from the textbook, practically verbatim. Thinking about missing social studies, I felt a little happier to be in the car in the middle of nowhere. Although my next class would have been English with Mrs. Ritchie, which I loved. The week before she had assigned an essay—"Describe a Branch of Your Family Tree"—and had read mine aloud to the class, along with Gretchen Baird's, as one of the two best examples. I felt a little guilty because I had made up a grandmother, my mother's mother, who was dead years before I was even born, but in my essay she was alive and well in Florida, where we visited her every winter. There was a kidney-shaped pool in her backyard, along with two orange and lemon trees, and she squeezed fresh orange juice for breakfast every morning and lemonade for lunch. "Very vivid use of detail," Mrs. Ritchie had written in red ink, "A+."

Mrs. Ritchie had read the essays anonymously, like she always did, but everyone knew who wrote them, like we always did. The instant she read aloud the title of the essay, the author's face would flush and then he or she (usually it was a she since the girls were the best writers) would stare down at the desktop, stricken by a mixture of pride and embarrassment. Gretchen's essay was about being adopted, and the class was so quiet as Mrs. Ritchie read it, you could hear the chalk screeching on the blackboard in the next room. "All my adoptive parents knew was that my biological mother was seventeen years old, blonde, blue-eyed, healthy, from West Virginia, and unmarried," Gretchen had written. "When I first found out, I hated her for giving me away, but then I started thinking about how if she had kept me, I would have had a whole different life. Nothing would be the same. I would not even be me." After Mrs. Ritchie finished reading, the class stared at Gretchen with silent awe, as if she had just revealed the fact that she was actually from Mars—a superior but alien being.

In the cafeteria that lunch period I had set my tray down next to where Gretchen was sitting by herself. Her family had just moved to Wisconsin from one of those little states back east, Delaware or Rhode Island, and she usually sat with another new girl, Judy Stoner, who must have been absent that day. We were both a little trembly from just having had our essays read out loud in class, and we smiled at each other, feeling this bond between us—even though I knew that her essay was real and brave, whereas mine was just fake and loaded with the sort of description that English teachers always eat up.

"I liked your essay," she said shyly. "I thought it was better written than mine."

"No way." I shook my head. "Yours was a million times better. I mean yours was so much more"—I was about to say "honest" but felt silly and said—"more original."

Gretchen blushed and stabbed a bite of hot dog. "I hope everyone doesn't think we're just sitting together because the teacher liked our essays the best," she'd said, surprising me since I was thinking the same thing.

"That's their problem." I'd shrugged indifferently, as if such a worry would never enter my mind.

My mother looked at me and said, "A penny for your thoughts."

"I was just thinking about school."

She nodded, obviously hoping I'd elaborate on the topic. We had barely spoken all morning. I unwrapped a butter rum Life Saver and popped it into my mouth and sucked noisily. After a minute my mother said, "I hate the smell of butterscotch. It reminds me of Nana."

I had thought about writing about my real grandmother for my essay, but it had seemed too depressing. Who wanted to read about false teeth and insulin injections?

We stopped for lunch at some restaurant with a fake Dutch windmill on the outskirts of Des Moines. It had a little gift shop with postcards and corny souvenirs and travel supplies. I thought about buying postcards to send to Kim and Gretchen, but it didn't seem like that sort of trip, and I figured I'd probably be back before the postcards even reached them. My mother bought a pack of Lucky Strikes and a bottle of Bufferin.

As we were walking back to the car, my mother arched her back and rotated her neck. "Too bad you're not old enough to drive."

"You could have brought Bonnie," I said snippily. "I didn't ask to come along."

My sister had gotten her driver's license last year. Even though she had passed drivers' ed, my father had insisted upon taking her out for private lessons with him until he was satisfied that she knew what she was doing behind the wheel. I think mostly he just used it as an excuse to make her spend some time with him. She was always out doing something with her girlfriends or with Roger, her boyfriend, whose ambition in life seemed to be to deliver pizzas in a series of more expensive cars. He'd bought a used Mustang and had to get a job delivering pizzas on weekend nights in order to pay back his parents. So on Saturday nights my sister would drive around with him, artfully sneaking bits of pepperoni and olives off the pizzas so as no one would notice. It drove my father crazy. His idea of a date was a boy arriving in a suit with a corsage. He said that when he was in high school he'd worked afternoons at a lumber store so that he could save a few bucks to take his girlfriend out to a decent restaurant on Saturday night. He would wear a sports coat and a tie and open the car door for her. Roger just sat in the driveway and honked.

"Times change," my mother would say whenever my father got himself all worked up over Roger's shortcomings. Or, "It's not as if she's going to marry him."

"Perish the thought," my father would groan. Or, "Thank God for small favors."

The radio stations kept fading in and out as we drove. I would fidget with the dial, trying to get something besides country western, until my mother finally ordered me to sit still. Just outside Omaha a heavy, slushy snow began to fall. As the road slickened and the traffic congealed, my mother's posture grew rigid, her lips pressed together in a grim line. Her tension communicated itself to me. I sat erect and alert like a copilot in heavy turbulence. My mother had slowed to a crawl, forcing other cars to pass us, splattering our windshield with a blinding veil of muddy slush.

"I must have been out of my mind," my mother moaned to herself, on the verge of panic.

"You're doing fine," I told her by way of a pep talk. We were crossing over a multilane bridge and I knew bridges made my mother nervous under the best of circumstances. As we slowed down to exit off the ramp, the rear end of the car fishtailed. A sickening, helpless sensation. I squeezed my clenched fists between my thighs—my mother's face was dead white—and I flashed on the highway patrol calling my father and informing him that we were officially deceased. Then I thought, How ironic: My mother takes a trip to her hometown, which she hasn't returned to in over twenty years, since her parents were killed in an accident, and ends up being killed in an accident herself. It was the sort of thing that happened in movie plots, only she wouldn't actually die, she would make a miraculous recovery—since movies always had happy endings.

Half an hour later we had made it through the city and were back on the open highway about fifty miles outside Lincoln. Once we had negotiated the Lincoln turnoff, my mother pulled the car over onto the shoulder of the road, rested her forehead against the steering wheel, and let out a long, quavery sigh of relief. If she were Catholic, like Mrs. Quave, she would have made the sign of the cross. Instead, I handed her a cigarette. She thanked me and punched in the car lighter with a shaky hand. It was still snowing. I knew you weren't supposed to park on the shoulder unless it was a bona-fide emergency, and I was worried that a policeman would pull over to see what the problem was. Somehow it felt as if we were two fugitives at large.

I turned the radio back on. Now that we were near a big city, there was a variety of decent stations to choose from. I found "Puff the Magic Dragon." My sister had a Peter, Paul, and Mary album she played practically non-stop. I knew my mother liked it. The music seemed to soothe her. She turned the motor back on and pulled back out onto the highway. There wasn't much traffic.

"We're on the home stretch now," she said.

I nodded. "The snow seems to be letting up a little."

She turned the volume up and began to sing along. After a couple of seconds, I joined in, purposely messing up the lyrics the way my father would do to make us laugh: "Puff the magic dragon lives by the sea/He stuffs himself with liverwurst in a land called Germany!" Our voices grew louder and stronger, reaching a rousing crescendo by the end of the song. Then we looked at each other and laughed, heartened by our spontaneous outburst.

A commercial came on. My mother edged the volume back down. We were passing a big billboard for Boys Town, which I knew from the movies was some sort of orphanage. And I wondered how my mother felt seeing the sign, being an orphan herself. I wondered if there was a Girls Town somewhere and whether if my mother's aunt and uncle hadn't taken her in, she would have ended up somewhere like that. I remembered that when my parents flew to Puerto Rico the year before—a long-belated fifteenth anniversary celebration—they had had a will drawn up in case the plane crashed. They told us that Uncle Carl and Aunt Ruth would be our guardians if anything ever happened to them, but not to worry because nothing would. My sister snorted and said it better not because there was no way she was going to live out in the sticks with a bunch of smelly animals.

The scenery in Nebraska was even more boring than in Iowa. Flat and treeless. Compared to Nebraska, Wisconsin looked like travel posters of the Swiss Alps. I kept looking at my watch and holding it up to my ear, thinking it must have stopped. It was 2:58 when we saw the first Lincoln exit. My mother surprised me by saying, "I figured we'd spend the night in Lincoln. We can see the university."

"It's not that late," I said. "It won't be dark for another two hours."

"So?"

"So, I thought we were going to Troy. I thought that's what this trip was all about."

My mother shrugged. "I'm exhausted. I'd rather wait till the morning." When I didn't respond, she added, "Hopefully the weather will be better tomorrow."

I felt let down. We had come this far, and now she wanted to stop when we were within half an hour of the place. It seemed as if she were just stalling, a sudden attack of nerves. "I think we should just keep going," I insisted. "We're so close."

"I can't."

"Why not?"

"I have a headache."

I looked at her to see if she was telling the truth. I could, in fact, see a vein pulsing in her temple, and her eyes had that bruised look. I sighed. Since we had moved to our new house, my mother's migraines had nearly disappeared. Now, this would be the third one in two weeks. Since the assassination. It was as if a fragment of the bullet had lodged itself in her brain.

She took the 9th Street Downtown exit. The highway ended, funneling us into town. Everything looked dull, squat, and ugly.

"Look, there's the capitol building." She pointed up ahead.

I could see a tall white building with a gold dome and some sort of statue. "What's that thing on top?"

"The sower," she said. "He's sowing grain."

I thought of my sister hunched over her sewing machine, whipping up some new fashion creation. I wondered if she even missed us.

We drove into the center of town, up O Street, and checked into the Cornhusker Hotel. The room was expensive, more than what my father would have paid, but money seemed to be no object to my mother on this trip. For all the attention she paid, she might as well have been spending Monopoly money. We rode the elevator up to the sixth floor. The room was large and luxurious. I had never stayed in a real hotel before, just motels. In the desk drawer I found embossed stationery, notepads, and postcards, which I tucked away in my suitcase. There was also a leather-bound menu for room service. I couldn't believe the price of a hamburger. My mother walked out of the bathroom holding a glass of water and two prescription pills that she downed in a single gulp. Then she lay down on the bed closest to the window and draped a warm washcloth over her forehead.

"You feel really bad?" I asked.

"I just need to rest," she said. "Unwind a bit. Then we'll go get some dinner."

"We could call room service," I suggested, testing the limits of my mother's extravagance. "Then you wouldn't have to go out."

"We'll see. Let's see how we feel in an hour." She closed her eyes. "If I fall asleep, wake me up when you're hungry."

I wanted to turn on the television but didn't want to disturb my mother. I knew from experience that this was the critical juncture: either the headache would just go away or it would turn into a full-blown migraine that could last for two days. I wished I'd brought a book to read. There was nothing to do. I lay down on the other bed and daydreamed about Kenny Snow, who sat next to me in home room. I wondered if he'd missed me and wondered where I was. Sometimes we passed notes. And sometimes he walked with me to my next class, which was right next door to his next class. Kim said he liked me, but I knew he had a crush on Corrinne Bell. Whenever she was around, he got all tongue-tied and the tips of his ears flamed bright red. Corrinne was a real snob, and I liked to create little scenarios in which Kenny would say to me, "Sure she's pretty, but she's so shallow. Not like you"—gazing deep into my eyes, then down at the ground, his ears burning crimson.

After a while my mother sat up and said she was feeling better, she just needed to eat something. She pulled back the heavy drape and looked outside. "It's stopped snowing. I feel like getting a little exercise."

We put on our coats and gloves and boots and rode the elevator back down to the lobby and walked out into the cold night air that seemed to shock us both wide awake.

"When I was in high school, we used to come here on the weekends. It was the big city." She paused at the corner and looked in both directions. "There used to be this great hamburger joint, but everything's changed so much. I hardly recognize it." She crossed the street and I followed her. "I think maybe it was down this way."

But she couldn't find the place. Three blocks later, after I'd pointedly mentioned the possibility of frostbite, we settled for a hole-in-the-wall Mexican restaurant with striped blankets and sombreros hanging on the walls.

"A margarita sounds good," my mother said, "but I suppose I shouldn't drink on top of those pills. They're pretty strong."

"One probably wouldn't hurt," I said. I liked my mother when she was slightly tipsy. She seemed to glow brighter, like a three-way bulb turned up a notch.

In the end she had two margaritas and one taco. I had a Coke, two tacos, and fried ice cream—something I'd never heard of—for dessert. The margaritas seemed to have rejuvenated my mother. As she paid the bill, she looked at her watch and said, "It's still early. Maybe we could find a movie to see."

"Great." I grabbed a handful of pastel mints from a bowl by the cash register. My mother and I both loved movies. It hardly mattered what was on the screen. We just liked sitting there in the dark enveloped by the smell of buttery popcorn.

We walked past one theater showing *Stolen Hours* with Susan Hayward, which my mother didn't think would be appropriate for me. And another showing *Vertigo*, which we had already seen years ago. Then a couple of blocks farther down we spotted a marquee that read "*Lilies of the Field* with Sidney Poitier." My mother's face lit up. "I wouldn't mind seeing that," she said casually, as if it didn't really matter, but I could tell she really wanted to see it.

"Me, too," I said, as if I really meant it, even though I didn't have a clue as to what it was about.

We had the theater practically to ourselves. As luck would have it, the opening credits had just ended as we walked in, groping our way down the aisle in the pitch-black. Sidney Poitier, driving an old station wagon, was rattling along a dry, dusty road. He pulled up to some nuns who didn't speak English and asked for some water for his radiator. The old German nun who was in charge of the convent or whatever was a real witch, but the younger nuns were sweet and giggly. In the end, Sidney Poitier wound up building a chapel for them and everyone pitched in and helped. In the beginning, I thought it was going to be pretty boring—this Negro guy helping a bunch of nuns—but it turned out to be really good. And my mother and I walked out of the theater in high spirits. "That was a very uplifting movie," my mother said. "I'm glad we saw it."

"Me, too." I was thinking that Kim would probably like it since she had nuns for Sunday school. For her confirmation, the year before, she got to choose a confirmation name. We had spent hours compiling long lists of our favorite names and then narrowing them down to a short list. I would have chosen "Hayley," like Hayley Mills, but Kim said it had to be a saint's name and there was no Saint Hayley. After changing her mind about a hundred times, she finally took the name "Annette" in honor of Annette Funicello.

When we got back to our hotel room, my mother went into the bathroom and ran the water in the tub. Then she shrugged her sweater off over her head and stepped out of her gray flannel slacks. I looked away as she stood there in her white underpants and bra. She had large breasts that both repelled and fascinated me. I had only seen them bared once, in the women's locker room at the community swimming pool. A quick, lurid glimpse as she lowered the top of her bathing suit, lifted her bra off the wooden peg, and hooked it awkwardly behind her back. Her flesh had been goose-pimpled, and, in my memory, her nipples jutted out as firm and pink as pencil erasers.

While my mother was taking her bath, I turned on *The Tonight Show*, changed into my pajamas, and climbed into bed. Since Johnny Carson had replaced Jack Paar, my father had taken to staying up later to watch Johnny. I felt bad that my mother hadn't called him. I thought about picking up the phone and dialing our number in Wisconsin, but I didn't really know what I could say. I figured it was between him and my mother, whatever it was. I was just along for the ride.

When my mother finally emerged from the steamy bathroom, fresh and fragrant in her pink nylon night-gown, I pretended to be asleep, curious to see what she would do if she thought she was alone and unobserved. She turned on a lamp in the corner and sat down in the armchair with the phone book in her lap. She sighed as if the book was almost too heavy to lift as she placed it on the table next to a notepad and pen. Through half-closed eyes, I watched as she seemed to flip through, looking for particular names. Then she shut the phone book and closed her eyes. She was so quiet, it took me a couple of minutes to realize that she was crying.

When I woke up the next morning, she was gone.

I couldn't believe it even when I found the note on the table with a fifty-dollar bill anchored in place by a jar of Ponds cold cream. "Dear Suzanne," it said, "Buy yourself some breakfast in the coffee shop and a new outfit at Miller & Paine. I'll be back by noon. Love, Mom." I looked at my watch. It was only 8:15. Where could she go at that hour? Nothing was even open yet. How could she just go off and leave me in a strange town? I couldn't believe it. I was so mad I called room service and ordered a large orange juice, a blueberry muffin, and an apple. The orange juice alone cost a dollar.

While I was waiting for my breakfast to arrive, I got dressed and turned on the TV to the *Today* show. They were talking about the Warren Commission's report on the assassination, which had concluded that Lee Harvey Oswald was just some lone nut. My mother didn't believe it. She thought Castro or Khruschev was behind it. I had heard her arguing with my father about it the day before we left. Only two days ago. It seemed like a month. Suddenly I realized it was Friday the thirteenth, which seemed like a bad omen. There was a knock on the door and a voice called out, "Room service!" A man in a uniform wheeled in a silver cart. Just like in the movies. Everything looked perfect. The butter was shaped like little seashells. There was a frilled paper hat on the glass of orange juice. There was a tiny jar of orange marmalade, which I put in my suitcase. The apple was so red and shiny it looked like one of Mr. Quave's wax apples. But I didn't have any appetite. I wanted to go home. My father would just be leaving for work. I walked over to the telephone on the table and picked up the receiver to call him, then noticed that my mother had written a phone number on the pad of paper next to the phone book. Maybe that's where she was, I thought. Maybe she'd left me the number on purpose. Maybe I should talk to her before I talked to my father. I dialed the number she had written down. It rang several times before a female voice answered, "Nebraska State Penitentiary."

"I must have the wrong number," I said, "sorry," and hung up. I dialed the number a second time, more slowly and carefully. This time it rang only once before the same voice answered. "Nebraska State Penitentiary."

I couldn't think what to say. Then I said, "You mean like a prison?"

"Yes," the woman answered impatiently, "this is the prison. How can I direct your call?"

I slammed down the receiver and sat there staring at the number my mother had jotted down, thinking maybe I had misread one of the digits, but her penmanship, as always, was neat and precise. It was one of the things she prided herself on. "Good penmanship," she would declare, "is next to godliness."

My mouth felt dry. I lifted the paper hat off my orange juice and drank it slowly. My mind was blank. The juice tasted fresh. I flashed on my essay about my fake grandmother with the orange trees in her backyard in Florida. Suddenly it occurred to me how easy it was to invent stories, to fool people into believing whatever you wanted them to believe. "Very vivid use of detail—A+!" And my mother hardly used any detail at all. She hardly ever mentioned her childhood, and when you asked her a question, she would say she didn't remember. Even though she had a remarkable memory for everything else—dates, names, things she read in books, little things that had happened to my sister and me when we were small. I remembered once, a couple of years ago, asking my father why he had fallen in love with my mother and his saying, "Your mother wasn't like the other girls I'd dated. She didn't like to talk about herself, but she had this way of getting others to open up. People, total strangers, would tell her anything. There was just something about her." He shrugged. "She was warm and cool at the same time. It's hard to explain." But I had known what he meant even then. "Like Baked Alaska," I'd said. He had laughed and nodded, and later I heard him repeating it to my sister, who didn't get it.

My mother's stiff white suitcase was sitting in the corner of the room, closed but not latched. A nylon stocking dangled out one side. I knelt down in front of the suitcase and opened it. A whiff of my mother wafted out and, for an instant, she seemed to materialize like a genie from a bottle, then drift off. I didn't know what I was searching for. Clues, evidence. But of what? When I was younger I used to search through my parents' bureau drawers, which were off-limits to me. My father's dresser was tall and narrow, my mother's long and low. It was the same in Mr. and Mrs. Quave's bedroom. The very shapes of the dressers themselves seemed to hint at some primal difference between men and women. My father's drawers were neat and spare, his balled socks lined up in rows as straight as an abacus. There was nothing much of interest. My mother's drawers were crowded and messy. I'd find a rhinestone earring stuck to a nest of nylon stockings, half of which had runs in them. Or a silk scarf that had wormed its way inside a girdle. But the most disturbing find was a tube of K-Y lubricating jelly nestled in a pile of brassieres. At the time I didn't know what it was for, exactly, but I knew it must have something to do with sex even though it looked as innocuous as a tube of Ben-Gay or Ipana. Otherwise it would have been in the medicine chest and not the bedroom.

My mother had not bothered to unpack much except for her toiletries and a couple of outfits hanging in the closet. I rummaged through layers of underwear, stockings, shoes, sweaters, belts, and scarves, finding nothing of interest. Then I slid my hand into the puckered satin pockets that lined the suitcase. I pulled out a fake pearl necklace, a matching gold cloverleaf brooch and earrings she had bought at a Sarah Coventry party hosted by Mrs. Crawford (like a Tupperware party for jewelry), a tortoiseshell barrette, and a pair of crumpled Peds. Nothing. But as I was cramming the Peds back into the satin pocket, I felt a hard lump in one of the toes and pulled out a tarnished silver locket on a chain that I had never seen before. Prying the heart open, I saw two tiny, grayish photographs. My mother as a young girl and a boy with dark hair and dark eyes. My mother's light hair waved softly around her face. She was wearing a pale cardigan with small pearl buttons up the front. I was unnerved by how much she looked like my sister. The boy looked nothing like my father. He looked serious, no smile, and movie-star handsome. Like Gregory Peck in *To Kill a Mockingbird* (which my mother and I had seen twice), only younger.

I put everything back in the suitcase and then paced

around the room, bored and restless, wondering what to do next. The department store wouldn't be open for another hour. And anyway, everyone would wonder why I wasn't in school. Maybe some busybody clerk would call a truant officer. I pulled the drapes back and looked outside. It was gray and ugly. A thin dandruff of snow was falling but not sticking. The weatherman had said it was ten below zero with the windchill factor. I didn't feel like talking to my father. I felt a million miles away, in some foreign country. Afraid to venture outside my hotel room.

I thought of Marta Jaspersen, our foreign-exchange student from Finland who had lived with us the year before last. My mother, all aglow with Kennedy's Peace Corps spirit, had volunteered us to take an AFS student despite my father's and sister's lukewarm response to the idea. Marta was in my sister's grade, and the idea was that Bonnie would befriend her and make her feel at home. Only Bonnie wanted nothing to do with Marta, who was plain-looking and studious and spoke perfect, stilted English. To add insult to injury, Bonnie and I had to share a bedroom so that Marta could have her own room.

"Why do I have to give up my room?" Bonnie protested. "Just because she's a foreigner."

"Ask not what your country can do for you," my mother had airily replied. "Ask what you can do for your country."

The whole thing had been a disaster from beginning to end. It might have worked out if Marta had been pretty and outgoing like Paola, the Andrettis' exchange student from Italy the previous year, in which case my sister might actually have warmed to her and taken her under her social wing. But Marta's idea of a good time was playing Scrabble with my mother and me or cross-country skiing in the fields behind our development. She had seemed relieved when June had come and it was time for her to return home. She still occasionally wrote to us and invited us to come for a visit. "Finland," my father had muttered, "is not high on my list of places I'd like to see."

Looking out the hotel window at the bleak, stingy Nebraska landscape, I might as well have been in Helsinki. I wished my mother had grown up in Florida or California. Somewhere warm and colorful. Somewhere you could send a postcard from and make people wish they were there.

After the war ended, my parents had actually up and moved to Honolulu with a vision of starting a whole new life five thousand miles away from the Great Plains. They were newlyweds unencumbered by furniture, appliances, children. My father's college roommate, an air force lieutenant stationed at Bellows Field, sent them a Christmas card boasting about Honolulu—the weather, the beaches, the business opportunities—and my parents, braced to endure another long, cold Chicago winter, thought, Why not?

They rented the bottom floor of a little white frame house on Oahu, and my father teamed up with another optometrist whose partner had moved back to the mainland. My mother found a part-time job filing and typing in a travel agency. In the photographs of that period, they are tanned, smiling, dressed in bright prints, pleased with themselves. But they only lasted a year. My mother developed island fever, just like my father's partner's ex-partner who had moved to Los Angeles. It wasn't, apparently, all that uncommon even though they had never heard of it before. People not used to living on an island would often become claustrophobic, panicked by the thought of being surrounded by thousands of miles of ocean, cut off from the rest of society. And then my mother discovered that she was pregnant. For a while they hoped that the island fever was just the result of her hormones being out of whack. But the nightmares and anxiety attacks only became more frequent and more severe. Accompanied by migraines.

Three months before my sister was born they gave up and moved to Madison. Bonnie was born in my grandparents' farmhouse. My father's family had thought the whole idea of moving to Hawaii was crazy to begin with, and weren't shy about saying "I told you so." According to my mother—when I overheard her telling Mrs. Quave the whole story of their brief sojourn in paradise—my father took the whole thing in stride, but my mother felt bad, the way Eve must have felt when she got them thrown out of the Garden of Eden.

My sister, who lived for summer and the perfect tan, never really forgave my parents for moving back to the Midwest before she was born. Whenever my mother complained about the cold, Bonnie would sigh and say, "It's your own fault. We could be living in Hawaii." She had learned to swim at the age of three. "My little Esther Williams," my father used to call her. And unlike the rest of our family, she never seemed to burn, no matter how long she stayed in the sun. Somehow, it seemed, she had managed to acclimate herself to the tropics during her six months as a fetus in Honolulu.

I looked at my watch. Only nine-thirty. The hotel room was hot and stuffy, but the windows didn't open. I lay in bed and watched *I Love Lucy*, followed by *Pete and Gladys*. Then, bored with TV, I washed my hair in the bathroom sink and set it on pink rubber Spoolies even though it would take forever to dry without a hair dryer. My hair was so thin and wispy that normally it dried in about two minutes when I didn't set it. Last summer I had talked my sister into giving me a Toni home permanent that looked pretty good at first, until my hair started to turn green from the chlorine in the swimming pool and break off. I refused to leave the house for two days. My mother dragged me to Verna's little basement beauty shop. Verna fingered my hair and shook her head. "Oh, you poor thing," she'd said, "what happened to you?" Then she cut my hair in a pixie. Six months later I was still growing it out.

Since I hadn't eaten much breakfast and I was bored, I called room service again and ordered a turkey sandwich and a Tab. We had skipped Thanksgiving this year. No turkey or pumpkin pie. My mother wasn't in the mood to cook or give thanks. The President had been dead less than a week. My sister ate dinner at her friend Melanie's house. They were rich Republicans with a Puerto Rican cook. My father and I ate Swanson's chicken potpies. I don't remember my mother eating anything.

I was still waiting for room service and watching *Father Knows Best* when the phone rang. Startled, I walked over and picked up the receiver, thinking it must be my mother. I was all set to bawl her out for leaving me alone when a voice I didn't recognize said, "Suzanne?"

"Yes?" I whispered, afraid that it could only be tragic

news. A traffic acccident. A nurse calling to inform me that my mother was in a coma.

"This is Peggy Lovejoy, an old friend of your mother's. I'm calling from the emergency room—"

"Oh no!" I choked, my throat clenching shut like a fist.

"She's fine, honey. Your mom's okay." She sighed and mumbled under her breath, to herself or someone standing right next to her, "Shit, I knew I was going to screw it up." In the background I could hear a Dr. Thompson being paged. "She slipped and broke her wrist, and she got a real bad chill, but she's going to be all right."

There was a knock on the door. Room service. I ignored it, but they just knocked louder. "Just a second," I mumbled, "someone's at the door."

"Don't open the door for any strangers," she said.

"It's room service," I told her, setting down the receiver. I opened the door and said, "I'm on the phone." The waiter set the tray down on the bureau and left, shutting the door behind him as I picked up the phone again. "Okay," I said.

"Well, the thing is, they want to keep your mom here overnight, just for observation, you know, just to be on the safe side—apparently she bumped her head a little, too, on the ice—and anyway, she wanted me to come pick you up and bring you back to my house for the night."

"Are you in Troy?"

"That's right. I can be there in half an hour, give or take a few, and—just a minute . . . "

I heard a little kid crying, then what sounded like two little kids crying. "Eric!" she scolded. "Give that little boy his truck back! Right now! You hear me?"

I could hear what sounded like a smack. One of the kids stopped crying. One started to whimper.

"Excuse me," she apologized, out of breath. "He missed his nap and he's real cranky." She sighed. "So how 'bout if you just get your stuff together, and wait for me in the lobby. 'Bout half an hour, okay?"

"Okay."

As soon as she hung up, I thought of about twenty questions I should have asked her. Now I would just have to wait until she got here. I didn't even know how I'd recognize her. I supposed she'd figure out who I was—a twelve-year-old girl (almost thirteen) sitting alone in the lobby with two suitcases. My legs felt rubbery when I stood up and started throwing our stuff into the suitcases. It only took about five minutes. Then I sat on the chair next to the bureau and nibbled a couple of slices of turkey and a lettuce leaf, checking my watch every minute or so. When twenty minutes had passed, I decided I'd better take the Spoolies out of my hair and head down to the lobby. My hair was still damp as I unwound each Spoolie and tossed it into the sink. I had already packed my hairbrush and had to rummage through my suitcase to find it. Even though I brushed it as vigorously as I could, my hair still looked weirdly dented and lopsided, with some sections straighter than others. I tried to make a ponytail, but my hair was still too short. Disgusted, I left the Spoolies lying in the sink. Then I put on my winter coat and half dragged, half kicked our two suitcases down the carpeted hall to the elevator. A Negro maid emerged from one of the rooms, carrying a pile of dirty towels, and said, "You all alone?" I nodded and pressed the Down button, trying to look calm and collected, as if I traveled alone all the time—one of those child prodigies: a concert violinist or maybe a chess whiz.

Peggy—that's what she told me to call her—drove a rusty, red pickup truck. I had never ridden in one before. When she pulled up in front of the hotel, she just ran into the lobby, grabbed my suitcases, and said to hurry, the baby was asleep in the car. Since there were only two seats in the truck, I had to sit in the passenger seat and hold the sleeping baby in my lap all the way to Troy. His drool slobbered onto my coat. From one side he looked like a blonde angel, but after we were on the highway, I let out a gasp when he rolled his head and I saw a maroon birthmark that started up under his hair and spread through his eyebrow down to his cheek. I pretended to cough, but Peggy looked over and said matter-of-factly, "It's called a port-wine stain. Nothing we can do. It's a shame. I don't even notice it anymore, but kids can be cruel." She reached over and stroked the hair out of his eyes.

I nodded. There was a girl at school with the same sort of birthmark on the side of her face. She parted her hair on the side and tried to let it hang in her face; she held her head at an odd angle so the hair would cover that side of her face as much as possible, but you could still see it. Except for the birthmark she was pretty, but she seemed really shy, and her only friend was a chunky girl with a brace on her leg from polio. It was sort of sad and pathetic, but touching, when you saw them together, and when I read *The Heart Is a Lonely Hunter*, I thought of them. It was my favorite book after *To Kill a Mockingbird*. They both made me cry.

"What happened to my mother?" I asked, partly to change the subject and partly because I wanted to know.

Peggy fished into her purse—a red fake-leather bag with duct tape on the strap—and lit a cigarette.

"My mother smokes Lucky Strikes, too," I said, thinking maybe she had bummed a pack from her.

"I know." Peggy winked at me. "We smoked our first cigarette together. Shared it. I sneaked it from my aunt Gloria's purse."

"How old were you?"

"Your age, more or less." She cracked the window open and fanned the smoke away from the baby's face. "I knew your mother from since before I can remember. Families lived right down the road from one another. Went all through school together." She held up two crossed fingers. "We were like this. People called us Cheng and Eng. You know who they were?"

I shook my head.

"Famous Siamese twins," she said. "From China."

"Oh, yeah," I said, vaguely remembering a gruesome photograph Marjorie had shown Kim and me from one of her gross science books. I had never met anyone who'd known my mother as a child, and for a moment I was so distracted that I forgot that she was lying in the hospital.

Until Peggy said, "I about died when she rang the doorbell and I opened the door and there she was. After all these years." She took a long draw on her cigarette and blew out three perfect smoke rings. "She was as white as a sheet, in shock, probably, holding onto her wrist. She'd driven out to her old house and gotten her car stuck in the snow. There was no one around. No one lives out there anymore. She'd tried to push the car, see-ing if she could just jog it a little, and she slipped. Broke her fall with her wrist."

The sleeping baby was heavier than a sack of potatoes and my legs were going numb. I tried to shift his weight without waking him. We were driving through flat, mostly empty countryside, a stray house here and there. The sun was trying to shine through the hazy gloom. Once in awhile it would break through and brighten everything up for a couple of seconds so that it looked almost pretty, then slide back under a cloud.

"How'd she get to your house?" I asked.

"Walked. It's about a quarter of a mile. She probably hoped someone would come by and give her a lift, but no one did. We're the closest house. She was about froze to death."

"You took her to the hospital?"

Peggy nodded. "She couldn't move her wrist. And she had a lump the size of an egg on the back of her head. Said she felt sort of woozy. I thought she might have a concussion."

"Does she?"

"Maybe a mild one, but nothing serious." She tossed her cigarette butt out the window. "It's been twenty-two years, but I recognized her right off. She hasn't changed that much. Still just as pretty."

There was a little edge to her voice, like maybe jealousy or envy, and I looked at her more closely. She was small and thin, with smooth skin, bright blue eyes, and shiny brown hair cut in an adult version of a pixie. She had on a red car coat and jeans rolled up at the cuff and rubber walking boots. She looked sort of like a grown-up kid. Cute rather than pretty. She had a nice, warm smile that made you feel as if she liked you and made you like her right back.

We passed a car dealership and an Alpo factory.

"We're almost there now," she said. "I thought we'd go back to my house first, get you settled in, then visit your mother after supper. How's that sound?"

"Fine," I said, although I would have preferred to go directly to the hospital. We passed a sign saying WELCOME TO TROY, NEBRASKA. POP. 5,911.

"You never been here before?"

I shook my head. She nodded to herself. We passed a Dairy Queen, an Elks lodge, and skidded to a stop at a stop sign. Unlike my mother, she drove with speed and confidence. "Well," she said, "you haven't missed much."

As if sensing that we were almost home, the baby opened his eyes and seeing me, a total stranger, started to wail. "Gramma!" he shouted.

"I'm right here, Squeezix." She reached over and tickled his tummy. "This is Suzanne. Can you say hello to Suzanne?"

He grunted and shoved his mittened thumb into his mouth and sized me up suspiciously. I was surprised. I had assumed that she was his mother. She was the same age as my mother. She didn't look like a grandmother. She must have seen my confusion because she said, "I take care of him while my daughter's at work."

"What about his father?" I asked without thinking.

"He's not in the picture."

The baby reached out and yanked on the silver button of my coat. "Button," he said.

We turned onto a long gravel driveway. The pebbles rattled off the bottom of the truck as Peggy barreled heedlessly up toward the house. I thought of how my father would have crawled along, wincing and cursing as stray pebbles nicked his shiny paint job. I saw a two-story white house with peeling paint and black shutters, one of which was missing, like an open parenthesis. We had just learned to use parentheses in school, and I was crazy about them. I used them a lot (too much, my teacher said), but I loved the idea of jamming extra little thoughts into sentences, making them as long and full as possible.

"This is it," Peggy announced, reaching over and hoisting the baby onto her shoulder. "Would you get my purse? We'll come back for your suitcase later."

I picked up her red plastic purse, which was amazingly heavy—my father would have said, "You got rocks in here?"—and followed them up the front walk, which hadn't been shoveled. The snow caved in over the tops of my boots. On the porch Peggy stopped and stomped her feet on the welcome mat. I did the same as she pushed open the front door, which wasn't even locked. I supposed there wasn't much crime in such a small town where everyone knew everyone else, at least by sight, like New Glaurus, my father's hometown, but then I remembered the Nebraska State Penitentiary. I wanted to ask Peggy if she knew why my mother might want to call the penitentiary, but I didn't have the nerve.

The inside of the house was a surprise. I would have expected it to look old and dark, with heavy furniture and patterned wallpaper, like the house where my father grew up. But all the walls were painted bright white. The wood floors were bare except for two deep-blue area rugs in the living room and dining room. The furniture was simple and modern, and there wasn't much of it. There were a lot of healthy-looking ferns—no brown edges like ours at home—sitting in baskets on the built-in bookcases with leaded glass doors.

"It's nice," I said, looking around as Peggy peeled off Eric's snowsuit and poured him some apple juice. I noticed a big wooden loom in the sunroom off the dining room, with a blue-and-purple weaving about half finished. "Did you make these rugs?" I asked, noticing that up close they contained an intricate but subtle pattern, sort of Indian-looking. I had never seen a real loom before, just those kids' kits for making pot holders that my sister and I got from Aunt Lucille one Christmas.

"It keeps me sane," Peggy said. "It's my form of meditation. And it pays for the groceries. My parents left me the house free and clear. Otherwise I'd have to get a real job."

I wondered about her husband but was afraid to ask in case he wasn't "in the picture" either. Even though she wore a diamond wedding ring and I had noticed a wedding photo on the mantle. Peggy with longer hair, in a simple white dress and veil standing next to a boy in a navy uniform who might have been sort of handsome if his ears hadn't stuck out so prominently. She saw me glance at the photograph and said, "My husband died in the war. He never even got to meet his daughter. Not that they would have gotten along." She wiped up some spilled juice from the counter. "Of course, she might have turned out different if she'd had a father." She stuck a finger down Eric's pants and said, "He needs a new diaper. You want to come upstairs while I change him? I'll show you where you'll be sleeping."

I followed her up the stairs and into Eric's room, which was filled with toys. She laid him on the kid-size bed, removed his shoes, and whipped off his trousers. I stood in the hallway and looked around as she washed his smelly butt.

"Your room's the one across the hall," she mumbled, clamping a diaper pin between her lips. Eric was wrestling around on the bed, squirming and kicking. "Be still!" she ordered him. "You want to get stuck with a pin?"

The room across the hall had a slanted roof and twin beds with matching pink chenille spreads. Two Siamese cats were asleep, nestled together, in an old wicker rocker. Upstairs things looked more old-fashioned. It looked like the original flowered wallpaper. It felt like a completely different house, a different lifetime.

"That used to be my room," she called across the hall to me. "Your mother and I slept in those beds when she'd sleep over."

"Wow," I said, "really?" I felt a little shiver up my spine, as if there were ghosts in the room. "Which bed was hers?"

"The one by the window." She stood in the doorway carrying Eric, who was dressed in a fresh pair of red corduroy overalls. "I still sleep here sometimes. In the winter it's warmer than the big bedroom."

"What are the cats' names?"

"Cheng and Eng," she shrugged and laughed.

I followed her down the hall to the big bedroom. "This was my parents' room, of course." She sighed and set Eric down on his own two feet. "It's strange living in the house you grew up in. Sort of sad and comforting at the same time. I never thought I'd stay in Nebraka, let alone Troy, let alone the same damn house. But"—she sighed—*"c'est la vie, n'est-ce pas?"*

I could see that the room had been transformed, like the downstairs. The wallpaper stripped. The room painted white, her parents' bedroom suite replaced by a bed with no frame and a simple, unfinished pine bureau. A handwoven bedspread in bright corals, reds, and yellows so intense it seemed to glow like the sun. And a small jewel-like rug woven in shades of turquoise like waves in the ocean.

"It's the most beautiful room I've ever seen," I said so fervently that she grinned and tousled my hair.

"Let's get your suitcases."

As I followed her back downstairs, I wondered why my mother had never mentioned Peggy, how she could have let such a wonderful friend slip away. Peggy reminded me a bit of Mrs. Quave, and I thought maybe that was why my mother had hit it off with her right off the bat, like a long-lost sister.

While we were hauling the suitcases out of the truck, a mud-spattered white VW zoomed into view, tooting its horn.

"Mommy!" Eric shouted, stumbling toward the car.

A stick-thin woman in skintight black jeans, a fringed leather jacket, and white cowboy boots emerged from the VW, handed Eric a doughnut, and walked toward us. A German shepherd in the backseat pawed at the window, eager to get out.

"That's Joyce, my daughter, as you've probably gathered," Peggy said. She didn't look all that thrilled to see her. "I keep telling her not to ruin the kid's dinner with junk food, but she never listens. Never did."

"Hey," Joyce greeted us. "How was he?"

"Fine," Peggy said. "He's a good boy. This is Suzanne."

Joyce smiled at me. She had her mother's same nice smile, but she wore too much makeup, so it didn't seem as genuine. Her eyes were outlined in black, her lashes stiff with clumpy mascara, and her lips were a ghostly frosty pink. From a distance, her dyed blonde hair, teased and sprayed, looked like a football helmet. My sister would have said she looked like "a hood." It was hard to believe she was Peggy's daughter. Eric dropped his doughnut on the ground and started to cry. Joyce bent over, plucked it out of the slush, and handed it back to him. Peggy shook her head and rolled her eyes at me.

"Suzanne is Helen Hansen's daughter," Peggy said.

"Really?" Joyce's raccoon eyes opened wide and seemed to scrutinize me more curiously. "Where's your mother?"

"In the hospital," I answered.

"The hospital?" Joyce's eyebrows shot up and she looked at her mother. "What's the deal? Did she—"

"I'll tell you about it later," Peggy said, cutting her off and shooting her a warning glance.

Joyce shrugged and said, "Well, we got to get a move on, anyway. Come on, Buster." She grabbed his sticky hand and tugged him in the direction of the car.

"'Bye, Gramma!" He looked back and waved with his soggy doughnut.

Peggy waved back. "See you Monday!"

As Eric was climbing into the passenger seat, the dog wolfed down the rest of his doughnut. Eric started to howl. Ignoring him, his mother threw the car into gear and rocketed off down the driveway, gravel flying, just like her mother.

"Where's she work?" I asked as we walked back inside the house. She hadn't looked like she was dressed for a job.

"She's a receptionist at the A-1 Animal Clinic. She's got a way with animals. I'll say that for her." Peggy opened the refrigerator and slapped a package of hamburger on the counter. "I always said it was too bad for Eric that he wasn't a puppy."

I looked at her, unsure whether it was a joke or not, whether I should laugh. To be on the safe side, I just smiled. Peggy winked at me and said, "You like spaghetti?"

Unlike my mother, Peggy made her own tomato sauce from scratch. While the sauce was simmering on the stove, we went into the living room and Peggy built a fire in the fireplace. The cats materialized out of thin air and warmed themselves on the flagstone hearth. I studied the photographs on the mantel while Peggy prodded the kindling with a brass poker. There was a photograph of Joyce on a tricycle, looking cute and fresh-faced. And another of her in a white nightgown rocking Eric when he was just a tiny baby. Without all the makeup, I could see that she looked a lot like her father.

"How old is Joyce?" I asked.

"Nineteen." Peggy's knees creaked as she stood up and dusted the ashes off her hands.

Holy cow, I marveled to myself, only two years older than Bonnie. If Eric was three, she must have had him when she was sixteen, a year younger than my sister was now. In high school! I couldn't imagine Bonnie with a baby. Not that Joyce seemed all that motherly.

"You want a Coke?" Peggy asked.

"Okay, thanks."

As Peggy went into the kitchen, my gaze slid down to the bookcases and skimmed over some of the titles. I recognized *Peyton Place*, and suddenly it dawned on me that Joyce was like Betty Anderson, who got herself "knocked up" by Rodney Harrington and had to leave town and pretend to be visiting a maiden aunt in Vermont even though the whole town knew. I remembered, word for word, how Allison MacKenzie's mother told her: "You see what happens when a girl lets some fellow paw her? The result is what happened to Betty Anderson. That is the way cheap behavior pays off. In trouble."

I was thrilled and curious. I had never, as far as I knew, met an unwed mother and an illegitimate baby before. When Peggy handed me my Coke in a bottle, the way I liked it, I wanted to ask her whether Joyce had left town to have the baby. I wanted to know what had happened to the boy who was "not in the picture." Did he still live in Troy? But I didn't want to be rude. I knew enough to know it wasn't the sort of thing you talked about. Even with Peggy, who seemed less prim and stuffy than most of the other mothers I knew.

She sat down on the sofa next to me. One of the cats roused himself to leap onto her lap. I reached over and petted him. "I have a cat at home," I said. "His name's Jack. Bonnie, my older sister, is supposed to be taking care of him while we're gone, but I don't really trust her."

"Bonnie." Peggy smiled. "Your mother always said she

was going to have a daughter named Bonnie and a son named Randolph. Randy, for short."

I felt weird hearing that I was supposed to have been a boy. Then I remembered about my mother's two miscarriages. Maybe one of them was supposed to have been Randy.

"What about you?" I asked.

"Me?" she laughed. "I was going to have two sons— Sam and Max—named after my two older brothers. I guess the best-laid plans, no pun intended . . ." She let the sentence trail off. I didn't get the pun. "You know, I didn't get much chance to talk with your mother," she continued. "The poor thing was in so much pain and then the doctors whisked her off. I don't even know anything about your father."

"He's an optometrist," I said. "He grew up in Wisconsin, on a farm."

"What's his name?"

"Glen. Actually it's Harold Glen Keller, but everyone calls him Glen." I wrinkled up my nose. "He hates Harold."

"Your mother always hated the name Helen, too. She always wished she could have a nickname like me, you know, for Margaret." Then suddenly she let out a little chuckle and clapped her hand over her mouth. "Helen Keller," she said. "Your mother's name is Helen Keller?"

I nodded. To us, it was a stale joke by now.

"Your mother and I used to make fun of this woman in town named Jean Peckham who married Charlie Harlow. So she was Jean Harlow. And the worst part was she weighed about three hundred pounds with mousey brown hair and bad teeth."

"Who's Jean Harlow?"

"Oh, Lord." Peggy sighed. "She was an actress. Back in prehistoric times. When your mother and I were growing up." She stared at the fire for a minute and then stood up so abruptly that the cat slid off her lap onto the floor with a shrill meow of protest. Then she walked over to a cabinet and pulled out a couple of leather-bound albums. "I thought you might like to see some pictures of your mother when she was your age."

As Peggy sat back down beside me with the albums, I was speechless with anticipation, holding my breath. She flipped the cover of the first book open casually, as if it were no big deal. Then, sensing something, she looked over at me and said, "You okay?"

I just nodded. I didn't want to tell her that I had never before seen any pictures of my mother as a young girl. I thought if she knew that, she might change her mind about showing them to me. She might not show me whatever it was that my mother didn't want us to see.

Peggy flipped the pages of the first album, pointing out the occasional snapshot of my mother. The early snapshots were black and white, actually muted tones of gray, with white wavy edges. There was a picture of my mother and Peggy wearing only white underpants, splashing around in a big tin tub of water. Peggy was spraying my mother with the garden hose. Looking at the picture, I could almost hear my mother's little shrieks of laughter as the cold water hit her. Most of the pictures were taken on holidays—a succession of birthday cakes, Christmas trees, Halloween costumes. There was a picture of the two of them in white dresses and veils. Sort of like brides. "What kind of costumes were those?" I asked.

"Our First Communion." Peggy looked surprised. "Didn't you make your First Communion?"

I shook my head and flipped to the next page, not knowing what to say. I didn't want to tell her that I never even knew my mother was Catholic. I couldn't believe it. But pictures didn't lie.

The phone rang. While Peggy answered it, I sat there looking through the album. There were exactly eight pictures with my mother in them—I counted them—and I kept flipping back and forth among them while Peggy was on the phone. I felt guilty, the way I used to feel when I sneaked into my mother's bedroom and searched through her drawers. Her features and body could have belonged to almost any pretty little blonde girl; it was in the expressions and gestures that I recognized my mother. And it was the first time I realized, really understood, that we are one person from birth until death. For the first time it hit me that all old people had once been young, like me, like my mother. And someday someone, maybe my own daughter, would look at pictures of me when I was young and feel like crying.

When Peggy came back, she opened up the second album. Junior high and high school. There were fewer pictures of my mother. In the best one, she was dressed in a beautiful long dress with a corsage around her wrist, standing next to a boy in a white tuxedo jacket who looked familiar. I glanced up to Peggy's wedding photo on the mantel.

"That's right," Peggy nodded. "That's Tom. Your mother and he went steady all through school. Then"— she hesitated—"afterward, after she moved away and all, we were both so upset, it was like this bond between us.

Then gradually, I don't know, things just sort of evolved into something else—or at least we wanted to believe they did—the war was going on, he was going off to France, who knew what would happen? So we got married. Just like in one of those old war movies."

It occurred to me that maybe that's why Peggy and my mother had lost touch. That maybe my mother was mad at her for marrying her old boyfriend.

"I don't think poor Tom ever really got over your mother," Peggy sighed. "She was so beautiful. Everyone thought she should be an actress. Like Ingrid Bergman. But she was smart, too. Straight As. She could have done anything." She shut the album abruptly and said, "I better boil the water and make a salad. Visiting hours start at six." She set the albums down on top of a bookcase and stood up. "You can watch TV, if you want. Or I've got all my old books from when I was growing up here." She pointed to the bookcase in the corner. "If you like to read."

"Okay," I said. "Thanks." I was still thinking about the photographs.

"Just make yourself at home. We should eat in about twenty minutes."

After a minute I could hear her bustling around in the kitchen, clanging pots and pans. I got up and walked over to the corner bookcase, thinking I would find a book to read, but my eyes kept straying back to the photo albums. Peggy had shut the album so suddenly, with such a strange expression on her face. I was about to reach for the album when Peggy appeared in the doorway and said, "Do you like radishes in your salad?"

"Sure," I said, although I didn't, but I didn't want her

to think I was a picky eater. I opened the door of the bookcase and slid out a hardbacked copy of Edna Ferber's *Cimarron*. I had seen the movie *Show Boat* with my mother and really liked it. The book flap said it was about a struggling pioneer family in Oklahoma.

Peggy walked over and set another log on the fire. "That was one of my favorite books. Do you like to read?"

I nodded.

"Your mother was always a great reader. Must run in the family."

"She still is. My sister hates to read, though."

"I never could get Joyce interested in books either." Peggy sighed. "Oops, water's boiling!" She ducked back into the kitchen.

I sat back down on the couch and started to read, but my mind kept wandering. I kept seeing the photographs and thinking about them. Especially the first communion picture. I couldn't wait to tell Kim that I was really part Catholic. I wondered if my father even knew. I doubted it. Then I felt guilty for not calling him. I decided I would wait until after I saw my mother in the hospital, and then I would call and tell him everything was fine, under control, there was no need for him to worry. Even though I wasn't sure it was true. But I felt a lot better now that Peggy was in the picture.

A few minutes later she called me to dinner. The table was set with bright purple and pink woven placemats and thick white china dishes. "It looks so pretty," I said, thinking of our vinyl tablecloth and plastic everyday dishes at home. My mother only used the china dishes for company.

Suddenly I realized I was incredibly hungry. I ate two helpings of spaghetti with three pieces of garlic bread and a small bowl of salad. Even the radishes didn't taste too bad. Peggy seemed hungry, too, and we didn't talk a lot while we ate, but it was a comfortable silence. It seemed to me that Peggy would have been a great mother and I couldn't figure out why Joyce had turned out so bad. I wondered if Peggy got lonely living alone and thought it was too bad she didn't have another husband since the first one had died so long ago. I thought maybe Catholics weren't allowed to remarry.

As I was helping her carry the dishes to the sink, she said, "Your mother's very lucky to have such a nice daughter." She squirted some dish detergent into the water. "Of course, she's had more than her share of bad luck."

"What do you mean?" I set the wooden salad bowl down on the counter.

Peggy turned her head around and looked at me, then looked away. "What do you know about your grandparents?" she asked after what seemed like a long pause.

"Nothing much. They died in an accident," I said. My heart was racing. I could tell that she was going to tell me something important and terrible, something my mother had never told me. But she didn't say anything. She just kept washing the dishes. "After they died she went to live with her aunt and uncle in Kansas City," I added, hoping to prompt her. "She was sixteen."

Peggy nodded, then shook her head, setting another plate in the dish drainer. "Did she ever mention anyone named Buck? Ballard Roebuck?"

"No," I said. "At least not that I can remember."

"You would have remembered." She shut off the water and dried her hands. "I'll do the rest of these later. We should get going." I could tell she wanted to change the subject. "I'll just freshen up and be right down." As she hung her apron on a hook, she paused and sighed, noticing my disappointed, downcast expression. "You should ask your mother," she said gently. "I've probably already said too much. I believe in talking about things, but different people have different ways of dealing with things." She rested her hand on my head for a second, like a blessing, then went upstairs.

"Buck," I whispered to myself, thrilled by the tough, hard sound of the name. And immediately the picture of the dark-eyed boy in the silver locket flashed into my mind as if the name had conjured him up. I put on my coat and gloves and stood outside on the front porch, in the cold, waiting. It was pitch-dark. No streetlights. And very quiet. A couple of seconds later Peggy flicked on the porch light.

"I can see you're anxious to get there," she said as I followed her down the snowy path to the truck.

It was a small, friendly hospital. The nurses and doctors didn't seem to be all that busy, unlike on *Dr. Kildare* and *Ben Casey* where everyone was always rushing around saving lives. Also, the nurses were not that young and pretty. My mother had a room to herself. The other bed was empty. When we walked in she was watching Walter Cronkite just as she would have been doing at home at this hour, only the TV was mounted on the wall. A tray of food on a metal cart was pushed aside. I saw that, as usual of late, she had hardly touched her dinner, but I couldn't blame her. It didn't look that appetizing. A slab of gray meat, pale-green peas, mashed potatoes, and orange Jell-O. It looked as if she had eaten a couple of mouthfuls of mashed potatoes and about half the Jell-O. Her left wrist was lying in a stiff white cast on top of the bed covers. She didn't hear us come in. I walked over and kissed her cheek and said, "Hi, Mom."

She turned her head slowly and smiled at me. "Hello, honey, it's so nice to see you." Her voice sounded slow and slushy. I looked at Peggy, who whispered, "It's the medication."

"Well, your daughter and I have had ourselves a grand time while you've been lying here suffering," Peggy said in the exaggeratedly cheery voice people use to talk to sick people. "I'm crazy about her. You wouldn't consider letting me adopt her, would you?"

I looked down at my feet, pleased and embarrassed. My mother sort of laughed and then winced. "Bruised ribs," she said. "I feel like such a clumsy fool."

"Have you talked to Daddy?" I asked.

She nodded and looked away.

"What did he say?"

"I don't remember." She waved her good hand vaguely. "They've got me so doped up it's just all one big blur."

I didn't really believe her but I didn't say anything. She looked pale and scared lying in the hospital bed, like a sick child. I didn't want to make her feel worse.

"Can I sign your cast?" I asked, thinking it might perk her up. "At school whenever anyone has a cast, everyone signs it. Like an autograph book."

"What a good idea!" Peggy exclaimed, handing me a pen from her purse. "You first."

I dragged the chair over to the bedside and wrote my

full signature—Suzanne Marie Keller—as neatly as possible, careful not to press too hard on my mother's injured hand. Then I handed the pen to Peggy, who scrawled her name with a flourish. I read it aloud to myself: "Margaret Kelly Lovejoy." I figured Kelly must have been her maiden name. Peggy had lowered the volume on the TV and an awkward silence now filled the room. There were so many questions in my mind that I wanted to ask but couldn't that I couldn't think of anything to say. I wondered if my mother had a plan. I wondered if she could drive with her broken wrist. I wondered when we were going home. Tomorrow was Sunday. On Monday, school would start again. I had a test in U.S. history. But most of all I wanted to know about Buck.

On the silent TV screen Lyndon Johnson and Lady Bird were standing in some official reception line shaking hands with dignitaries. There was a Christmas tree, as tall as a skyscraper, in the background. My mother started to cry, staring at the television. She seemed to have forgotten that we were in the room. I was alarmed and embarrassed. I figured she was thinking about Jack and Jackie. I wondered what kind of Christmas Caroline was going to have. John-John seemed too little to understand.

Taking charge, Peggy said, "We're just going to get a Coke from the machine. Back in a minute."

I followed her out of the room and down the corridor. At the vending machines I said, "I'm not really thirsty."

Peggy plugged in some coins and got herself a cup of black coffee. As she blew on it to cool it off, I said, "My mother was crazy about Kennedy. She hasn't been herself since the assassination." Then I surprised myself by adding, "I think maybe she's having a nervous breakdown."

Peggy took a cautious sip of coffee and nodded thoughtfully. "I'm not surprised," she said. "That's how it works sometimes."

"How what works?"

She shrugged. "Life."

As we walked back toward my mother's room Peggy stopped at the nurses' station and talked to a short, busty woman with kinky gray hair. I stood off to the side, eating some M&M's I'd found in my coat pocket, trying unsucessfully to eavesdrop over the Muzak. After a minute Peggy came back and said, "She's going to be released tomorrow morning. That's good news, isn't it?"

I nodded, thinking, Then what?

Peggy squeezed my arm and said, "It'll be all right."

"What will?"

She didn't answer me.

When we returned to my mother's room, she was asleep. Or maybe just pretending to be. Either way, she looked exhausted, worn-out. Peggy picked up the remote control and blipped off the TV. Then we walked back out into the bright corridor as an elderly couple emerged from the room opposite my mother's. The man was holding the woman's arm. She was smiling and waving good-bye to someone. The instant she shut the door and turned around, her face crumpled. The man handed her his handkerchief.

"We'll come back in the morning to pick her up," Peggy told me. "Ten A.M."

"Do you think she can drive with one hand?" I asked anxiously as we rode the elevator down to the lobby. "She just got her license a couple of years ago. She's kind of a nervous driver."

"Well, fortunately it's her left hand," Peggy said, not really answering my question. "Brrr." She shivered as we walked through the revolving door into the freezing night wind. "I don't know why anybody lives in this climate."

As we hurried across the parking lot I said, "Did you know my parents lived in Hawaii for a year?"

"No. Really?" Peggy stopped in her tracks.

"Really. When they were first married." I opened the door to the pickup and climbed into the passenger seat. A second later Peggy climbed in beside me and turned on the heat and the defroster.

While we were waiting for the truck to warm up, she said, "Why did they move back to the Midwest?"

"My mother got island fever. She was pregnant with my sister."

"Hmmm." Peggy seemed to be thinking about something as she turned the key in the ignition. "I've missed your mother," she said as we drove out of the parking lot. "I tried to keep in touch with her, you know, but she just kind of disappeared."

I yawned, covering my mouth with my gloved hand. I was suddenly so sleepy I could hardly keep my eyes open. Peggy hummed to herself as she drove. A song I didn't recognize. As we passed through town, I noticed the Christmas decorations suspended like tinsel tightropes across Main Street. Twinkly colored lights seemed to twitter like nervous birds in the branches of the bare trees. It seemed a sad attempt at festivity.

When we got back to Peggy's house, she made us some hot cocoa. I felt tired and confused and worried. Peggy was asking me about school, making conversation. I didn't feel much like talking even though I really liked her. And was glad to be in her house instead of the hotel.

"Would you like to watch TV for a while?" she asked, setting our empty cups in the sink and running water in them.

I nodded but didn't get up. I was staring at the yellow phone on the wall. Peggy seemed to follow my eyes. "Would you like to call your father?" She took the receiver off the hook and stood there holding it out to me. I could hear the anxious hum of the dial tone. I walked over and took it from her. As I started to dial, she left the room. The phone rang a couple of times before my sister answered. "It's Suzy!" she hollered to my father. I could picture her standing in the upstairs hallway yelling down to the family room. "Boy, you guys are really going to get it," she whispered before he picked up the phone. "He's fit to be tied."

"Suzanne?" He snatched up the other phone.

The instant I heard his voice I started to cry.

After the phone conversation, which was short and tense, I walked out to the living room, where Peggy was sitting on the sofa reading *The Feminine Mystique*. I recognized it right away because my mother had been reading it for her book group when Kennedy was shot. I don't think she ever finished it. The book was still lying in the same spot on the coffee table with an old postcard from Helsinki marking the same page.

"My father is flying here tomorrow," I announced. "He's going to drive us back home. My mother and me."

Peggy nodded.

"He said he'd call and tell me what time his plane was

arriving. He was hoping maybe you could pick him up at the airport."

"Of course," Peggy nodded again. She was petting one of the cats curled up beside her. "I'd be happy to."

"My mother's going to be mad at me," I said, trying not to cry. My voice quivered.

Peggy looked at me so sympathetically I thought maybe she was going to cry herself. "You did the right thing," she told me. "Your mother will understand."

I picked up *Cimarron*, which was lying on the table where I had left it. "I think I'll get into bed and read for a while," I said, sounding like my father, who would make the same announcement nearly every night at ten-thirty on the dot.

"You just need a good night's sleep," Peggy agreed. "Things always seem better in the morning."

She followed me upstairs and turned down the bed while I brushed my teeth and washed my face in the bathroom. She had also plumped up the pillows and added an extra blanket. Once I was in bed, she came to the doorway and said good night. "If you need anything, just help yourself or holler," she said. "I'll be right down-stairs."

"Thank you."

She walked over and planted a kiss on my forehead. "Sleep tight, don't let the bedbugs bite."

It was what my father always used to say when we were little. For the first time I realized how much I missed him.

A couple of hours later I heard Peggy's footsteps creaking on the stairs, the sound of water running in the bathroom, and saw the light blink off in the hallway. I hadn't been able to concentrate on my book, so I'd turned off the reading lamp on the night table and burrowed under the covers, waiting, willing myself not to fall asleep. Fortunately, Peggy wasn't a night owl like my mother. It was only nine-thirty. I made myself wait ten more minutes, then tiptoed downstairs in my socks. I felt like a burglar. My heart was ticking like a bomb in my chest, ready to explode if I was caught. A stair creaked and I froze for a moment, but nothing happened.

Downstairs, it was cold. The fire had long ago died out, and Peggy must have turned down the thermostat for the night. The moonlight filtered in through the windows. In the semidarkness the wood floors and sparse furniture looked stark and spooky. I turned on the pole lamp. Standing on tiptoe, I slid the photo album down from on top of the bookcase. The refrigerator suddenly buzzed on in the kitchen, startling me so that I nearly let the album slide out of my hands, but I managed to keep a grip on it. I sat on the sofa and opened the album, quickly flipping the pages past the photos I had already seen to the spot where Peggy had slammed the cover shut.

There was a yellowed newspaper article with the bottom part folded up. I unfolded it carefully. The headline said "Troy Couple Die in Fire, Police Suspect Arson." There were two fuzzy photographs, one of a gutted house and one of a fair-haired, middle-aged couple that looked like a posed studio portrait.

I stopped before reading the article and crossed myself, the way I'd seen Mrs. Quave and Kim do on occasion to ward off evil. The gesture came naturally—as if, having just found out that I was part Catholic I had suddenly tapped into some hitherto untapped reservoir of faith.

I knew, more or less, even before I turned the page and saw his face staring out at me that Buck would be involved somehow. So I wasn't really surprised when I read in the second article that the police had arrested Ballard (Buck) Roebuck, age 18, who had confessed to the double murder. He had admitted he'd done it, but he wouldn't say why. However, police had questioned the victims' daughter, Helen, age 16, who had been spending the night at her girlfriend's house when the fire occurred. The distraught daughter told police that she had gone out on a couple of informal dates with Roebuck before her parents found out and forbade her to see him again. She had informed Roebuck that she was not allowed to see him anymore a week before the fire was set. Mr. and Mrs. Hansen, asleep in their bedroom when the fire broke out, were trapped on the second floor. The daughter's friend, Margaret Kelly, told police that Roebuck was obsessed with Helen Hansen; Kelly had observed him following them on several occasions during the month preceding the fire.

There were several more articles about the trial and Roebuck's subsequent conviction. Sentenced to life imprisonment. Spared the death penalty on account of his young age.

Half frozen, I shut the album and slid it back on top of the other album. Then I sneaked back upstairs and into bed. My hands and feet and heart felt like blocks of ice. Right before I fell asleep I suddenly remembered who it was that Buck really reminded me of: Warren Beatty in *Splendor in the Grass*. The same wavy dark hair and tortured dark eyes. Last summer, while my father was away at an optometry convention and Bonnie was spend-

ing the night at a friend's house, my mother had taken
me to the drive-in on the outskirts of town. It was a hot
summer night, humid and buggy, and my mother had
sprayed us with mosquito repellant before we left the
house at dusk. I had asked if Kim could come along, but
my mother said it wasn't really an appropriate movie for
kids. We both knew that Mrs. Quave read some Catholic
newspaper that rated movies and wouldn't let Marjorie
or Kim see anything the Pope deemed immoral. My
mother threw some pillows and a lightweight blanket in
the backseat of the Rambler and said I could just go to
sleep when I got tired.

It was a Saturday night. The drive-in was packed with
teenagers and adults with small children. The little kids
were dressed in summer pajamas, playing in the swings
and slides, the way Bonnie and I had when we were little.
My mother and I found a good spot not too far back or
too far to the side of the gravel lot, then went to the con-
cession stand for Cokes and popcorn. As it grew darker
outside, we waited in a long, snaking line, slowly inching
our way toward the counter. The teenage girls, hanging
on their boyfriends' arms, were all dolled up with
makeup and cute color-coordinated outfits. The boys
reeked of English Leather and Jade East. I could imagine
Bonnie and Roger fitting right into the crowd, and if
Roger hadn't been stuck delivering pizzas on Friday and
Saturday nights to pay for his car, they probably would
have been here.

The coming attractions were playing when my mother
and I finally trudged back to the car carrying our snacks
in a flimsy cardboard tray.

"Why don't you stretch out in the back?" my mother

said to me. I knew she was hoping I'd fall asleep since she knew my father would object to her bringing me to such an adult movie.

"I'd rather sit up front," I said. Only little kids lay down in the backseat.

"Okay, suit yourself." She was busy hooking the car speaker onto the window and adjusting the tinny volume. It was so hot that her skin gleamed with perspiration and her underarms exuded a mixture of Emeraude and Ice Blue Secret deodorant. "You know, we don't have to tell your father we saw this movie," she suggested casually. "He doesn't need to know everything."

"Okay," I agreed, stuffing a handful of buttered popcorn into my mouth.

My mother smiled and winked at me as the credits started to roll. I loved Natalie Wood. If I could have looked like anyone in the world, it would have been her. In the movie she was madly in love with Warren Beatty (Bud), who loved her, too, but then he stopped seeing her for some reason and she tried to kill herself in a waterfall and then got sent off to some sort of mental institution that looked like a beautiful Southern plantation. I fell asleep while she was at the institution, even though I liked the movie, and when I woke up the screen was dark and the huge parking lot was empty except for us. I didn't know how long we had been sitting there like that. My mother was using one of the pillows from the backseat to muffle her sobs. I was alarmed and embarrassed. I pretended to still be asleep. Then a guard from the drive-in pulled up with a flashlight and shined it in the car. He seemed surprised, as if he'd expected to see some necking teenagers. He snapped off the flashlight and apologetically told my mother that we had to leave. As she turned the engine on, I pretended to wake up, stretching and rubbing my eyes.

"What happened?" I pretended to yawn. "Did they get back together?"

My mother shook her head. Our tires crunched loudly on the gravel. The parking lot was littered with empty paper cups and candy wrappers. It looked unreal and alien, like the surface of the moon.

The next day, I remember, it was all over the news that Marilyn Monroe had killed herself. My mother and the neighbor women stood out on their lawns discussing it.

"I always felt sorry for her," Mrs. DiNardo said. Her hair was set in pink plastic rollers and she was wearing a baggy shift and terry-cloth slippers, her meaty arms folded underneath her baggy bosom. "There was just something sad about her. I always felt that."

Mrs. Crawford, in a tight, low-cut sundress with spaghetti straps, stared at Mrs. DiNardo as if she were crazy. She admired Marilyn the way my mother admired Jackie Kennedy.

I thought of Natalie Wood throwing herself into the waterfall the night before. The more beautiful you were, it seemed, the more likely you were to meet with a tragic end. My father always said that my mother was the most beautiful woman he'd ever seen. I was glad she had put on a few pounds and had crow's feet around her eyes. Besides, Marilyn didn't have any children. Mothers were different.

The next morning my father called Peggy's house at the crack of dawn to say he would be taking a United flight that landed in Lincoln at 11:05 A.M. Peggy spoke to him—I was still in bed—and told him we'd be there at the gate, waiting. I could hear her voice across the hall, talking on the phone in her bedroom. She assured him that I was fine and that my mother's injuries were not serious. She said she was looking forward to meeting him.

At ten o'clock we drove to the hospital to get my mother, who was already dressed and waiting for us, sitting on the edge of the bed smoking a cigarette. She looked like hell. Her hair was limp, her clothes rumpled, and she had dark circles under her eyes. When she saw us she seemed anxious to get out of there, as if afraid the doctor might suddenly change his mind and make her stay. Peggy carried her suitcase as the orderly wheeled her outside in a wheelchair—hospital policy—while I tagged along behind them, dreading the moment of truth that was about to arrive. In the car on the way to the hospital Peggy had suggested that we wait to tell my mother that my father was coming until after we were on the road. I had readily agreed, anxious to postpone telling her news that I suspected would only upset her. I was hoping against hope that she might actually be relieved, at least a little, to hear that my father was coming to take us home, to take care of us, but somehow I doubted that she would be.

Outside, the sky was the color of ashes and a biting wind was blowing. Peggy had driven my mother's Nash Rambler, which she'd had Triple A tow over to her house the afternoon before.

"I hope you don't mind my driving your car," she said to my mother as the three of us climbed in. "There's only room for two in the truck."

"Of course not," my mother said. "I appreciate all the trouble you've gone to for us."

The two of them were in the front seat; I was in the backseat biting my fingernails. While the engine was warming up, with her good hand my mother fumbled clumsily in her purse for a cigarette. On the other hand she was wearing a sock for a mitten since her leather glove wouldn't fit over the edge of the cast. Peggy punched in the lighter and lit two Lucky Strikes—one for my mother and one for herself. Our suitcases were loaded in the trunk just in case my father wanted to leave right away or stay the night in Lincoln, in which case, Peggy had explained to me, she would get Joyce to come pick her up and give her a ride back to Troy. As Peggy shifted the car into reverse, her eyes met mine in the rearview mirror, as if prompting me to say something, but I just sat there like a bump on a log, unable to speak. In order to crack her window for ventilation, my mother had to clamp her cigarette between her lips and grab the window handle with her one good hand, an awkward maneuver that seemed to require all her energy. The blast of icy air was too much for me in the backseat but I didn't complain. We were passing by a big, low, grim-looking complex surrounded by a high concrete wall topped with rolls of barbed wire. A sign read NEBRASKA STATE PENI-TENTIARY. The hair on the back of my neck shivered. There were tall guard towers with tinted glass; I looked for guards armed with rifles, but the towers appeared to be empty. I wondered if Buck were in there, making license plates or eating in the cafeteria or lying on a cot in his cell like movie prisoners.

My mother turned her head stiffly toward the backseat

and said, "I thought we could visit your grandparents' graves, then go out to lunch somewhere nice."

I nodded, caught off guard. This seemed like a real turning point of some sort—my mother taking me to the cemetery to see where her parents were buried—and I wanted to go. She probably planned to tell me the whole story about the fire and Buck and the trial. I knew that my father's coming would ruin everything. I wished I'd never called him. I was racking my brain for some way to postpone meeting him at the airport even though I knew his plane was due to land in less than half an hour. I was fantasizing that Peggy could drop us off at a motel, then go on to the airport alone and tell my father that we had disappeared while she was in the rest room at the airport. She had looked all over and figured that we must have taken a flight somewhere since the Rambler was still in the parking lot. Meanwhile, my mother and I would rent a car from Hertz and return to Troy, having thrown my father off our track. I was thinking it could work, maybe, if I could get Peggy to go along with it, when my mother suddenly seemed to wake up and notice where we were. "Where are you going?" she said. "I thought we were going back to your house."

"We're going to the airport." Peggy flashed me a pointed look in the rearview mirror.

My mother turned to me and said, "What's going on?"

"Dad's coming," I mumbled. "He's going to drive us home. Because of your wrist."

"And whose idea was this?" My mother was staring straight ahead, her jaw clenched, her voice chilly and clipped.

"Mine," Peggy said, taking pity on me. "I thought he should know. I persuaded Suzanne to call him last night."

"Great." My mother turned her face toward the window.

"She's just a kid, Helen. Don't take it out on her."

My mother didn't say anything, just stared straight ahead at the road. After a couple of minutes she said, "I'm sorry. It's not your fault." I didn't know who precisely she was apologizing to. Then she shut her eyes and rested her head against the window.

Peggy turned on the radio and we listened to music the rest of the way.

There were Christmas carols playing in the airport. "Joy to the World," "O Little Town of Bethlehem." Just the piano melodies, no singing. But as we sat at the gate waiting for my father's plane to land, the familiar lyrics kept running through my brain. "Hark the herald angels sing/Glory to the newborn king/Peace on earth and mercy mild/God and sinners reconciled!" My father's plane was ten minutes late. We were fifteen minutes early. I couldn't sit still. I wandered over to the gift shop and bought some Milk Duds and cherry-flavored Chap Stick, then browsed through the magazines. Most of the news magazines had issued special memorial editions. Portraits of the dead president lined the rack, staring out from the covers of *Life*, *Look*, *Time*, *Newsweek*, the *Saturday Evening Post*. There were two issues of *Life*, side by side, one with Jackie Kennedy in her black veil flanked by Caroline and John-John in pale blue coats, and one of Lyndon Johnson standing behind the desk of the oval office looking serious and official. My mother still refused to refer to LBJ as President Johnson. The women's magazines were different. Looking at their covers, you wouldn't even know that Kennedy was dead. They were still filled with the usual recipes and makeovers and Christmas crafts. In *McCall's* there were two paintings by Jackie that were going to be made into Christmas cards and the proceeds donated to some charity. One was of three wise men on a deep-red background and the other was of an angel with a trumpet on a heavenly-blue background. They were very pretty. I didn't even know she knew how to paint. I bought the magazine for my mother, a sort of peace offering. As I was paying for it at the counter, I heard the loudspeaker announce that my father's flight had landed.

In the gate area a stream of passengers was straggling off the plane into the terminal. My mother was still sitting in a chair, smoking a cigarette. I figured that was a bad sign. If she had wanted things to go smoothly, she would have hidden the fact that she had started smoking again—at least for a little while. Until the ice was broken. Peggy was standing off to the side as if she didn't want to be in the way. I don't know what she was thinking. She probably thought my parents fought all the time, which they didn't. They hardly ever fought. At least not big fights where they raised their voices or threw things. Sometimes they bickered over little things, but that was about it. My mother just hadn't been herself since the assassination. As far as I could tell, it didn't really have anything to do with my father. It wasn't anything personal.

He was one of the last ones off the plane. I knew he

liked to sit in the back because he'd read that that was supposed to be the safest spot. He was carrying a small suitcase and his brown tweed overcoat. When he caught sight of me, he hugged me tight, then looked around for my mother, who nodded coolly and exhaled a thin stream of smoke. Holding his hand, I led him over to my mother and Peggy. "This is Peggy," I said. "And this is my father," I said, even though it was obvious. They shook hands. I tried to imagine whether Peggy would think he was handsome. My mother always said he looked "distinguished," meaning like a college graduate, a successful breadwinner. It occurred to me that if his hair were clipped shorter and he were wearing a navy uniform, he would have looked something like Tom Lovejoy, Peggy's husband, my mother's old childhood sweetheart.

My father bent down and embraced my mother somewhat stiffly, I thought, although it might just have been the awkward angle. My mother stubbed out her cigarette and stood up.

"How's the wrist?" he asked.

"Broken," she said.

"Did you have a nice flight?" Peggy chimed in, trying to ease the tension as we stepped onto the Down escalator to the ground floor. "Do you have any more luggage?"

"Nope, this is it," my father said. "There was snow in Chicago and . . ." He and Peggy kept up a polite conversation while my mother and I followed them silently out to the parking lot.

When we reached my mother's car, we stood there awkwardly for a moment, realizing we didn't have a plan.

"Why don't you drive, Glen?" Peggy handed my

mother's key ring to my father. It was a gold letter "H" studded with simulated sapphires (her birthstone) that I had given her for her last birthday.

My father thanked her, unlocked the doors and chivalrously held them open for us—"Ladies first"—then climbed into the driver's seat, adjusted the seat for more leg room and the angle of the rearview mirror. As he fiddled with the mirror, he caught my eye and winked at me in the backseat with my mother. Peggy had protested that she'd sit in back but my mother had ignored her and climbed in behind me. It felt weird, as if my father and Peggy were the ones who were married. My father turned the key in the ignition and said, "Where to? Just give me directions."

"Just drop me off downtown. I've got some Christmas shopping to do and I'm meeting my daughter for lunch," Peggy said in a rush. I knew this wasn't true and my mother probably did, too, but we didn't say anything. I figured she was just anxious to be rid of us and what was obviously a tense situation.

"We'll drive you home," my mother said flatly. "It's the least we can do."

"That's right," my father seconded, anxious to seem helpful and gracious.

"No, really." Peggy shook her head. "It's more convenient this way."

My mother sighed and shrugged. I thought about suggesting that my father and Peggy have a cup of coffee at her house while my mother and I visited the cemetery, but I didn't have the nerve. I sensed that whatever mood had prompted my mother's earlier offer had passed. The window of opportunity had shut.

Peggy directed my father out of the small airport and in the direction of downtown Lincoln. It was only a ten-minute ride, but it still seemed long. My mother seemed to feel no need to hold up her end of the conversation. Mostly Peggy asked my father questions about his work, nodding breathlessly, as if he were a secret agent or a lion tamer instead of an optometrist. I knew that she was just trying to lighten up the atmosphere in the car, but it irked me anyway. Especially that he seemed to think she was genuinely fascinated by cataracts and glaucoma. My mother, off in her own world, didn't seem to notice. At the corner of O Street and Thirteenth, Peggy directed my father to pull over to the curb and said, "I'll get out here."

We got out of the car and hugged each other good-bye, promising to keep in touch. My mother managed to snap out of her trance and come to life, briefly, as she told Peggy how good it was to see her again. They both had tears in their eyes. My father stood at a discreet distance on the sidewalk, studying a window display of office supplies. Then Peggy said, "It was a pleasure to meet you. I hope next time it's for longer." My father gallantly agreed and nodded his head alertly as Peggy gave him directions for getting back on Route 80 East. My father hated to be lost; he thought only women and foreigners got lost. He believed men, at least American men, were born with a natural sense of direction.

We waved good-bye to Peggy and watched as she disappeared into a jewelry store, no doubt relieved to be on her own again, even if it meant being stranded in Lincoln with no ride home. I wanted to run after her.

"Well," my father cleared his throat, "what should we

do? How about some lunch?" He sounded as if he were talking to two mental retards, upbeat and uptight. I wished he would just yell and get it over with. It was obvious he was attempting to control himself, to pretend as if this were nothing out of the ordinary.

"Let's just get on the road," my mother said.

My father looked at me. I nodded. He shrugged and said, "I'm just the chauffeur." When the light changed to green, he pulled out, drove around the block, and headed back toward the interstate, following Peggy's directions. Looking at the back of his head, I could tell that he was miffed.

At the next red light I got out of the car and joined him in the front seat. It seemed only fair. And my mother, sitting ramrod straight in the backseat with her eyes closed, like some yogi hermit in a cave, didn't even seem to notice that I was gone.

Out on the interstate it started to snow, a light dusting of confectioner's sugar. It didn't look like much but I knew from quizzing my sister with the Wisconsin drivers' handbook that the most dangerous time was right after it started snowing. That was when the roads were slickest. It gave my father an excuse to concentrate on driving, which was just as well, since there didn't seem to be much to say. Or rather, there was too much to say. Probably if my father and I had been alone we would have talked, but it felt awkward with my mother in the backseat. Her silence seemed louder than words. I leaned over and turned on the radio, which my father had turned off when he got in the car. He didn't protest.

Since this clearly wasn't going to be a pleasure trip my father felt free to make good time. We stopped for a quick lunch at a McDonald's in Council Bluffs, eating in the car. At least my father and I ate. My mother only nibbled on a few french fries. My father ate her cheeseburger. ("No use letting good food go to waste.") At the gas station next door, my mother and I used the rest room while my father got the tank filled. As we were washing our hands I said, "Are you mad at me?"

My mother shook her head but didn't say anything.

Outside, my father was sitting in the car waiting for us with the motor running. I wanted some gum and candy, but he seemed so impatient that I just got in the car. My mother, however, took her time. She strolled inside the gas station. "What the hell's she doing now?" My father fidgeted and sighed. A couple of minutes later she got back in the car and dumped a Snickers, an Oh! Henry, a pack of Juicy Fruit, and a roll of cherry Life Savers into my lap. I knew this was her way of telling me she wasn't holding anything against me. Or if she was, she forgave me.

We stopped for dinner at a Kentucky Fried Chicken outside Dubuque. It had already been dark out for two hours, and I was starving. It was too cold to eat in the car, so we trooped into the brightly lit restaurant. My father and I wolfed down chicken, mashed potatoes, and biscuits while my mother pecked at a small coleslaw and sipped a Tab. "How about dessert?" my father asked her. She shook her head. "At least she's a cheap date," he muttered to me. He looked at his watch and yawned. "ETA is nine-fifteen. We're on the home stretch now."

We trudged back out to the car.

"Why don't you let your mother sit in front this time?" my father said, holding the door open for her. I thought she was going to balk, but she just shrugged and slid in, as if it weren't worth making a fuss over. Relieved, I settled into the backseat. My mother lit a cigarette awkwardly with her one good hand as we pulled out onto the dark highway.

"I'm sorry to see you smoking again," my father said, unable to contain himself any longer. "After three years." He shook his head. "Seems crazy."

"Feel free to take the car back," my mother snapped.

He sighed and grumbled something to himself. I don't remember any other conversation. I must have fallen asleep. When I woke up, we were sitting in our driveway and my father was rolling up the screechy garage door. "Home sweet home," he said as he maneuvered the car into the garage next to his new LeSabre. I couldn't tell if it was supposed to be a joke or not. My mother got out of the car and swept herself silently and majestically into the house, leaving my father and me to unload the suitcases. My sister was waiting for us in the kitchen eating a Twinkie and drinking a glass of milk. My mother was nowhere in sight. I could hear her heavy footsteps overhead.

"So," Bonnie said, "did you have a good time?"

PART THREE

The neighbors missed my mother. They were always asking me about her and I made up various lies about how busy she was with this or that project, assuring them that she was fine. I don't think they believed me—at least, the other mothers—but they didn't seem to know what to do. In those days, the early sixties, at least in the Midwest, people still believed there was a line between sane and crazy. Hand them a ruler and they'd draw it for you. Normality was still considered a virtue. No one had heard of the nuclear family since we didn't know there was any other kind. Ozzie and Harriet, David and Ricky. That was a family. In only five years there would be the Manson family on TV—Charles, Tex Watson, Susan Atkins, Patricia Krenwinkel—but by then it was a whole different world.

My father kept predicting that my mother would catch

the holiday spirit, but she didn't. The DiNardos' life-size crèche was on their front lawn as usual except for the fact that Mr. DiNardo had nailed the baby doll into the cradle, crucifixion-style, since last Christmas some smart-ass punk had stolen the baby Jesus in the middle of the night. Santa smiled and waved from his sleigh atop the Gusdorfs' roof. The Matsumis' yard was the usual fairyland of twinkling white lights. The inside of the Quaves' house boasted the traditional plastic profusion of holly swags, mistletoe, wreaths, and poinsettias. But my mother remained unmoved. Finally, on his own initiative, my father nailed a pathetic-looking strand of colored lights over the porch. When he asked my mother to come outside and tell him what she thought, she said she was sure it was fine and continued reading her book. She had gone to the library and checked out half a dozen books on Buddhism. She had become interested in the subject through Dr. Matsumi's book on the internment camps in which he described how their Buddhist beliefs helped to sustain the Japanese-Americans during their imprisonment. Whenever my sister or I complained about something, she had taken to quoting the first of the Four Noble Truths: "Life is suffering."

My mother's New Years Eve's party had become an annual tradition for which she planned all year, collecting recipes and clever ideas for decorations or party favors from the women's magazines, trying to outdo herself each year. In the three years between the time we'd moved into our new house and Kennedy's assassination, my mother had blossomed into a social butterfly. The phone rang for her almost as much as for my sister. Everyone was crazy about my mother, who was witty and creative and attractive without being too showy or flirty like Mrs. Crawford. My father approved of her newfound popularity. He never complained when she spent money on a new cocktail dress or crystal punch bowl. His business was flourishing, his wife was flourishing, his daughters were happy and healthy. We were all leading the life of Riley.

But this year when my father asked if it wasn't time to send out the invitations for New Year's Eve, my mother just looked at him as if he were out of his mind. I think he knew the answer before he asked the question but couldn't help himself. His way of coping with my mother's abnormal behavior was to pretend that everything was normal. He still believed she was going "to snap out it." I wasn't so sure. I debated whether to tell him or Bonnie what I'd discovered in Troy, in the newspaper articles. On a couple of occasions I came close to blurting it out and then didn't. I'm not sure why. Maybe I just liked knowing something that they didn't know. I had not even confided in Kim that I was half Catholic.

My father went to a couple of holiday parties alone. He made excuses for my mother. At the Gusdorfs' Christmas get-together, he said my mother's broken wrist and bruised ribs were still causing her a lot of pain. At the Crawford's New Year's Eve party he told them that she had the flu. I was busy baby-sitting. I made sixty-five dollars from December fifteenth through January first. I was saving up for a real weaving loom like Peggy's. A good one cost a lot, at least twice what my sister's zigzag sewing machine had cost. And my father thought it seemed like a weird idea. You couldn't make clothes with it, at least not normal clothes. And he said it seemed like a lot to spend for a few placemats. But I was determined. When I was upset or anxious, I liked to close my eyes and imagine myself working with a bright pattern of threads, calmed by the soothing, regular rhythm of the shuttle.

A week before Christmas my sister reported that she had searched everywhere and was 99 percent certain that my mother had not done any Christmas shopping. Sometimes she got in her car and disappeared for a couple of hours and we thought maybe she was shopping in secret, to surprise us, but that didn't appear to be the case. Usually, by now she would have mounds of presents wrapped and stashed in various hiding places, as well as under the tree. I tried not to let on that it bothered me even though it did. I couldn't imagine my mother not giving me a Christmas present no matter how lousy she felt. For the first time I didn't tell my sister to shut up when she complained for the umpteenth time that our mother was selfish and self-absorbed and didn't give a damn about anyone except herself and some dead president who never even knew she was alive. Jackie and her kids, my sister pointed out, were spending the holidays in Palm Beach, Florida, having a nice time. They weren't sitting around moping. I didn't really think it was the Kennedy thing anymore—I sensed it had gone beyond that—but I didn't know to explain it.

On the Saturday before Christmas our father took us to the mall to buy gifts and bought us pizza for lunch. He was doing his best for us. The weekend before he had gone out and bought a Christmas tree and set it up all by himself. The trunk was crooked and there were a lot of spindly branches toward the top. My mother looked at it sadly but didn't comment. My sister and I took charge of decorating, squabbling over what went where until my father yelled at us to knock it off.

It wasn't as if my mother had completely ground to a halt. She still cooked simple, bland dinners and did the laundry and vacuumed the carpet and watered the plants. The basic duties. More like a maid than a mother. Or a wife. She was there but not there. She had made herself a little nest in the corner of the living room, which we never used except for company, which we never had anymore. She had dragged one of the matching armchairs over next to the end table where there was a lamp and a stack of books and some pens and paper. Like a little study carrel. And she spent most of her time in the armchair, feet propped up on an old ottoman she'd retrieved from the basement, reading with a red pen in hand, like a college student. She stopped going to her book club but once or twice she invited Mrs. Matsumi over for tea and they talked about the books my mother was reading. She hardly ever talked to Mrs. Quave anymore, which made me sad. When I was over playing with Kim, Mrs. Quave would holler out from her bed and ask me how my mother was doing. I could tell she missed my mother. The baby was due any day. They had decided to name it Christine Louise if it was a girl and Michael Charles if it was a boy. They were all hoping for a boy, except for Kim, who wanted a little sister.

Once, while my mother was taking a bath, I went into the living room and picked up the book she was reading. *Essays in Zen Buddhism* by D. T. Suzuki. Passages were starred and underlined in red ink, which shocked me because it was a library book. The fact that she would deface a library book shook me up; I figured she must not know what she was doing. She had underlined the first sentence: "Zen in its essence is the art of seeing into one's own being, and it points the way from bondage to freedom." I read that sentence to myself twice. Then my eyes skipped to the next paragraph, where she had bracketed a brief passage and starred it: "This body of ours is something like an electric battery in which a mysterious power latently lies. When this power is not properly brought into operation, it either grows mouldy or withers away, or is warped and expresses itself abnormally. It is the object of Zen, therefore, to save us from going crazy or being crippled." The author went on to talk about "the third eye" that allows us to see through "the cloud of unknowing," or ignorance, both of which phrases my mother had underlined. I had never read anything like it and it scared me. I shut the book and petted Jack, who liked to curl up in the armchair when my mother wasn't there, as if waiting for her to return. I knew exactly how he felt.

The thing that finally seemed to snap my mother out of it was a second tragedy. Like one of those amnesia victims who loses her memory after a blow to the head and then regains it after a second blow. On January third, almost two weeks early, Mrs. Quave gave birth to a baby boy. Charlie spoke to my father after he got home from the hospital that evening. "It's a boy," he told us. "Seven pounds, ten ounces." He looked exhausted and sounded subdued as he accepted my father's hearty congratulations.

"What's the matter?" my mother asked, suddenly

appearing in the kitchen doorway, clutching to her chest the book she'd been reading in the living room.

My father looked exasperated. "What kind of question is that?" He frowned at her. "How about a drink?" he asked Charlie. "Scotch? Brandy?"

But Charlie just shook his head and looked at my mother and started to cry. My father and I stood by in shock while my mother put her good arm around Charlie's shaking shoulders and led him over to a chair. My heart pounded in my chest like a baby kicking in its mother's womb. Once Mrs. Quave had called Kim and me over and had put our hands on her big belly so that we could feel the baby kicking. I figured the baby must be dead or deformed. No arms or legs, like those thalidomide babies in England. My mother glanced over at my white face and told me to go upstairs. For once I didn't protest; I was glad to get away from the terrible sound of Mr. Quave's crying. As I ran upstairs to my room I thought of the first noble truth—"Life is suffering"—and for the first time it occurred to me to wonder what the other three noble truths were.

My sister was in her room cutting out a new pattern for a jumper. "Something's wrong with the baby," I said. "Mr. Quave's crying."

Bonnie gawked at me for a moment as if trying to decide whether I was making it up, then set down her pinking shears and tiptoed out onto the landing. A minute later she came back and said, in a hushed voice, "He's a Mongoloid."

I gasped and clapped my hand over my mouth. I remembered the first time I'd seen one. My mother and I were sitting in the dentist's waiting room and a mother walked in with a little girl about my size in a pink snow-suit with a hood. My mother was reading a magazine. I was restless and nervous; it was only my second visit to a dentist. I didn't notice anything until the mother took off the little girl's jacket and then she turned to me and smiled and I knew right away that something was wrong with her. She didn't look like anyone else I'd ever seen and she was making strange noises. I jabbed my mother, who looked around to see what was the matter and then shot me a warning look not to say anything. She smiled at the little girl and said something pleasant to the mother about the weather. A minute later the dentist's nurse walked in and ushered them into the back, even though we'd been sitting there for at least half an hour and the nurse had apologized, saying that Dr. Collins was running late. Once they were out of earshot my mother leaned over and whispered, "She's mentally retarded, poor little thing. She's a Mongoloid." From one of the examining rooms in the back we could hear loud moaning noises and the mother trying to shush her. That night I had a nightmare.

Since then I'd seen one every now and then in a gro-cery store or the library or playground. And a girl in my English class, Shelley Nelson, had a retarded older brother. She had written an essay about him, saying what a great kid he was even though he was fifteen and still had, always would have, the intelligence of a first-grader. Once I had seen him sitting in the car with her mother, waiting to pick Shelley up after school. When he spotted Shelley he clapped his hands and smiled, jumping up and down in the seat, as if he hadn't seen her for a year.

"Do you think Kim knows?" I asked my sister.

"Probably," Bonnie said. She hadn't gone back to cutting out her pattern. She was just sitting there on the floor trimming split ends off her hair with the pinking shears.

I couldn't imagine. Here she was all excited about having a new baby sister and now this. Her parents had warned her to not get her heart set on a girl because it might be a boy, but no one had ever said anything about it maybe being a Mongoloid.

"At least they're Catholic," I said.

"What's that have to do with it?" Bonnie looked at me as if *I* were retarded.

"I don't know." I shrugged. "They have faith, which helps them get through tragedies. Look at Rose Kennedy." After I said it I suddenly remembered that, in fact, one of Kennedy's sisters was in an institution for the mentally retarded. I almost told my sister that we were half Catholic, but it didn't seem like the right time.

My mother knocked on the door even though it was open. "Girls," she said. "Are you okay?"

"Is Mr. Quave gone?" I asked.

My mother sighed and nodded.

"Is something wrong?" Bonnie asked innocently.

At which point my mother explained about mongoloidism and older women being statistically more at risk. Mrs. Quave was forty-one. She tried to sound matter-of-fact, like it wasn't really all that terrible to be retarded. "At least he's healthy. It could be worse," she added unconvincingly.

"What's his mental age going to be?" Bonnie asked. She had studied this stuff in biology.

"They can't tell right away," my mother said. "We just

have to hope for the best. After all, intelligence isn't everything."

"That's for sure," I snorted, looking pointedly at my sister.

"Suzanne," my mother said sternly, "that's enough. Kim is going to need your support. You're going to need to behave maturely." She straightened her shoulders. "We're all going to have to be our best selves. Can I count on you two?"

We nodded.

She smiled and said, "Well, we all better get a good night's sleep." But she looked more awake, more like her old self, than she had in weeks.

By the end of the week, Mrs. Quave and the new baby came home from the hospital. And by the end of the month, my mother and Kim's mother were like best friends again. Everyone—but especially my father, sister, and I—was amazed by my mother's tireless strength and competence. She just took charge and set a positive tone so that the neighbors, unsure how they should act, simply took their cue from her. The baby, Mikey, had a soft nest of red hair like chicken fuzz and was actually pretty cute and cuddly, like any other baby. The first time I'd gone over there after they brought him home from the hospital, I was afraid. I was worried that I'd find him repulsive and that it would show in my face even though I was determined to be a tower of strength. I was relieved when Kim led me over to his bassinet on tiptoe and gently slid down his blue blanket so that I could get a better look, and my involuntary response was to reach out my finger and stroke his little fist, just like I would with any baby.

After Kim shut the door softly behind her, we went into her new room. Since Marjorie was living in the dorm, Kim had inherited her sister's room, the bigger of the two bedrooms, and the baby had inherited her room. It felt strangely disorienting to see Kim's furniture and stuff in Marjorie's old room. Marjorie seemed like some distant relative now that she was away at college, even though she was still in Madison, and I wondered if that's how it would be next year when Bonnie started college. If anywhere was dumb enough to accept her. I had the impression that Marjorie was embarrassed by the whole notion of her mother having a baby at her age and was trying her best not to give off any "I-told-you-so" vibrations. Oddly enough, my mother, who had told Mrs. Quave in no uncertain terms that she thought she was making a big mistake, now rallied loyally to her defense. And when Mrs. Quave tried to blame herself, my mother told her to stop punishing herself for something that was nobody's fault. Any sort of talk about "God's will" drove her crazy. "That's like saying a flopped cake is God's will," she muttered to me once after some pious, well-meaning visitor had left. "These things just happen."

Kim and I never talked about the baby being a Mongoloid. She didn't bring it up, and I didn't think I should unless she did first. Until one afternoon a few weeks after the baby was born when we'd both stayed home from school with head colds and scratchy throats. Kim was staying at my house so as not to spread germs to the baby. We were camped out in the family room on blankets and pillows watching one TV show after another. *Love That Bob*, *Day in Court*, *To Tell the Truth*, *Queen for a Day*. This was our favorite daytime show.

Now we liked to joke around and make sarcastic com-
ments, but when we were younger we used to drape a red
blanket around our shoulders like a velvet cape and take
turns telling the saddest story we could think of. I was
the best at it. I could even make myself cry. We joked our
way through the first contestant's tale of woe—a husband
with a bad back who couldn't work, six kids, and a trailer
destroyed by a tornado. "Uh-oh, Toto, we're not in
Kansas anymore!" Kim said, referring to the tornado. We
were still laughing when Jack Bailey introduced the second contestant, a slender, pretty woman with soft eyes
and a nervous smile. The first thing she said was, "My
husband committed suicide six months ago and I have a
one-year-old son who is Mongoloid and needs special
care and medication." As she went on to describe the
desperate details of her situation, Kim and I fell silent. I
didn't know where to look. Finally Kim reached out and
changed the channel to *The Edge of Night*.

"Do you think everyone can tell Mikey's a
Mongoloid?" she asked after a couple of minutes.

"No," I lied. "I don't think so."

Kim was looking down at the carpet.

"He's really cute," I added. "And so good-natured.
That's all people notice."

"Really?"

"Really."

She sighed and her voice quavered when she said, "I'm
just worried the other kids will make fun of him, you
know, like when he's old enough to go out and play and
stuff."

I was going to say something fake and reassuring but I
couldn't. I knew as well as Kim what it would be like.

How the meaner kids would call him names and the nicer kids would just pretend not to notice him. I thought of Peggy's grandson with the port-wine birthmark. I thought of the first noble truth: "Life is suffering." But it wasn't fair. Some people, through no fault of their own, suffered more than others.

"He's probably never even going to learn to read," Kim said. "Can you imagine?"

I shook my head. I really couldn't. I tried to remember what it felt like before I knew how to read but I couldn't remember. "Of course, not everyone likes to read," I said, trying to be helpful. "Look at Bonnie. She never reads a word unless it's going to be on a test."

"That's different," Kim said. "It's not the same."

"Well, maybe he'll be a concert pianist. I saw something on TV about a . . . a person with a very low IQ who could play Mozart without any lessons or anything. Like a genius."

"My father says there's lots of things he can learn to do." Kim seemed to brighten up a little. "He says there are all kinds of excellent vocational schools nowadays for kids like Mikey. It's not like in the old days."

I had no idea what it was like in the old days but I nodded enthusiastically.

"He's just so sweet." Kim's voice trembled and her eyes brimmed over. "I just wish he never had to find out he's different."

"I know." I hung my head and felt on the verge of tears myself but held them back because my mother had said Kim needed me to be strong. I handed her a Kleenex. When she finished blowing her nose, I said, "There's something I never told you." She looked up at me. "I'm part Catholic," I confessed. "I just found out last month."

Kim frowned in confusion. "I don't get it."

"My mother was Catholic. I saw a picture of her making her First Communion when I was in Troy. At her friend's house."

"But why isn't she Catholic now?"

"I don't know," I said. "I think maybe when her parents died, it was just such a shock that she stopped believing in God."

"But my mother says that's when faith counts the most, when something awful happens." She looked shocked and upset. I thought maybe I shouldn't have told her after all.

"You can't tell anyone," I said. "She doesn't even know I know."

"But if you're Catholic and you don't go to mass, it's a mortal sin. And if you die with a sin on your soul, you go to hell."

"Even if it's not really your fault?" I couldn't believe that. There had to be some sort of loophole.

"Yup."

"Are you sure?"

She nodded. "Even little babies who die before they're baptized go to limbo instead of heaven."

"Well, I'm sorry, but that just doesn't seem right," I said, thinking maybe my mother knew what she was doing when she decided not to be a Catholic anymore. I was sorry I'd brought it up, but at least Kim had stopped crying.

By the weekend we had recovered from our colds and were in a fever of anticipation over the Beatles' appearance on *Ed Sullivan* that Sunday evening. My sister, a total Beatles fanatic, had invited her girlfriends over for a TV party. Their near hysteria was infectious. Melanie, Jill, Laurie, and Janet arrived at six o'clock. My father had sprung for pizzas for the whole crowd. Bonnie had brought her portable stereo down to the family room and they played Beatles' records, the same ones over and over, until it was time for *Ed Sullivan*. My father thoroughly enjoyed himself; he loved it when my sister brought her friends home instead of going out as she usually did. My mother was at her book club, the first social gathering she had attended since the assassination. They were discussing *The Silent Spring*, some depressing book about how pesticides were ruining the planet. My father asked why they couldn't ever read something upbeat—his favorite author was James Thurber—but he was glad she was going out.

At seven o'clock my sister turned off her stereo and turned on our old Magnavox console. She and her friends sat with their noses practically touching the screen. Usually my father didn't let us sit so close because he said it was bad for our vision, but this time he didn't say anything. My father, Kim, and I sat on the sofa behind them. When Ed Sullivan introduced the Beatles, they all squealed and poked one another. Melanie knocked over her glass of Tab and didn't even seem to notice. My father told me to get a paper towel and wipe it up.

"Why can't Bonnie?" I grumbled.

"Because I'm asking you."

I heaved a put-upon sigh and stomped out to the kitchen. When I got back, the Beatles were already singing. My sister and her friends were going nuts, except for Janet, who appeared to be more composed than the others. The Beatles sang "Till There Was You," "She Loves You," "I Saw Her Standing There," and "I Want to Hold Your Hand." After they had finished, my father shook his head and said, "Well, they have a lot of pep, I'll say that much for them." My sister groaned and rolled her eyes as if he'd just dismissed Albert Einstein as being clever. "Come on," she said to her friends, leading them upstairs to her bedroom, where they could swoon in private. My father shrugged at Kim and me, a little hurt by their abrupt departure as they stampeded overhead. Kim had to go home, since it was a school night. My father and I stayed in the family room and watched *Bonanza* and then *Candid Camera* until my mother came home.

By ten o'clock, Mr. Klein, Laurie's father, had already picked up Laurie, Melanie, and Jill, who all lived close by. Janet, who lived on the other side of town, in our old neighborhood, was still waiting for her father to pull up. All the Andrettis were notoriously late for everything. She said it was part of the Mediterranean temperament. When Janet walked downstairs to wait near the front window, she saw my mother reading in her usual armchair in the living room and walked over and said hello. My mother smiled at her and set her book aside, pleased to see Janet, who hadn't been over in quite some time. Janet noticed all my mother's books on Buddhism—long overdue from the library—and said, "Have you read *Franny and Zooey*? It has to do with Buddhism."

"Really?" My mother shook her head and looked interested. Janet was the only one of my sister's friends who could actually talk with adults. It irritated my sister, who announced, loudly, that she would be in the family room watching *What's My Line?*

"Yeah," Janet said to my mother. "I read it because I loved *The Catcher in the Rye*, but it was much weirder. I liked it, but I'm not sure I understood it all."

"I know what you mean," my mother said as if she really meant it. "I'll have to read it."

"I can lend it to you," Janet said. "I'll bring it by if you'd like."

"That would be great, but you don't have to do that. I can get it at the library."

"I don't mind," Janet said. A horn tooted out front and she drew back the drapes and waved at her father. "That's my father."

My mother nodded. "Better not keep him waiting."

"Tell Bonnie I said thanks and I'll call her," she said, gathering up her scarf and gloves. "And I won't forget about the book." She looked over at me as she wrapped the scarf around her head. "'Bye, Suzanne."

"'Bye," I said, thinking she looked just like Natalie Wood in *Splendor in the Grass*, with the white scarf tied under her chin, contrasting with her dark hair and eyes.

"'Bye, Bonnie!" she called out as she opened the front door, but my sister must not have heard her.

As my mother got up to walk Janet out the door and wave to Mr. Andretti, a scrap of newspaper fluttered to the carpet from the book she'd been reading. I picked it up. It was a photograph of a bald monk sitting in a cloud of flames. The caption said "Buddhists Hold Fiery Protest in Saigon." The article explained how the monk had doused himself with gasoline and then set his own robes on fire. The picture made me queasy. I stuck it back in the book and slammed the cover shut. It was a library book, so there was a chance that someone else had left the article in the book, I told myself. I didn't want to think of my mother cutting out the gruesome picture and saving it. Then I flashed on the other article in Peggy's photo album—"Troy Couple Die in Fire." It was too coincidental. Even if I didn't really understand the connection.

On Valentine's Day my mother's cast was removed and the doctor gave her some exercises for her wrist. She still wasn't sleeping or eating regularly. Once or twice I got up in the middle of the night and saw her sitting in her chair in the dark, smoking a cigarette with one hand and doing her wrist exercises with the other. It looked spooky, like something out of *The Twilight Zone*. My father seemed to have given up on trying to get her to quit smoking again. In fact, he seemed to have given up on her, period. It seemed to be enough for him that she got up every morning and got dressed, that she washed and set her hair twice a week, that she helped out Mrs. Quave, that she went to her book club, that she had polite conversations with the neighbors in passing, that she grocery-shopped and cooked (more or less) and chauffered my sister and me to our various appointments and activities or let my sister borrow her car. He no longer seemed to expect much more from her. I rarely saw them touching or talking or even sitting in the same room except at supper time. After we got a second smaller TV for upstairs, he would cloister himself in the master bedroom watching sports events while my mother and I watched *The Defenders* or *Burke's Law* or a movie.

My sister was usually out. On a couple of occasions I even noted them watching the same show on their separate TVs. They both liked Jack Benny. Sitting in my room doing homework, I could hear them laughing at the same jokes on different floors. Even though they were laughing, it sounded sad.

In mid-April Bonnie received letters of acceptance from UW, Beloit College, and Loyola University. My father wanted her to stay in Madison and my sister wanted to go to Chicago, so they compromised on Beloit, a small college about an hour away. My mother did not offer her opinion and they did not ask for it. Janet Andretti, on the other hand, asked my mother's advice about whether she should go to Mount Holyoke, Stephens, or Mills College, all of which had offered her scholarships. The two of them spent a long time poring over the catalogs, comparing the pros and cons of each school. Ever since Janet had dropped off her copy of *Franny and Zooey*, as promised, she and my mother had developed this odd relationship, almost as if they were friends. Janet's parents were not the intellectual type. Their house was always in an uproar—full of music, guests, the clatter of pots and pans—and she seemed to enjoy quiet conversations about books with my mother over a cup of tea. More and more, my sister wasn't even at home when Janet came over. It was one of the only issues on which my sister and I saw eye to eye: Bonnie was insulted by Janet's devotion to my mother and I was jealous of my mother's devotion to Janet.

It was an early false spring. The shrubs started to bud the first week of April, and the crocuses sprouted. Even

though she knew you were not supposed to plant anything before May, my mother couldn't wait. She went to
the nursery and came home with two rose and two lilac
bushes. My father told her she was crazy, it was too early,
so she dug the holes herself. It was her first burst of
enthusiasm in months and I thought he should have been
more encouraging, even though, as he predicted, it
snowed the next week and the fragile shrubs suffered permanent frostbite. They survived but never truly seemed
to flourish. By the time it finally warmed up for good, my
mother had lost interest in the yard and it was my father
and I who ended up planting the edges of the front walkway with the usual impatiens, petunias, and marigolds.

That spring my father bought himself a set of golf
clubs and joined the country club. Dr. Matsumi was a
golf nut. Every Saturday and Sunday morning before the
rest of us were even awake, the two of them were out on
the golf course. One afternoon a week my father took off
from work early for his lesson with the golf pro. In the
evenings after supper, he took to practicing putting on
the little putting green next to the Timberlake
Community swimming pool. We hardly ever saw my
father anymore unless it was raining or dark out. He
became tanned and fit and took to wearing jaunty polo
jerseys in bright colors instead of his old short-sleeved
shirts. He had a collection of sporty golf caps. My sister
started calling him "Bing," for Bing Crosby, and the
name caught on. He seemed to like it. He'd mentioned
once how all the men he knew had nicknames—Bob, Bill,
Ed, Ted, Dick, Chuck—except for him. What could you
do with a name like "Glen"? A couple of months later, at
the club, I heard him introduce himself to a new mem-

ber. "Glen Keller," he said, shaking the man's hand, "but people call me Bing."

Mrs. Matsumi, who also played golf, tried to persuade my mother to take up the game. She said the fresh air and exercise would do her a world of good. But my mother wasn't interested. Occasionally she would play a game of croquet with me in the backyard if Kim was busy and I whined long enough that I was bored and that she never did anything with me anymore. Her heart never seemed to be in it, though. She always let me win.

Peggy had sent us a Christmas card with a long note enclosed, but as far as I knew my mother had never answered her. I sent her one of the cards I'd made in art class and told her that I was saving up for a weaving loom. My mother never mentioned our trip to Troy, and when I tried to bring it up, she would change the subject or find some excuse to leave the room. It began to seem like a dream. If it weren't for my souvenir bars of soap from the Hawkeye Motel and the marmalade, notepad, and pen from the Cornhusker Hotel, I might have wondered if I'd made the whole thing up. I often thought of confronting her with what I knew, but I was afraid. I thought about asking Dr. Joyce Brothers for some psychological advice and actually drafted a letter but never sent it because it sounded crazy.

Then, as luck would have it, I was sitting in the beauty parlor, waiting to get my hair trimmed while my sister browsed through the stores. Verna had retired and we now went to a new place in the mall called The Mane Attraction. There was a pile of magazines on the table beside me and I picked up the tattered March issue of *Redbook* and flipped through it until I came to an article entitled "The Day the President Died" by Dr. George R. Krupp. The caption under the title read: "A psychiatrist reports of its meaning in his own life and the lives of his patients . . ." I sat up straighter and started reading as fast as my eyes could move, as if, at last, everything would become clear to me. I didn't understand every word but I understood enough to know that what he was saying was true. "I saw how each person's response to the terrible event," he wrote, "not only revealed an objective sense of loss, but revealed as well the subjective nature of that person's emotional problems." He went on to give examples of various patients who had reacted in different ways because of what had happened to them in their own lives. One woman mostly felt sorry for little Caroline because her own parents had been killed in a car accident when she was very young. Another patient, a lawyer, mostly worried about Lyndon Johnson and how scared he must feel taking on this heavy burden of responsibility so suddenly because this man's father had just died of a heart attack and he was worried about having to run their law practice all by himself.

I was so deeply involved in my reading that the beautician had to come over and tap me on the shoulder with the handle of a hairbrush to get my attention. I jumped as if I'd been shot. "Sorry," she said, "I called your name but I guess you didn't hear me. What's so interesting?" She tried to peek over my shoulder but I slammed the magazine shut.

"Nothing," I said. "A new diet."

"You don't look like you need to worry any about that," she declared as she led me over to the sinks. "Now I, on the other hand . . ." Her huge breasts mashed against my face as she bent over to fasten the plastic cape around my neck and tilted my head back at an uncomfortable angle against the hard rim of the sink. I hated this part—the base of my skull always felt sore the next day—but the spray of warm water and her strong fingers scrunching the shampoo into my scalp felt good. I closed my eyes and thought about what the doctor had said. Something about how if we could recognize and admit our true feelings about the assassination, then maybe we could trace them back to their true origin in our own lives and then maybe we could come to understand *why* we feel the way we do and move on with our lives.

The beautician wrapped a towel around my hair and led me over to the salon chair in front of the mirrored wall. She yanked the tangles out and then started whacking away at my bangs as if the scissors were pruning shears. She didn't even ask me how much I wanted off. I hated short bangs, but I was too much of a shrinking violet to say anything until it was too late. "What do you think?" she asked, whisking off my pink plastic cape with the flourish of a matador.

"They seem a little short," I mumbled, pulling at them.

She was busy sweeping up the skimpy pile of pale hair on the floor and didn't respond. I handed her the fifty cents my mother had told me to give her as a tip. She thanked me and slipped it into her pocket. I paid the cashier and then walked back to the waiting area for my jacket. The old *Redbook* was lying on the table. On an impulse I glanced around to see if anyone was looking, then slipped the magazine inside my jacket and hurried out into the mall, my blood racing in my ears, expecting to be nabbed by a security guard. But nothing happened. It wasn't as if it were the current issue, I told myself. Nobody would ever miss it.

When I got home I ran up to my room and read the rest of the article. I especially liked the part where the doctor said, "In losing John F. Kennedy we lost a father or a son, a brother or a husband, a friend or a foe. But we lost more than the man: we lost the family. Together they were absorbed into our lives—father, mother and children . . . Thus we have lost much. We have lost a beautiful family and none of us can easily give up beauty." In the Kennedys, he concluded, we saw the ideal family, the family we all wanted to be part of, and then, in an instant, it was gone. The article made me feel better since it seemed to be saying that my mother's behavior was not so abnormal after all; it was, in fact, understandable. But toward the end of the article the doctor said that by now most Americans had worked through their mourning period and had accepted the loss and achieved "emotional separation." According to him, that was the sign of good mental health. But I wasn't so convinced about my mother. I wondered where Dr. Krupp lived and wished he could talk to my mother. I thought that he would know just what to say or do to help her. Unfortunately, I figured, he probably lived far away—in New York or Los Angeles—since no one I knew had ever gone to a psychiatrist. So I did the next best thing I could think of. I left the magazine lying on the kitchen table where my mother was sure to see it.

The magazine disappeared, and my mother never mentioned it. I thought maybe she had thrown it out without reading it, and I kicked myself for not just show-

ing her the article. What would have been the big deal?
Hey, Mom, here's an article that's sort of interesting. But
then, several days later, I found it torn out of the magazine and tucked into one of the cookbooks she never
used. I looked through the six-page article to see if I
could see any visible proof of her having read it and, sure
enough, on the very last page I came across one sentence
underlined in red ink: "Feelings of *guilt* seek relief in
punishment, either of oneself or others; feelings of
responsibility seek relief in restitution, the righting of a
wrong." I read the sentence over several times, commit-
ting it to memory. I didn't see what it had to do with the
assassination, but I was glad that my mother had read the
article.

In June we all got dressed up and went to my sister's
graduation ceremony and then out to dinner at her
favorite restaurant, Porta Bella's. My sister looked beautiful, almost adult. She was wearing a white eyelet dress
with spaghetti straps that she had designed herself. She
was growing her hair long and setting it on orange juice
can rollers to get it to look straight and smooth. My parents gave her a Lady Bulova watch. I couldn't even
remember the last time we had all gone out to dinner
together. My father was feeling particularly well-disposed
toward my sister because she had dumped Roger the
week before, the day after the senior prom. She offered
no explanation for the sudden breakup—my father
assumed that she'd just finally seen the light—but I overheard her talking to one of her friends on the phone and
I knew it was because she had a crush on some college
guy who worked at a record store on State Street. She
had abruptly stopped listening to the Beatles and started

buying folk music—Bob Dylan, Joan Baez, Judy Collins. My father was also pleased with her new musical tastes. He liked Joan Baez and Judy Collins although he was less keen on Bob Dylan who, he said, sounded like Mr. Ed.

My mother was smoking and nibbling on a breadstick. She had lost a lot of weight and was super thin, like a fashion model. Her old watch, which used to fit snugly, slid up and down her wrist whenever she moved her arm. She was wearing a black sheath that was so baggy on her now that she'd had to cinch it in at the waist with one of Bonnie's wide belts. I noticed the man at the next table staring at her while his plump wife toddled off to the ladies' room. We were all making an effort to be peppy and festive, our voices and gestures exaggerated like bad actors.

"I was thinking maybe we could take a little trip to the World's Fair this summer," my father said. "Maybe see a Broadway show."

The Quaves had driven to New York for Easter in order to see the Vatican pavilion's unveiling of Michelangelo's *Pietà*. Kim had sent me a postcard of the statue which, she wrote on the back of the card, had made her cry.

"My job starts this weekend," Bonnie said. She was going to work at Fabric World in the mall to save money for college.

"I'm sure they could give you a few days off." He cut a precise bite of his veal marsala and chewed contentedly.

"I thought you were always lecturing us about taking work seriously," she said, "being dependable."

I could tell that this idea of a little family trip wasn't going over. And that although my father should just let the idea drop, he wouldn't.

"What do you say?" He looked at my mother, who stopped sipping her wine and gave him a blank, flustered look like a student who hasn't heard the teacher's question.

"About going to the World's Fair," I prompted.

"Oh," she nodded vaguely. "Well, it's certainly an idea."

My father rolled his eyes and snapped a breadstick in two. "We're a family. Families are supposed to do things together now and then. Enjoy each other's company." He bit off the top of a breadstick and started to choke. My sister pounded him on the back while he reached for his water glass.

When he stopped sputtering, she said, "Oh, Daddy, that's only on TV."

For the first time all day, my mother laughed spontaneously.

My father glared at her. "I don't see what's so funny."

My mother shrugged, as if it were his problem.

The waitress came and asked us if we were ready for dessert.

When we got home, there was a brand-new lemon yellow VW parked in the driveway. Yellow was my sister's favorite color, and I knew even before my father handed her the keys that it was her big graduation surprise. She looked as if she were about to faint from shock and joy. "I don't believe it!" she kept squealing like a contestant on a game show. She threw her arms around my father and then ran over and opened the door of the car and bounced up and down in the driver's seat with her hands tugging the steering wheel back and forth the way we did when we were little kids pretending to drive. My father stood in the driveway all teary-eyed. My mother reached over and put her hand on his arm.

"Seems like just yesterday . . ." he said, shaking his head and letting the sentence trail off.

My mother patted his cheek and went inside the house. A minute later I could see her through the upstairs window slipping the black dress off over her head. My sister had turned the key in the ignition and was blasting the radio and tooting the horn of her new car like a one-woman parade. Denise and Dianne DiNardo came running from their backyard to the curb and stood there shyly trying to figure out what all the commotion was about.

"It's my sister's new car!" I called across the street to them. "Her graduation present."

They nodded and waved. They were wearing my sister's and my old baby-doll pajamas with the polka dots. My sister's (now Denise's) were yellow with pink butterflies. Mine (now Dianne's) were pink with blue butterflies. Mr. DiNardo opened the screen door and walked across the street to admire the new car. Then Hank Crawford appeared, shirtless in his Bermudas, carrying a couple of beers, which he offered my father and Mr. DiNardo. The three men stood there talking and drinking while I walked across the street and said hi to Denise and Dianne, who were finishing off some Popsicles. Denise's lips were purple (grape) and Dianne's were dark brown (root beer), and a trail of sticky syrup was running down her wrist to her elbow.

"Neat car," Denise said. "I want one just like it when I'm sixteen."

"Me, too," Dianne said.

A minute later my sister backed out of the driveway and puttered down the street, waving to everyone like a queen on a Rose Bowl float. I walked back over to our house and asked my father where she was going.

"To show off the car to her friends," he said. "Where else?"

I could see my mother out back dressed in a flowered shift and rubber flip-flops, watering her blighted rose and lilac bushes. I walked around back and said, "Did you know about the car?"

She shook her head.

"Me neither," I said.

The water droplets sparkled on the bright-green leaves. The sun was just starting to sink in the sky. In English class the last week of school we had read Walt Whitman's "When Lilacs Last in the Dooryard Bloom'd." Which our teacher explained was about Abraham Lincoln's assassination. When Mrs. Ritchie read the poem aloud, her voice shook. In the seat behind me, Fred Resnick snickered. I turned my head around and hissed, "You're a moron!" Mrs. Ritchie looked up from the book and noticed me turning back around in my seat. She gave me a disappointed look, as if to say she would have thought I would have appreciated the poem. I wanted to explain, but I couldn't.

When I walked around to the front lawn again, Keith Matsumi was out in front of their house pruning their azaleas. Their yard was a work of art. In the back they had a little fishpond with a footbridge and lanterns. I waved to him and sat on our front steps, hoping he might walk over and talk to me. Unlike the other boys, he was reserved, almost formal, and seemed older than his age. He was notoriously smart, but no one seemed to hold it against him because he was so modest and was the best tennis player in the school. He never flirted or asked girls out on dates. He was planning to be a surgeon. The one time I had managed to have a conversation alone with him, at a neighborhood barbecue, he had talked passionately about artificial hearts. He seemed to me a romantic figure, mysterious and self-sufficient. I sat on the porch, pretending to read a book in the deepening twilight, until he put the pruning shears away in the garage and went inside. A few minutes later, I could hear him practicing his violin, the clear, birdlike melody soaring down to me from his open bedroom window.

My sister was in love. She worked at the fabric store five days a week, Tuesday through Saturday. Sundays and Mondays she devoted to catching up on the prime tanning hours she had to miss during the week. She took it as a personal affront whenever it happened to be cloudy on one of her days off. But mostly she just waited impatiently for evening, when she could go hang around the record store on State Street where Greg worked until he got off at 9:00 P.M. Then they would drive around in her Volkswagen or go to his apartment, which he shared with two roommates, and do whatever. My father fretted over her going to his apartment. I think he almost regretted the breakup with Roger Braindead, who at least lived with his parents. "What do you do over there?" he asked her.

"Listen to music, talk, et cetera," my sister replied airily.

"Et cetera," my father muttered. "That's what I'm worried about."

During the days, Kim and I would hang out at the swimming pool after Kim finished practicing her flute. We would cram our sandwiches, beach towels, suntan oil, and books into our beach bags and trudge the two blocks to the pool and camp out until supper time. There were a couple of boys we liked to flirt with. We would pretend to ignore them and they would splash our books until we had to look up in mock protest. That summer I read *The Diary of Anne Frank* twice. Inspired by her, I bought a white leather diary with gold-edged pages and wrote in it every night with a special fine-point pen before I went to sleep. I asked my mother if she ever wrote in her journal anymore, the one that she'd started years ago during the presidential campaign, and she said she had stopped once Kennedy won the election. That summer the Republicans nominated Barry Goldwater to run against LBJ, but my mother was no longer interested in politics.

In the warm evenings after supper and before his bedtime, Kim and I would take Mikey for a walk around the neighborhood in his stroller. He loved the motion and would kick and gurgle with excitement. His favorite toy was a ring of bright plastic keys that he liked to rattle and was always throwing onto the sidewalk. We had to stop and pick them up and hand them back to him about a thousand times each block. I suggested tying them to his wrist, which we tried, but he didn't like it and cried until we untied them, then immediately smiled and threw them on the ground. The other kids' parents had explained to them about Mikey being a Mongoloid, but the kids still stopped whatever they were doing and stared at him when we strolled by. Once Dianne

DiNardo stopped jumping rope and said, "Hi, Mikey." Then she looked up at me and whispered, "Can he hear me?"

"Of course he can hear you," Kim snapped at her. "He's not deaf, he's just retarded."

Dianne's lip trembled and she burst into tears and ran inside her house.

On the Fourth of July, as we had done every year since we'd moved to our new house, we went next door to the Quaves' for a barbecue. Only this time Marjorie was in Mississippi with a bunch of college friends who had gone down there together on a bus to help register Negro voters. And Bonnie was at a party in the country with Greg. Mikey was sitting in his stroller beside the picnic table gumming his plastic key ring. While the coals heated up, our parents stood together looking glum and worried, talking about the three white college boys in Mississippi who were still missing after their burned-up car had been discovered.

"I want her to come home," Mrs. Quave was saying. "I sympathize with what she's doing, but it's just too dangerous."

Mr. Quave reached for his wife's hand and held it tightly. "Of course she's all fired up with idealism. We'd have to go down and physically drag her back." He shook his head. "It's a war zone."

My mother sighed and said, "Well, I have to say I admire Marjorie's courage and social conscience. I can't imagine Bonnie doing something like that."

"Thank your lucky stars." My father glared at her as if she were out of her mind. My mother shrugged and looked away. She was wearing her dark glasses, but I imagined that she was glaring back at him. Or else looking right through him, as she seemed to do a lot lately.

Mr. Quave put his arm around his wife and kissed her cheek. "She'll be okay," he said. Mrs. Quave nodded and squeezed his hand. Ever since the baby was born they seemed more tender and solicitous toward one another. My mother had noticed it, too. She had commented that a terrible blow was the true test of a marriage. You either turned against each other or joined forces. Most couples, she said, turned against each other.

Mikey started to fuss and Mr. Quave bent down and picked him up and bounced him around until the baby was grinning and burbling little bubbles of happiness. Mrs. Quave smiled and pulled a Kleenex from her pocket and wiped the drool from his chin. It seemed to me that they loved this baby even more than a normal baby, maybe because they knew they had to make up for all the love he wouldn't get from the rest of the world. I almost wished my parents could have a retarded baby to bring them closer to one another again. But I knew in my heart that it wouldn't work that way. They would be the other sort of couple. My father would blame my mother somehow, although he wouldn't come right out and say so. Her smoking, for instance. He would have to fix upon something as the logical cause of such a catastrophe. And my mother would blame him for blaming her and for having such a small heart.

After we ate dessert—vanilla ice cream and bluebery pie on red paper plates—it started to get dark and fireworks started exploding around the neighborhood. Loud firecrackers popping like machine-gun fire and showers of sparks falling from the sky. Startled and frightened, Mikey started to shriek and wail. Nothing they could do would calm him. Finally Mrs. Quave took him inside, shut the doors and windows, and turned on the stereo and air conditioner. Kim and I went out to the front yard and lit some sparklers with the other kids. Kevin Crawford had a whole arsenal of fancy fireworks—Stinging Ants, Fire Dragons, Comet Tails, Rainbow Rockets, Shooting Stars, Atomic Blasters. My father had never allowed us to play with fireworks because of his eye accident when he was four years old and a firecracker had nearly blinded him. I had always been terrified of them. But when Keith Matsumi offered to let me light a special Chinese Joy Blossom that his relatives had sent from Tokyo or Hong Kong or someplace on the other side of the world, I summoned up all my courage and thanked him. He held the lantern as I struck the match, hands trembling, and lit the wick. As the shower of sparks fizzed and flickered all around us, he smiled at me. Then, without a word, he walked back to his house as if he'd suddenly remembered he had something important to do. I picked up the dead Chinese Joy Blossom and slipped it into my pocket like a wilted corsage.

"Come on," Kim said, tugging me away. I knew she thought he was a hopeless case. And I thought he had a crush on her because she played the flute so well and he always seemed a little tongue-tied and fidgety when she was around. But she thought I was crazy and didn't care anyway because she had a crush on a boy she'd met at music camp who lived in Green Bay.

We climbed out my bedroom window onto a roof ledge where we could just barely get a glimpse of the big fireworks display over Lake Mendota. It was a warm, clear, breezy night. The distant explosions and flashes of light seemed like a war produced by Walt Disney. Down below I could see my parents sitting side by side in lawn chairs, not talking or even looking at each other while Mrs. Quave was inside with the baby and Mr. Quave was busy mixing drinks.

"I don't think my parents love each other anymore," I blurted out before I could stop myself.

She opened her mouth as if to contradict me but closed it again. I had the feeling that she knew something she wasn't saying. I waited. After a minute she said, "I heard your mother talking to my mom about it."

"About what?"

"About how she didn't think things could go on like this much longer."

"What things?"

"You know." She looked down at my parents sitting there. My mother was lighting her hundredth cigarette. My father was polishing the lenses of his glasses with his white handkerchief.

"What did your mother say?" I felt strangely calm, as if the conversation were happening at a distance, like the fireworks.

"She said just to wait it out. She said lots of couples went through bad patches and came out okay in the end."

"And what did my mother say?"

"Nothing. She didn't say anything."

A particularly spectacular series of explosions lit up the horizon. Huge red, yellow, green, and white flowers that bloomed in a bright gaudy flash and then wilted abruptly, their petals falling to the ground in a shiver of sparks.

That night Jack wasn't there when we got home. He usually stayed with me until I fell asleep and then curled up wherever my mother happened to be sleeping that night. The living-room sofa, the family-room sofa, the lounge chair on the screened-in porch. Or sometimes she just fell asleep, reading, in her armchair. He didn't show up all night or the next morning. We figured he must have been unnerved by all the fireworks and had slunk off somewhere to hide. Usually he stuck pretty close to home.

Later that afternoon, around supper time, a woman a couple of blocks away on Blue Spruce Lane called and asked if this was the Keller residence. When I said yes she asked to speak to my mother or father. I called my mother, who was applying a clear coat of Hard as Nails, trying to get her fingernails back in shape now that she had started smoking again and had stopped biting them. She picked up the phone awkwardly, trying not to smudge her wet nails. "I see," she said in a hushed voice, "well, thank you for calling. No, no, I'll send my husband over when he gets home." Then she picked up a pen and wrote down an address and hung up. I knew even before she told me.

"It's Jack, isn't it?"

She nodded.

"What happened?"

"Her kids found him in the empty lot behind their house. She thinks someone hit him with their car and dumped him there." My mother's voice broke. "The woman was very nice. She saw the tag on the collar and called here."

I started to cry.

"I'm sorry, honey," she said as if the loss were all mine even though the cat was more attached to her than to me. And vice versa.

We heard Bonnie's car putter up to the front curb and the front door bang open and shut. She burst into the kitchen, happy to be home from work, took one look at us and turned pale. "What happened?"

"The cat," I sobbed. "He's dead."

"Oh," she said and let out a sigh of relief. "I thought something'd happened to Dad." She grabbed a Tab from the refrigerator and ran upstairs to change her clothes.

"Don't mind her," my mother said, stroking my hand on the sticky vinyl tablecloth. "Sensitivity is not your sister's strong suit."

"I want to go get him," I said.

My mother shook her head. "I told the woman your father would be over later."

"But I want to go now. Us."

My mother hesitated, screwing the cap back on the Hard as Nails. "Okay. Maybe you're right." She stood up and fished her car keys out of a bowl on the sideboard. "We should bring a cardboard box," she said gently. "Could you get one out of the garage?"

I held the box on my lap during the short drive over to Blue Spruce. It was the box that my father's golf shoes had come in. My mother and I didn't talk. It was suffocatingly hot in the car. The woman turned out to be young and very pretty. She carried a blonde baby girl in a pink ruffled sunsuit in her arms as she led us out to the edge of the backyard, where Jack was wrapped in an old towel, under a shade tree. There were black flies buzzing all around him. "I'm so sorry," she kept saying, as if it were her fault. She seemed ready to cry herself. They had a cocker spaniel puppy, chained to a stake in the yard, who yipped at us as my mother and I stooped down and lifted Jack's body into the box. His stiff tail stuck out over the edge.

When we got home my mother and I got the spade and took turns digging a grave in the back corner of our yard under a red maple tree my parents had planted the first summer we moved in. I ran inside and brought out Jack's fur mouse and tucked it into the grave next to him, along with a can of his favorite Pacific salmon with gravy. In school we had studied the Egyptians and how they would bury all the pharoahs' most treasured belongings with them in the tombs, the pyramids, for use in the afterworld.

My father strode out into the yard, frowning at his watch, and said, "I don't see anything for dinner. Were you planning to eat tonight?"

"Jack's dead." I pointed to the freshly dug earth.

"Oh no." His face fell and he put his hands on my shoulders. "I'm sorry, pumpkin. Are you okay?"

I shrugged.

My father looked at my mother and said, "I'll go get some subs. Don't worry about dinner." I could tell that he felt bad even though he had never been particularly fond of the cat. Or vice versa.

That night I felt too depressed to write in my diary. Before turning out the light I dug the diary out from under my mattress, where I kept it hidden from my sister—not that she was particularly interested in my life but she still liked to humiliate me on occasion when she had nothing better to do: "Jack's dead. Hit by a car. The whole house feels dead without him."

It was around that time—sometime between Jack's dying and my father's moving out—that I discovered my mother was writing letters to Buck Roebuck in care of the Nebraska State Penitentiary. I found his letters to her, two of them, tucked into a box of Kotex on the floor of my mother's side of the closet. I had started my period at the beginning of the summer. Usually I used tampons, but when I took the blue box out of the linen closet, it was empty. My thoughtful sister had used the last one and left the empty box in the cupboard. So I stuffed a wad of toilet paper in my underpants and hurried to my mother's closet, where I knew she kept a spare box of sanitary napkins. My father was at work and she was at the dentist's. As I yanked a Kotex out of the box, an envelope poked up. The purple stamp in the corner caught my eye. There was no return address. I found a second letter at the bottom of the box.

I took the letters into the bathroom along with the Kotex and locked the door. My first thought was that my mother was having a secret affair and that these were love letters. The idea both scared and thrilled me. But when I unfolded the first letter, the first line read: "I was surprised and pleased to hear from you after all these years. 24 years, 2 months, and 8 days to be exact but then who's counting?" I turned to the second page and read the signature: "Ballard Roebuck." He had nice handwriting but the language sounded stiff and awkward, as if it had been written by a foreigner, and his grammar was not the best. The letter wasn't very long. It was mostly about how he was glad to hear that my mother had forgiven him and how he had prayed that she would. He said he had found Jesus in prison, read the Bible every day and was doing the best he could to atone for his sins before he had to face his maker. He was glad to hear that she was married and had two girls and that he hadn't ruined her life. At least not completely. He said he'd spent many hours talking to the prison psychiatrist about his childhood and trying to understand how it had all come about the way it had. He said he'd gone from feeling sorry for himself to hating himself and finally was coming to some sort of acceptance. He said the trick was to accept responsibility for your actions and at the same time forgive yourself, if that made any sense. He concluded the letter by saying that he still liked to think that what he felt for her was love, the real thing, even though his shrink said it wasn't. At the bottom of the letter was a scrawled P.S. "Thank you for the picture of your daughters. They look like lovely girls. The older one looks alot like you."

The thought of my picture being in a prison, being looked at by a murderer, shocked me. I couldn't believe my mother had done that. It gave me the creeps. I imagined other prisoners, other murderers, picking up the photograph and staring at it and asking who we were and where we lived. He hadn't mentioned my father, and I wondered if he just didn't want to or if my mother had deliberately chosen a picture that didn't include him.

The second letter was longer and harder to follow because it seemed to be written in response to some things my mother had written to him. It was like listening to only one half of a telephone conversation. From what I could gather she had written an apology, a confession of some sort, asking him to forgive her for something. "It's crazy for you to blame yourself, Helen. You were only sixteen. I guess you were right to be scared of me. As for things maybe having been different if youd of told me the truth, who can say? Maybe I would of killed you instead of your parents. Or all three of you. And I'd still be sitting here today."

Downstairs, I heard the door open and shut and my mother's voice calling "Suzanne?" I flushed the toilet so she'd know I was home. I was too shaken to talk. Then I folded the letters back in their envelopes, crept back into her room, and slid them back into the Kotex box where I'd found them. When I straightened up and turned around, my mother was standing in the doorway looking at me. I jumped when I saw her.

"What are you doing?" she asked.

"I needed a Kotex," I said, realizing that I was standing there empty-handed. Caught red-handed.

My mother set the new toothbrush and container of dental floss she was holding down on the dresser. Her left cheek was still swollen from the novocaine and her face looked out of kilter. I couldn't bring myself to say anything. I was feeling mad and guilty at the same time. Finally I said, "You sent him my picture. Mine and Bonnie's. I think that stinks."

My mother laughed. More from nervousness than amusement.

"It's not funny!" I protested even though I could tell she didn't think it was. Not really.

"No, it's not," she agreed, hanging her head meekly.

"You lied to me," I said, knowing that the best defense was a good offense.

"I lied to everyone," she shrugged. "Including myself. Don't take it personally."

"Does Dad know?"

"What do you think?" She looked at his precise dresser top. Comb set squarely in brush. Loose change arranged in neat stacks according to denomination. "He'd be the last person I'd tell."

"Then tell *me*," I said.

She looked at me for a second, as if trying to make up her mind about something, and then said, "Okay. Go get my cigarettes. They're on the kitchen table."

As I ran downstairs, my heart jumping in my throat, she called after me, "And an ashtray, too!"

That night I wrote it all down in my diary, as much as I could remember, word for word, like a court reporter. Like a cross-examination. It seemed both more real and less real that way.

Me: How did you meet him?

Her: He lived in an old run-down farmhouse way out of town with his father and two older brothers. The mother had died in childbirth, giving birth to him. The father was German, spoke with a heavy accent. They didn't have much money. The boys were always scrambling for odd jobs. His two brothers had enlisted in the army, so Buck was the only one left at home, trying to make enough to live on. The father had terrible emphysema—bedridden. Buck was dying to go into the army like his brothers, but there'd be no one to take care of the father. As soon as his father died, he planned to enlist. It was Christmas 1941, right after Pearl Harbor. My mother hired him to make some built-in bookcases for the living room. The whole family did beautiful wood-working.

He was around the house for a week working on the bookcases over Christmas vacation. My vacation. He had dropped out of high school the year before. He was very handsome, known as something of a loner, a little mysterious. I was going out with Tom Lovejoy, had been forever, but I hung around the house while Buck was there, making excuses to be in the living room. He seemed shy even though he had a reputation for being wild. Before he dropped out of school he played on the football team and once he broke the leg of the other team's quarterback.

Me: On purpose?

Her: No, no. During a tackle.

Me: So did he ask you out?

Her: No, he wouldn't do that. He knew I was going with Tom. And no one ever saw Buck with any girls. We thought it was sort of odd since he was so good-looking. Anyway, after he finished the bookcases, that was it for a few months, till spring. I didn't see him again. But then I found out he was building a fence for the Steins, about a mile down the road. I started riding my bike out there, trying to pretend it was just a coinci-dence the first time I saw him. He had his shirt

off and was already tanned even though the
weather had just turned warm. I thought he
looked like Gary Cooper.

Me: Or Warren Beatty.

Her: (confused) How do you know?

Me: I saw his picture in your locket. And in the newspaper, in Peggy's photo album.

Her: And you never said anything all this time?

Me: (no answer)

Her: So I started bringing him little things to eat—a
cupcake, a Bartlett pear, a kolache, a—

Me: A what?

Her: Like a sweet roll. My mother made them. And we
started to talk. And one afternoon he asked me to
meet him some evening and I said okay. I lied to
my parents and to Tom and snuck out and met
him where he was waiting for me in his father's
truck just down the road. We drove out farther
from town and parked in a field behind an abandoned farmhouse. We talked—I asked him questions and got him to open up some. He was so
intense. His hands would grip the steering wheel
until the knuckles turned white. He didn't lay a
hand on me until I told him he could kiss me if he
wanted to. After that . . . (she closed her eyes). I
couldn't even bring myself to kiss Tom good
night when we went out even though I'd been
kissing him since sixth grade and liking it well

enough. After Buck it was like kissing a little boy. He's all I thought about and dreamt about, but I didn't say a word to anyone. Not even Peggy.

Me: Why not?

Her: I knew it was wrong. My parents would put an end to it if they found out. They'd lock me in my room if they had to. He was too old for me. There was something about him. They loved Tom. They assumed we'd get married when we graduated.

Me: But they found out anyway?

Her: (She shook her head.)

Me: What happened?

Her: I got scared. I was crazy about him, but he scared me. I was a virgin, of course, and he seemed like he was dying when I'd tell him to stop. I thought he was going to explode. Once he ran out of the truck and lay down in front of the wheels and told me to run him over, put him out of his agony. Then he started following me places. Everywhere. Just watching, not saying anything. He didn't want me to see Tom anymore. I said I had to or my parents and everyone would be suspicious. He started talking about running away together. At first I'd talk about it, too, until I realized he was serious. He was making plans. Setting a date.

Me: What about his father? I thought he had to take care of him.

Her: He didn't care. It was like nothing else mattered, like we were the only two people in the world as far as he was concerned. I felt like that, too, when I was with him—I really did—but when I'd go back home, it seemed insane. I couldn't just leave. I was only a junior in high school. I was my parents' only child, the center of their universe. Then Peggy got nervous about his following us. I couldn't tell her I was seeing him, so she just thought he was some weirdo stalker, only we didn't have the word "stalker" in those days. And she said she was going to report it to the police. I didn't know what to do. I was afraid about what would happen if the police questioned him. So I told her I'd talk to my uncle, Frank Carlson, who was a policeman. She said okay. I knew something bad was going to happen if I didn't do something. I was nuts about him, but I was just a kid, what did I know?

Me: Like Bonnie.

Her: Even younger. Girls were younger in those days, I mean, for their age. Less knowledgeable. More sheltered.

Me: Did you talk to Frank Carlson?

Her: No. No way. He would have told my parents for sure. So the next night when I saw Buck, I lied. I said my parents had found out about him and had forbidden me to see him again. And if they heard he was following me they were going to get him arrested. I said my mother's brother was a cop and she could just snap her fingers and that would be that. He'd be in jail. And they'd send me away to some Catholic girls' boarding school—a convent—in Minnesota. I made that part up, about the girls' school, but Buck believed me. He believed it all. Why wouldn't he? He believed I loved him. I did love him. But I guess I was too scared to be really in love and he was too in love to be really scared.

I didn't see him for a week. That Saturday I was spending the night at Peggy's house. In that same little room where you stayed. In the middle of the night the police pounded on the door. Mr. Kelly walked outside and talked to the policemen on the front lawn for a couple of minutes. When he came in, his face was dead white. He asked his wife, Peggy's mother, to step outside and he whispered to her for a couple of minutes. I had no idea what was going on, but I was nervous, I had a bad feeling. A guilty conscience. Then she came in and sat me down and told me there'd been a fire and that my parents were dead.

Me: Did you know? I mean, that it was Buck?

Her: I think it was one of those things you know right away but spend the rest of your life trying to believe—

It was at that point that we heard my father's car pull into the garage. My mother looked at her watch and said she hadn't realized it was so late. She said she'd better see about dinner and went downstairs. After she left, I emptied the ashtray and opened the bedroom windows wider. She wasn't supposed to smoke upstairs. I felt strange, as if I'd just walked out of a movie that had stayed with me. The way I felt after seeing *To Kill a Mockingbird*. When we walked out of the theater, even though there was snow on the ground, I'd felt warm, like I was still back in that stuffy little Southern town. I heard a crash and ran downstairs. My father had picked up the package of frozen hamburger and thrown it across the kitchen, knocking the spices off the spice rack. "Jesus Christ!" he muttered. "What in God's name do you do all day? Look at this place."

My mother walked out the screen door into the back-yard and lay down in a chaise longue with her eyes closed. My father sat down at the kitchen table and held his face in his hands. I tiptoed over and started to pick the spices up off the floor and set them on the counter. There were little anthills of cinnamon and paprika and oregano on the linoleum from where my mother hadn't shut the lids of the red tin boxes tightly. My father opened his eyes and saw me kneeling there. He looked sad and sheepish.

"It's not just dinner," he said. "It's more than that. It's everything. Can you understand that?"

I nodded, not wanting to commit myself one way or the other.

He picked up the frozen hamburger and put it in the refrigerator, then helped me pick up the spice tins, most of which were ancient and sticky. He looked out the window. My mother was still lying on the chaise longue as if she were on the deck of a cruise ship. His jaw tighted. He dumped the old spice tins in the trash and clapped me on the shoulder and said, "Let's go to McDonald's."

Shortly after that incident, maybe a week later, my father rented a two-bedroom apartment in a new complex over near his office. Bonnie and I referred to it as "the brown place," since when he showed it to us for the first time everything in it was brown. Beige walls, brown wall-to-wall carpeting, brown tweed furniture, fake walnut dinette set, and a brown plaid comforter. When Bonnie said it was depressing, he bristled and said he liked "earth tones." The next weekend she brought over some throw pillows she'd made in vivid reds and oranges to brighten up the place. My father seemed touched by the gesture. He said he wanted us to feel at home there. He gave us each fifty dollars and told us to go to the mall and buy ourselves new bedspreads and whatever for our bedroom, which had twin beds and matching fake French provincial bureaus and night tables. The vanilla veneer was already peeling off the edge of one of the night tables. Bonnie and I had not shared a room since Marta, the Finnish exchange student, had left, and we didn't take to the idea with any enthusiasm. At the mall we separated, knowing that any attempt at compromise was useless. She bought a wild purple, yellow, and black Indian-type comforter and I bought a white quilt with sprays of violets and an eyelet border. When we put them on the twin beds, the effect was disturbingly schizoid but my father didn't seem to notice.

My father's moving out seemed to affect my mother like shock therapy. For the first few days she cleaned the house from top to bottom and made an appointment to get her hair cut and styled. She took to the kitchen in a desperate attempt to salvage our respectability. In those days, at least in Wisconsin, divorce was still something mostly associated with other people, movie stars or trashy types, people with winter tans or criminal records. All of our friends had two parents, and after my father moved out, the neighbor kids seemed to look down on us, as if we'd had to sell one of our cars or something. So my mother began preparing these dull, well-balanced meals from the four basic food groups. "You are what you eat," she'd say, smiling her new fake Betty Crocker smile. As if eating all these boring all-American meals would make us just another boring all-American family. I missed the pizzas and subs and Big Macs.

I heard my mother arguing on the phone with my father, accusing him of trying to buy our loyalty with Chinese takeout, pizzas, and Dairy Queen sundaes after we came home on Sunday afternoon too full to eat the meat loaf, Rice-A-Roni, and string beans my mother had prepared for dinner. Before the separation my parents hardly ever fought—they rarely talked to one another— but now they were always shouting at each other on the phone. I thought maybe it was a good sign. Maybe they would get back together.

I sent a postcard to Peggy telling her about my parents' separation. "My father is no longer in the picture," I wrote, "at least for the time being." I told her I was still saving up for a weaving loom like hers. She sent back a catalog of weaving supplies and a note telling me that I was welcome to visit any time and stay as long as I wanted. She said she knew it must be painful, but that maybe a separation was for the best. I hadn't mentioned anything about my mother's correspondence with Buck Roebuck.

In the days following my father's departure, my mother seemed to zigzag between bursts of energy and sudden paralysis. On one of her energetic days she drove to the pound and got a dog. A small, scruffy terrier mix with perky ears and Brillo pad fur. She had always wanted a dog, ever since she was a little girl, she said, looking like an excited ten-year-old as she led the puppy into the house on his new leash. He yapped and wriggled and peed on the floor when I bent down to pet him.

"What are you going to call him?" I asked.

"It's a she," she said. "And I haven't decided yet."

We made lists of names and tried out a couple that didn't stick. In the end the only name that felt right was Jackie. The dog trailed her everywhere. She even lay on the bath mat while my mother soaked in the tub for hours.

Jackie and Pickle hit it off right away. Kim and I said it was too bad that Pickle had been fixed; otherwise they could have had puppies together. Ever since the separation, my mother and Kim's mother seemed to have drifted apart again. I think my mother was avoiding Mrs. Quave because, being Catholic, she didn't believe in divorce and the whole subject was an uncomfortable one for both of them. Mikey had learned to sit up and to flop himself over from his back to his stomach, although he had yet to master the move in reverse. Marjorie had returned from Mississippi safe and sound, and with a boyfriend for the first time in her life. He was from Boston, a law student who planned on becoming a civil rights lawyer. My mother told me that Kim's parents were upset because he was Jewish. "That's the problem with religion," she said. "Love thy neighbor as thyself— unless, of course, he wants to marry your daughter, heaven forbid."

"How would you feel if Bonnie wanted to marry a black guy?"

My mother laughed. "Your sister? You've got to be kidding."

"You know what I mean."

"Remember *Lilies of the Field*?" she said dreamily.

I nodded. It was one of the few times she'd referred to our trip to Troy.

"You could do a lot worse than Sidney Poitier," she sighed. "A lot worse."

"Why did you marry Dad? Were you in love with him?" It was something I had been wondering a lot lately. Especially since I noticed that she had taken down the wedding photograph she'd had colorized right before we moved into the new house, which wasn't so new any- more. In fact, before he'd moved out my father had been talking about re-wallpapering some of the rooms and painting the exterior. I couldn't imagine my mother por- ing over wallpaper sample books with the same fervent enthusiasm as the last time. I had a feeling she'd just flip the book open randomly and point to something and say "That will do."

We were sitting at the kitchen table. She lit a cigarette. She had a smoker's cough now that really bothered me. I could hear her coughing in bed in the mornings. Since my father had moved out she'd gone back to sleeping in their bedroom, across the hall from my room.

"Your father seemed very safe and sane," my mother

said. "He made me feel safe, like everything was under control. That's what I needed. He reminded me of Tom Lovejoy."

"Why didn't you just marry Tom? Peggy said he still loved you."

"She said that?" My mother blew out a lungful of smoke and picked a fleck of tobacco off her bottom lip.

"She said he never really got over you."

"I didn't want to go back," she said. "After I went to live in Kansas City, that was that. I wanted a new life." She shook her head. "I didn't know then that there's no such thing as a new life. You only have one life. Remember that."

I nodded.

"Say it," she ordered.

"You only have one life."

She got up and took a bottle of Gallo Chablis out of the refrigerator and poured herself a glass. Since my father had left, she always had an open bottle of wine sitting in the refrigerator. She didn't get drunk. She just used it to calm her nerves.

"It bothered your father not to be in uniform. To be declared unfit for service because of his bad eye, but not like Buck. It ate away at him, not being able to fight for his country. Being stuck at home. All this frustration just built up in him, like steam. And then I came along and made it worse. More frustration. But I think it was the war, really. He listened to the war news on the radio and read the papers. He knew all the battles and the generals and the casualty statistics. He read his brothers' letters over and over. Since he couldn't go anywhere, the war was raging inside him. My parents were casualties of the war. Civilian casualties. He should have been court-martialed, tried for war crimes. 'A crime of passion,' the prosecutor called it. Meaning me, of course. But I was only part of it. The passion was already there, bottled up, waiting to explode."

She stubbed out her cigarette. "Your father, on the other hand, was not a passionate man. And when I was with him, I felt calm and content. Affectionate, tender, but not stirred up inside. It was what I wanted. I felt very fortunate. I *was* very fortunate. He was a good husband and a good father."

"But you don't love him," I said flatly, trying to sound more matter-of-fact than I felt.

"I didn't say that."

"Well, you didn't say you did. Do."

"Do you think *he* loves me?"

"I think he would."

"If what?"

"If *you* loved him."

"That's not the way it works," she said. "Someday you'll see that." She drained her wineglass. The doorbell rang. "See who that is, okay?"

I walked into the foyer and could see Mrs. Bowman, the Avon lady, through the screen door. I was actually glad to see her standing there. The conversation with my mother had depressed me even though I'd asked for it.

"Come in," I said, opening the door and ushering her into the living room. "Mom!" I hollered. "It's the Avon lady."

My mother walked out smiling and said, "Hello, Evelyn, how nice to see you again." She sounded perfectly normal and charming.

The three of us sat down around the coffee table and Mrs. Bowman began pulling samples of perfumes and creams and cosmetics out of her case. We sprayed and dabbed, oohing and ahhing over the pretty little jars and bottles. By the time she left, we had bought seventy-five dollars' worth of cosmetics and had absolutely nothing to show for it except a lingering bouquet of scents hovering like a cloud in the room. Our purchases wouldn't be delivered until the following week, by which time my mother would feel guilty for having spent the money.

After only a couple of weeks of our going back and forth between our house and my father's new apartment, my sister announced that she had decided to move in with my father for good. Earlier in the week she had fallen asleep with her contact lenses in and had suffered corneal abrasions. For some reason both she and my father seemed to think it was my mother's fault, as if she should have gone into Bonnie's room every night after she was asleep and lifted up her eyelids to check to see whether or not she'd taken her contacts out. Even though my sister had never forgotten to take them out before. It was almost as if Bonnie did it on purpose to have an excuse to stay with my father, the optometrist, for a few extra days so he could keep a closer eye on the healing process. She was in a foul mood from having to wear her old glasses for a week, and the three of us—my mother, sister, and I—were sitting on the screen porch eating broiled chicken breasts, mashed potatoes, and peas. A sweltering, humid evening.

"I've decided to move into Dad's," Bonnie said. She was pelting peas at the birds in the yard. "It's right by the mall. I can walk to work in five minutes."

My mother set down her glass of iced tea and said, "Over my dead body. You belong here with your sister and me. This is your home."

My sister got up and left the table without finishing her dinner. My mother sighed and looked across the table at me. I was feeding Jackie bits of my sister's untouched chicken under the table. "Don't worry," she said. "Your sister's not going anywhere."

That weekend she was gone. My mother and I came home from the library and her room was stripped bare. Closets empty, vanity table cleared off. Stereo and record albums gone.

About the only thing she hadn't taken was her Singer sewing machine. Since she'd started seeing Greg, she had lost interest in sewing and had taken up the guitar. Even though my father was constantly complaining about money since the separation, he had bought her a new guitar with a beautiful rosewood inlay. She had a Joan Baez and a Judy Collins songbook. Greg was teaching her the chords.

My mother didn't say anything. She just shut my sister's ex-door behind her and went downstairs and started to read one of her new library books. *Siddhartha* by Herman Hesse, something that Janet had recommended. She still went to her book group, trying to keep up appearances, but mostly she read the books that Janet was reading. *Cat's Cradle*, *One Flew Over the Cuckoo's Nest*, *The Dharma Bums*. Janet had decided to go to Mills College in Oakland, California, and the school had sent her a summer reading list, which both she and my mother were diligently plowing through.

At dinnertime that night my mother said, "Let's just

order a pizza," even though she had a package of minute steaks defrosting on the counter.

"Okay," I said. "I'll call the pizza place."

My mother nodded. "And maybe I'll give Janet a call, see if she'd like to join us. You know how she loves pizza."

And that was it. My mother seemed to lose all interest in the four basic food groups after my sister defected to my father's apartment. She ended up giving the minute steaks to the dog. One night all we ate for dinner was canned peaches and Eskimo Pies. And once my sister was gone, Janet started spending more and more time at our house, just hanging out with my mother and me. It was as if my sister had left this vacancy and Janet had decided to fill it.

I hated spending the weekend at my father's apartment after my sister had permanently installed herself there. She treated me like a not-so-welcome guest. She acted like she was my mother—or rather, not *my* mother, but *a* mother. She had already taken to doing the grocery shopping and cooking for my father. Instead of going to China Palace, we had to eat what she cooked. Revolting recipes she got out of vegetarian health food cookbooks. Glop with brown rice and tofu. I could tell that my father didn't much like it either, but he didn't complain the way he did about my mother's cooking, or lack of it. Before the separation, my father hadn't paid much attention when my mother talked; he never asked her about her day. But now, suddenly, he was all ears.

"So how's your mother doing?" he asked me almost every weekend.

"Fine," I'd mumble, looking down at my plate. She

had given me strict instructions not talk about her. "Just tell him I'm fine if he asks," she had told me. "By the way, does he ask about me?" she had asked, trying to sound casual and unconcerned. When I said he did, she seemed gratified. She never asked about him because she never had to. I told her everything, in a censored version, so that she would not have to lower herself by asking. I told her when he went shopping with my sister and bought himself a new, more youthful wardrobe. He wore suede Hush Puppies now instead of his usual spit-shined loafers. And soft corduroy slacks instead of khaki. Under my sister's tutelage, he was wearing his hair differently, too, for the first time in twenty years. A little fuller and more windblown. No more Brylcreem. And he was dating a divorcée who lived in his building and had a five-year-old boy named Stone, which my mother and I agreed was a ridiculous name. I didn't tell her about how I'd heard him tiptoeing into the apartment, holding his shoes, just before dawn.

My mother didn't seem interested in men. One evening she asked me to run next door for Hank Crawford when she turned on the air conditioner upstairs and blew a fuse. The Quaves were on vacation in Wisconsin Dells, at a rented cottage for a week; otherwise she would have asked Charlie for help. I ran next door. Mr. Crawford was mowing his lawn with his shirt off. He had rigged up this holder for a can of beer that he could swig from as he mowed and I could tell that he was half bombed. He'd already mowed down the GOLDWATER-MILLER campaign sign in the front yard and had to hammer it back into the ground.

"We blew a fuse," I shouted over the lawn-mower

racket. I had to repeat it three times before he finally comprehended what had happened and that I was asking him for help. Then he ran inside for a shirt, which he put on but didn't bother to button, and followed me back to my house.

It took him only about five minutes to replace the fuse, but he hung around until my mother offered him a glass of wine. She didn't have any beer. He said, "Don't mind if I do," and settled himself in a lawn chair on the screen porch. In the kitchen, my mother whispered to me, "Don't leave us alone." My sister and I had been instructed not to say anything about our parents' separation but everyone knew anyway. Our houses might as well have been made of glass. We all knew about Mrs. Gusdorf's mastectomy, Mr. DiNardo's tax problems, Mr. Crawford's two DWIs.

"Maybe Gloria would like to join us?" my mother asked. "Suzanne could run over and ask her."

"She's at her sister's," he said. "Bridge night."

"Oh." My mother sounded resigned. "How's Kevin? I hear he's quite an athlete."

Mr. Crawford perked up and bragged about his son's batting average for a couple of minutes. Then there was an awkward silence. My mother lit a cigarette—or tried to. He reached out and took the pack of matches from her and lit it for her like something out of an old Bette Davis movie. As my mother inhaled, he touched her arm and said, "Glen's a real moron leaving a woman like you all alone." My mother pretended to having a coughing fit, trying to wriggle away when he patted her on the back. She shot me a desperate SOS look, at the kitchen table where I was pretending to read a magazine. I couldn't think what to do that wouldn't be too obvious. He was probably harmless—I didn't think he'd try to force himself on her or anything—but it was really disgusting. Even at parties he never knew when to leave. Once the Matsumis, too polite to ask him to leave, had actually fallen asleep in the living room while he was droning on about something, at which point Gloria finally succeeded in dragging him home. I was still racking my brain trying to think of a way to save my mother when I heard her start to cry. Quietly at first, then escalating into shuddering sobs. At first I thought maybe she was faking it, but then I could tell it was real. Heartfelt. Embarrassed and confused, Mr. Crawford clumsily patted her hand, saying "there, there" the way you would to a child. Then he stood up, noticed me sitting in the kitchen, and said, "I didn't do anything. I swear to God."

"She's just tired," I said. "She hasn't been feeling well. Stomach flu."

He looked relieved. "She should have said something."

I shrugged.

"Well..." He set his glass down on the kitchen table. "I better be going." He glanced back toward the porch. "She going to be all right?"

"Fine," I said. "She's fine."

He hesitated, unsure what to do.

"Really," I insisted. "My father's coming back later," I lied. "Around nine o'clock."

He looked surprised but said, "That's good."

I walked him to the front door. "Thanks for fixing the fuse," I called after him as he cut across the grass, making a beeline for home.

That night my mother stayed up late drinking the rest of the wine. She was still sitting on the dark porch when I said good night and went upstairs to bed.

Sometime later I woke up from a deep sleep. My mother was shaking me and shouting my name. The dog was barking shrilly. "There's a fire," my mother said, dragging me onto my feet and across the room to the doorway. Suddenly I could smell the smoke. My mother was coughing. We stumbled down the stairs and out onto the front lawn.

"Run next door and tell them to call the fire department!" She gave me a little shove in the direction of the Crawfords' house. "Hurry!"

Jackie was barking and running in circles. I could see the flames shooting out from the screen porch as I cut across the pitch-black yard. A terrifyingly beautiful sight.

By the time the fire truck screamed into view, a small crowd of neighbors dressed in summer robes had gathered out front, watching the smoke and flames. I was wearing a flimsy nightgown you could see through and I felt naked, but no one was paying any attention to me anyway. My mother had on the same shorts and shell she was wearing when I went to bed. As the firemen connected the hoses to the fire hydrant in front of the Quaves' house, I wished that Kim was home. It was a hot August night, and the heat from the fire was suffocating. I didn't see how the firemen could stand to go inside. But they did. We could see the arcs of water shooting up and the flames sputtering. It was like watching it on the news. Those poor people, you'd think to yourself. What must they be feeling? In a matter of minutes they had the fire under control. My mother seemed to be in shock. She wasn't crying or screaming. She just stood there holding the frantic dog in her arms, watching as the firemen dragged their long hoses back outside. The house was still standing, at least most of it. There was a gaping hole where the screen porch had been. You could see right into the gutted kitchen. It reminded me of a dollhouse where you could reach inside the rooms and move the people around.

Mrs. DiNardo put her arm around my mother. "It doesn't look too bad," she said, trying to sound comforting. "At least no one was hurt, thank God."

My mother nodded numbly.

"Why don't you spend the night at our house?" Mrs. DiNardo suggested kindly. "We have a sleeper sofa."

My mother set the dog down on the sidewalk and started walking up the front path as if she were going to go inside but a fireman stopped her and told her not to go in yet, it wasn't safe. She looked lost. I walked up to her and said, "I can't believe it."

She turned to me and said, "Well, it's bad, but it's not the worst thing that's ever happened. Just don't tell your father."

I gaped at her like she was nuts. "He's going to know. How can he not notice that half the house is gone?"

"It's not that bad, mostly in the back. The front looks okay. He hardly ever comes inside anyway. Just drops you off."

I shook my head. "What about the insurance? The repairmen. The neighbors. There's no way he's not going to know."

"We'll see." She looked around and walked over to

Mrs. Gusdorf and bummed a Viceroy. Everyone was offering their condolences and assistance.

"I think we'll just go to a motel," my mother told them. Then she remembered that her purse was in the kitchen and was probably a charred lump.

"We could stay at the Quaves'," I said. They always left us their key to water the houseplants and collect the mail.

"That's a good idea." My mother smiled gratefully at me. I could tell that she wanted to be alone.

One of the firemen called my mother over and talked to her for a couple of minutes. Then they started loading up the truck to leave.

"What did they say?" I asked her. She looked shaken up.

"Just something about the insurance investigators coming by."

Hank Crawford walked over and said, "I hope you don't think it had anything to do with that fuse I replaced."

"No, of course not," my mother assured him. "It never crossed my mind." He looked relieved.

"Hell of a thing," he said. "Jesus Christ."

The neighbors patted us on the back or shoulder and started to drift home to their intact houses. My mother and I walked next door. The Quaves' spare key was hidden under a geranium pot on the porch. I opened the door and turned on the lights. It felt strange to be in their house with no one home. Jackie skittered around in a frenzy, sniffing everything. My mother went into the bathroom. I felt like calling my father but knew that my mother wasn't ready to face him. I knew that she must have fallen asleep on the screen porch with a cigarette burning. Something my father fretted about frequently. Which was part of the reason she wasn't supposed to smoke upstairs. And she had promised him she would never, ever, smoke in bed. I wanted to run next door and remove the wine bottle from the scene of the crime. I didn't want them to think she was a drunk on top of everything else. But I figured the firemen had already seen it there. Unless it had melted in the fire.

We decided to sleep together in Kim's room, which had twin beds. I had slept in the room countless times but it felt completely different with my mother lying in the other bed instead of Kim. Especially under the circumstances. It took me a long time to fall asleep. The house felt hot and stuffy—they had left the windows closed. I wondered what my mother was thinking. I could hear her sigh now and then. I wondered if she was remembering the other fire, years ago. She had told me about driving to the house in the detective's car the next morning, after her parents' bodies had been removed. He had offered her a stick of Black Jack gum as they parked in front of the gutted house. It was a brick house, so it didn't look so bad from the outside. The inside was another story. And that's what the detective wanted to hear. That story. "Kerosene," he had said. "Arson. Do you have any idea who might have done this?" She had cried and cried while the detective waited patiently in the seat beside her, snapping his gum.

When my father found out about the fire, the next day, he marched through the house with a grim expression on his face. I accompanied him on the tour. My mother stayed out of the way. The screen porch and kitchen were a disaster. The rest of the downstairs was mostly a mess from smoke damage and water. The upstairs seemed eerily untouched except for the inextinguishable odor of smoke that clung to everything even with all the windows wide open. As we walked from room to room surveying the damage, I thought of my mother agonizing over the wallpaper samples, the carpeting, the drapes—all of which would have to be replaced. Even before the insurance investigator talked to him, the first thing my father had said to my mother was, "I suppose it was one of those goddamn cigarettes."

"She wasn't upstairs," I said. "She wasn't in bed."

"You're just lucky you're both still alive," he told her. "Think about what could have happened."

My mother turned her back and walked away from him.

"She feels really bad," I whispered to him. "It's not like she did it on purpose."

"I know," He removed his glasses and massaged the bridge of his nose. "I realize that. But still . . . I mean, look at this place. What next?"

"It was an accident. I'm sure she'll be more careful from now on," I said. "In fact, she told me she was going to quit smoking." Which wasn't true.

"It's too late." He shook his head firmly. I didn't like the look in his eyes.

"What do you mean?"

"You're coming to live with me." He ripped a strip of scorched wallpaper off the wall like a Band-Aid off a scab and examined what was underneath it. "Your mother needs help."

"What kind of help?" I thought maybe he meant a maid.

"Professional help." He tapped his index finger against his forehead. I thought of Natalie Wood in that beautiful institution with the sloping green lawns and art classes. It seemed like something my mother might actually enjoy. At least for a little while. A month maybe. Until the house was all repaired, as good as new.

When my father told my mother I was going to live with him for a while, she looked at me and said, "Whose idea was this?"

"His." I stared at my feet, feeling like a traitor even though it wasn't my fault.

She looked at him for confirmation, and he nodded.

"It's only temporary," I said.

"*Life* is only temporary," she sighed. I wondered if that was one of the Four Noble Truths.

With the insurance settlement, my father hired a small army of workers to strip away the old stuff and rebuild, repaint, retile, re-carpet. This time my sister picked out the colors in her quick, decisive, and confident way. It took about a month, and when everything was done, the house looked better than new. It looked like one of those model homes builders use to lure people in.

My mother did not go away to some plantationlike sanitorium after all. She rented a small apartment near the campus, in an old house that had been subdivided. The other tenants were college students. It was the only place she could find that would allow pets. She had confided in me that it was Jackie who had saved us. When the fire broke out, the dog had barked and nudged my mother awake just like an episode of *Lassie*. Once a week, she talked to a psychiatrist for an hour. Once a week, my father let me spend the night at her apartment. I slept on a fold-out Murphy bed that she kept in the closet. She didn't even protest when my father told her he was putting the house up for sale.

My sister was lucky that she had already moved most of her stuff out of the house before the fire. I went back to the house with my father and salvaged what we could: photo albums, papers, knickknacks, some furniture and clothes and miscellaneous stuff. I also packed some boxes for my mother, who refused to go back to the house. Most of the stuff we threw out or gave to the Salvation Army. I only took my favorite things. Even after we had the clothes dry-cleaned I could still catch faint whiffs of smoke. We rescued my sister's sewing machine and sewing table. In the top drawer were the remaining few labels I'd bought her for her birthday years ago— "Fashions by Bonnie." Nowadays, under Greg's influence, she mostly wore baggy jeans and his old T-shirts. At the end of August, just as the repairs were finished and the "For Sale" sign went up in the front yard, my sister left for college, her yellow VW piled high with her belongings. And I was left alone in my father's brown apartment all day while he was at the office. Sometimes I would ride my bike over to Kim's and hang out but it sort of depressed me being back in my old neighborhood, next door to my empty house. So mostly I met her at the pool.

In my white leather diary that I had salvaged from under my mattress, I worried for page after page about what was going to happen. I missed my mother. In the evenings, my father and I would go out to various cheap restaurants and try to make conversation, try to pretend we were enjoying ourselves. I could tell he missed my sister. Sometimes his girlfriend, Lois, and her son, Stone, would come with us, which made things both harder and easier. It was hard to see my father with another woman, but trying to keep a squirming three-year-old occupied took the pressure off our conversation. Plus, he made us laugh by doing stupid kid tricks.

My mother's apartment was in another school district. When school started right after Labor Day, it was somehow understood that I would stay with my father "for the time being." Even though my mother seemed to be doing better. Her migraines were less frequent and less severe. Since parking was a problem in her area, she had bought a secondhand bicycle, which she used to get around downtown. She became friendly with the college students in her building and started auditing a lecture class on comparative religion that her upstairs neighbor, a graduate student from Pakistan, was taking. Like my mother, Chandra felt displaced and lonely. She loved to cook and often invited my mother, who never cooked at all, to supper. The whole building always smelled of exotic spices. Once, when I was spending the night, she brought down some dessert wrapped in foil for us. Some sweet, sticky pretzel-shaped things that tasted like honey. Chandra wore bright saris and lots of gold bangles that tinkled when she moved her arms. Her shiny black braid reached to her tailbone and I noticed that she didn't even have to fasten the tip with a rubber band. She smelled of jasmine and spoke with a British accent. I thought she was the most glamorous creature I'd ever met. And she seemed to genuinely enjoy my mother's company.

Like Janet, who lived not far from my mother's new

apartment (our old neighborhood) and visited her several times a week. She was leaving for California, for college, the second week in September. A couple of nights before she left, my mother had a little going-away party with a store-bought cake. Just the three of us. Janet bummed cigarettes from my mother, who didn't seem to mind. They were talking about Tibetan lamas and something called the third eye. My mother read us a bizarre passage about these older monks driving a wood splinter into a younger monk's forehead and leaving him alone in a dark room for two weeks. Some sort of rite of passage. Later that night, after Janet had gone home, I picked up the book and read a passage she had underlined and starred in red. "One evening the Lama said: 'Later we will show you how to shut the Third Eye at will, for you will not want to watch people's failings all the time, it would be an intolerable burden.'" In the margin my mother had scribbled, "Sounds like Dr. Miller." Dr. Miller was her psychiatrist.

My mother seemed depressed over Janet's leaving, going so far away, even though Janet had made us promise to come visit her. My mother had never been to California except for the Los Angeles airport on her way to and from Honolulu years ago. She got up and turned on the late news. Bobby Kennedy was running for the Senate in New York. My mother sat there watching him for a minute as he gave a speech. For an instant I thought I recognized the old spark of passion in her face—her new apartment was right around the corner from the Kennedy campaign headquarters where she used to volunteer when we first moved into the new house—but then she sighed and changed the channel. I wondered if she had written to Buck Roebuck again. Or heard from him. And what her psychiatrist thought about all that. She never talked about it, and I was afraid to ask. She seemed to be doing okay. Even my father seemed relieved and surprised. She had found herself a part-time job filing and typing at a travel agency on State Street—just like her old job in Honolulu when my parents were still newlyweds.

After a few weeks, my father agreed to let me spend three nights a week at my mother's—Tuesday, Friday, and Saturday. I knew my presence had put something of a damper on his romance with Lois. Even though she pretended to be crazy about me. My mother said my father was a good catch.

On Tuesday nights, my mother would pick me up after work and take me back to her place. We would order a pizza and then I would do my homework until *Peyton Place* came on. It was our favorite show. I thought Mia Farrow, who played Allison MacKenzie, was angelically beautiful and I couldn't believe it when Lois told me that Mia Farrow reminded her of me. I was letting my baby-fine hair grow long, hoping it would get as long as Mia's. Grace Metalious had died earlier that month. "She was only forty years old," my mother told me. My mother's fortieth birthday had just passed. Chandra had made a special dinner, and I had baked a chocolate cake from a mix. My mother hardly had any cooking utensils. She hadn't bothered to replace what had burned up in the fire since she never cooked. I had to borrow a cake pan and mixing bowl from the girls who lived downstairs and nearly bruised my knuckles pounding on their door until they finally heard me over the Rolling Stones blasting from their stereo.

For my mother's birthday, Janet had called from California and had sent a strange little black-and-white paperback book of poems entitled *Howl* that she said was from a bookstore in San Francisco named City Lights, which my mother would just love when she came to visit. I skimmed through a few poems—I'd never seen anything like them, they seemed to have been written by a madman. My mother took the book to bed with her. The next morning on the drive to school, I asked my mother, cautiously, what she thought of the poems.

"Well, they're a long ways from Robert Frost." She winked at me.

"He sure uses a lot of curse words," I said. "I didn't know you could do that."

My mother laughed. Then a minute later, out of the blue, she burst out with "'I saw the best minds of my generation destroyed by madness . . . !'"

I figured, I hoped, it was a line from one of the poems.

She pulled up in front of the junior high. I sat in the car for a minute watching the kids milling around outside, enjoying the last days of summer before the first bell rang. For the first time, I wasn't really enjoying school. Kim's parents had decided to send her to a Catholic school, probably because they were still upset over her sister's boyfriend being Jewish. It was lonely without her even though I had become closer to Gretchen Baird. Since she was adopted and my parents were separated, I felt we had some sort of bond. My mother deposited a peck on my cheek and said, "See you Friday, my dear." She glanced at her watch. I could tell she was worried about being late for work. I opened the car door and got out. I turned and waved at her as she drove away, but she must not have seen me because she didn't wave back.

In late September, our house was sold. When I told my mother the news over the telephone, she didn't have much of a reaction. I hung up and cried. In the back of my mind I always thought that as long as we still had the house, maybe my parents would get back together and we'd move back in. But now I knew they were going to get a divorce. That weekend when I went to my mother's apartment, she said she had suddenly remembered the Zuni wind chimes in the backyard that she'd bought in Arizona on our family vacation to the Grand Canyon. They had been expensive, but their sound was so exquisite and otherworldly that she had fallen in love with them. I could still remember the look on her face, standing in the souvenir shop, as she gave them a little push with her hand and listened to the silvery ripple of music. She looked transported, like a woman in love. My father must have noticed it, too, because he had whipped out his wallet and bought them for her.

On Saturday afternoon, we drove over to the old house to get the wind chimes. My mother had not, as far as I knew, been back since the fire. It was an unseasonably hot day for September. "Indian summer," my mother said, rolling down the car window. And I flashed on the opening to *Peyton Place* I had read so many times that I'd apparently committed it to memory for life: "Indian summer is like a woman. Ripe, hotly passionate, but fickle, she comes and goes as she pleases so that one is never sure whether she will come at all, nor for how long she will stay."

As my mother turned onto our old street I could feel her muscles tensing beside me; she gripped the steering wheel tighter. "Maybe we should have come at night," she said. "I don't really feel like seeing anyone." She seemed to be embarrassed about the fire. Or maybe the divorce.

Fortunately, only a few kids were outside. The adults must have been inside enoying the air-conditioning. I saw my mother glance over at Mrs. Quave's car, which was parked in the driveway. There was an LBJ-Humphrey bumper sticker on the rear fender. Mrs. Quave had asked my mother if she was interested in doing any campaign work, but my mother had declined. The realtor had pasted a big red SOLD over the FOR SALE sign. We parked in our old driveway and got out of the car and hurried around back, like burglars, as if we had no right to be there. My mother stood on tiptoe and unhooked the wind chimes from a branch of the red maple she and my father had planted four years earlier. It had grown from a scrawny sapling into a good-sized shade tree.

"Let's go inside," I said when I saw my mother staring at the house. The whole porch area had been rebuilt and repainted. The trim was now yellow instead of black. My mother hesitated, weighing the keys in the palm of her hand, then shrugged and said okay. The back door was new and her old key didn't fit, but the front-door key still worked. When we walked inside, the freshly papered walls and new wall-to-wall carpeting reminded me of the picnic we'd had in the empty house, just my mother and me, right before we'd moved in. If I closed my eyes, I could smell the tuna sandwiches. I remembered how dazzled and thrilled my mother had seemed as we walked through the large, sunny, empty rooms. And how happy we had been there for a while, the happiest years of our lives. As if some curse had been lifted just long enough to let my mother think she might live happily ever after after all. Even if she had to watch the ball on TV and the prince was married to someone else. It didn't matter. True love was generous, openhearted. Ask not what your country can do for you, ask what you can do for your country.

I walked upstairs and looked in my old bedroom. The walls had been re-papered in a pastel plaid, appropriate for either a girl or a boy, but I felt as if I had X-ray vision and could see the ballerinas buried underneath, spinning and leaping, making the curtainless room quiver in the bright light. The master bedroom was beige, a true beige. I could almost hear my parents' voices bickering over whether or not the old wallpaper was, in fact, pink. Through the open window I could hear Mikey Quave crying in his room, which used to be Kim's old room, probably just waking up from his afternoon nap. Normally he hardly ever cried. He was the happiest baby I'd ever seen.

Downstairs, my mother was standing in the new kitchen. My sister's favorite colors: yellow and orange. She opened the empty refrigerator, looked inside, and shut the door. "Do you know who bought the house?" she asked, attempting to strike a tone of mild curiosity.

"A family from Ohio. He was transferred here by some big insurance company. They have a little boy and a girl. Five and two." I repeated what the real estate agent had told my father and me. "They love the house. They said it was just what they were looking for."

My mother nodded. "It seems so big," she said, looking around. "After my apartment. I can't believe I ever lived here."

The remark wounded me because I could tell she really meant it. "Are you senile?" I snapped. "How can you say that? It was only a couple of months ago." I wanted to slap her. Instead, I marched out through the front door and slammed it behind me.

Across the street Denise and Dianne DiNardo were out in their front yard, taking advantage of the last gasp of summer, in matching ruffled bathing suits that I immediately recognized as having once belonged to my sister and me. They were running through the sprinkler, shoving and shrieking. It was like watching an old home movie of ourselves, of some dumber and happier time. When they saw me they stopped dead, as if they had seen a ghost. I walked across the street and said, "Those bathing suits used to be my sister's and mine." I was still in a bad mood. They stood there looking at me, waiting expectantly for me to tell them something else, something really important, but I couldn't think of anything more to say to them—they looked so young and trusting.

Finally Dianne said, "Are you going to move back in?"

Denise jabbed her in the ribs with her elbow the way Bonnie used to do to me when I said something wrong. "The house is sold, stupid."

Dianne started to cry. I glared at Denise and then suddenly remembered the day that they sent us home from school early because the president had been shot and I had walked Denise home from the school bus, holding her hand while she cried, because she knew that something terrible had happened even though she was still too young to understand it. I wanted to ask her if she remembered that. But for some reason I couldn't.

EPILOGUE

The year after Jackie married Aristotle Onassis and the real Helen Keller died in her sleep at the age of eighty-seven, my mother met and married Leo Krieger and moved to Israel. A mild-mannered, whirlwind courtship. She met him through her work at the travel agency. After the divorce, she had taken some courses and become a bona-fide travel agent although she never traveled, never took advantage of all the discounts that were supposed to compensate her for the low salary. When she wasn't working she read travel literature—Lawrence Durrell, Thor Heyerdahl, Paul Theroux, Peter Matthiessen—but never went anywhere.

Leo was a visiting professor from Tel Aviv, in the history department. He happened into my mother's travel agency and she arranged two or three trips for him to various conferences. They chatted. He was impressed by the breadth and depth of her reading. By her good looks. They talked. Gradually she learned more about his life. He was a widower. A grown son, a physicist, back in Tel Aviv. From Heidelberg originally. A concentration-camp survivor. Buchenwald. She saw the number tattooed on his wrist long before he ever spoke of it. Like my mother, the only surviving member of his immediate family. A living embodiment of the first noble truth.

I visited them in Tel Aviv that summer, the summer before my freshman year at Berkeley. They had only been married a few months, but I couldn't believe the change in my mother. The serenity in her face, the tenderness in her body when she held Leo's hand. It was not passion, exactly. Leo was short, bald, stocky. His clothes always looked as if he had fished them out of the laundry hamper. But his eyes were extraordinary. Deep-set and golden brown. The keen energy of a hawk combined with the weary devotion of a dog. My mother told me that he was only sixteen when his family was rounded up and sent to the concentration camp. I liked to imagine him befriending Anne Frank even though I knew she had died in Bergen-Belsen.

That my mother had confessed to Leo all about her past— about Buck Roebuck, her lie, the fire—didn't surprise me. But for the first time I was amazed to hear her offering up casual little anecdotes from her childhood, funny little stories of those years she had always insisted she couldn't remember. The time the goat ate her mother's brassieres hanging on the clothesline. The time she'd tied her father's shoelaces together while he was reading the newspaper and he'd fallen flat on his face like Charlie Chaplin when her mother had called him to supper. Inconsequential little memories that I strung together in my mind like a strand of pearls: my mother's childhood. She had gained maybe ten pounds since her marriage, as if those reclaimed memories had actual weight. She looked both softer and stronger. I didn't once see her take a single aspirin during the six weeks I was there in their cramped apartment. And I remembered how when I was growing up she would have bottles of Bufferin stashed in every room and I would collect the empties even though I had no use for them. "What do you want all those for?" my mother asked me once, seeing them lined up on my dresser. "For my dolls," I'd answered vaguely. I didn't know why I saved them.

When I returned from my trip to Israel, my father picked me up at the airport in Madison. "How's your mother doing?" he asked on the drive home. He had just bought a new Lincoln Continental. White with pale-blue seats, the color of Caroline and John-John's funeral coats.

"Fine," I said. As if my mother's gag order to us just after the separation were still in effect. "She seems great," I added, more for her sake than his.

"Hmmm," he nodded. "That's good." At that time his brief marriage to Lois, mother of Stone, had just ended in divorce. He joked that he felt like a boulder had been lifted off his shoulders, meaning Stone, the hyperactive demon child, his mother's pride and joy.

"Doesn't she miss the States?" he asked as he squirted windshield fluid and turned on the wipers, attempting to clean a microscopic speck off the windshield, a nervous tic he had developed in recent years that drove me crazy.

"I don't think so," I said. "She says she feels at home in Israel."

"Really." He shrugged, baffled. "On the news it looks so foreign. But then your mother was always a little strange, wasn't she?" He glanced over at me as if asking for reassurance.

"She was," I agreed.

He smiled and winked at me. He seemed relieved. "So," he said, "where would you like to go to dinner? Anywhere your heart desires. Your wish is my command."

"I can't think," I said. "You choose."

He sighed, disappointed by my lack of enthusiasm, of pep. "How about Smokey's?" It was a crowded, noisy, steak joint he'd been partial to ever since I could remember.

"Fine." I yawned, jet-lagged. I didn't have the heart or energy to tell him that I had become a vegetarian.

Over dinner, while I poked at my salad and baked potato, my father sprung the little plan he had cooked up: He wanted me to drive his six-year-old Buick LeSabre out to my sister in Phoenix. To sweeten the deal he would give me five hundred dollars "mad money" and pay for my plane ticket from Phoenix to San Francisco. My sister, at the time, had fallen upon hard times. Her husband, a belated hippie, had left her for another woman and moved to a commune in Taos, leaving behind both his wife and his three-year-old son. My father was sending her money every month, urging her to go back to college, and now he wanted to give her his car. "That VW of hers has to be on its last legs," he worried aloud as he polished off the last of his prime rib.

Eventually I agreed to do it—not so much for Bonnie's sake as for my own when it occurred to me that it would give me the opportunity to retrace my mother's and my route to Troy. The brief, ill-fated trip we had taken six years earlier, just the two of us. I thought of the trip often; little details, moments, would come back with a sort of surreal clarity. As if every moment of those two days alone with my mother, before my father came to the rescue, was perfectly preserved. I thought of it as a window of opportunity that had opened and shut. Maybe if I hadn't panicked and called my father, our whole lives would have been different. Maybe my mother would have made her peace and then we'd have driven on to California, where eventually my father and sister would have joined us, where we would have started over, fresh, a new life in a kinder, gentler climate. The older I got— the more I came to see my parents more clearly—the more unlikely this scenario seemed. About as likely as President Kennedy having been kept alive in a coma on a Greek island for all these years. Still, I couldn't completely relinquish the notion that there was a moment, a turning point, when our family might have saved itself.

Before I left Madison, my father loaded me down with presents for Bonnie and her little boy, Travis. It killed him to see what a mess she had landed herself in, his golden girl so full of pep and confidence. Then he warned me not to get mixed up with any of those anti-war radicals in Berkeley, handed me a wad of cash, and told me to drive carefully. He had taken the car to a car wash the day before and had had it washed, waxed, and vacuumed. He snapped a picture of me as I sat in the driveway, engine running. He seemed reluctant to let me go. A little lonely and at loose ends and slightly embarrassed by his short-lived marriage to Lois.

"Maybe I'll take a trip out west this winter. Visit your sister in Phoenix and then go on to San Francisco," he said, chipping away with his thumbnail at a speck of bird shit on the roof of the car.

"Sure," I said, trying not to imagine my father on Telegraph Avenue, appalled by all the trash and chaos, which I loved. The ubiquitous dog shit and the panhandlers out in front of Cody's bookstore, a heady mixture of crap and culture. Since his separation from Lois, he had returned to his old barber.

He thumped the hood of the Buick affectionately, like the rump of an old, sturdy horse, as I pulled out of the parking lot of his new apartment complex. In the rearview mirror his expression looked bereft. I tooted the horn and he waved. It occurred to me that at the moment of his death, where your whole life is supposed to flash before your eyes, my father would see a quick, shiny parade of all the cars he had ever owned and cared for.

It was a bright, warm, summer day, ideal for a road trip. I stopped for lunch in Iowa City. A friend of mine from junior high school was living there and I thought about calling her, but I didn't really feel in the mood for company. I walked around the small downtown area until I found the Italian restaurant my mother and I had eaten in. It was dark and empty inside, not particularly inviting, but I went in and took a seat anyway. When the waitress came I ordered fettuccini Alfredo, the same as my mother had. I would have ordered a glass of Chianti but I was underage. Then, on impulse, I walked back to the cigarette machine and got a pack of Marlboro Lights. They didn't have Lucky Strikes—I didn't even know if they made them anymore. None of my friends smoked them. I was only a sporadic smoker, bumming cigarettes now and then at parties when I felt nervous, but I sensed that something vital would be missing without my mother's cloud of smoke. Both Leo and my mother were chain-smokers. It was a bond between them, with lots of little rituals involved, a form of intimacy. Every morning through the thin apartment wall I could hear them hacking as they woke up. Neither of them could climb the two short flights of stairs to their second floor apartment without wheezing and pausing for breath on the landing. Even my mother's poor dog, Jackie, now going on five years old, wheezed asthmatically at the slightest exertion.

Back in my booth I lit up and smoked a cigarette before the waitress brought my food. I remembered the bearded professor my mother was so certain must have been a writer. My friend Gretchen, who was going to school here, did, in fact, want to be a writer. I was planning to major in art, even though my father was not keen on the idea. When the waitress set my plate of steaming fettuccini in front of me, I stubbed out my cigarette. Although I'd been starving, I felt full after only a few bites, as if my mother's ghost had expanded inside me like smoke.

On the way out of town I stopped for gas at the Kum and Go and bought some gum and candy bars even though I wasn't hungry and had renounced sugar along with meat, under the influence of my then boyfriend's older brother, who would subsequently become my first husband. For Christmas he had given me a copy of *The Tassajara Bread Book*. If I were allowed to impart only one bit of romantic advice to my daughter it would be, "Beware of ascetics bearing gifts."

By dinnertime I was in Lincoln. Instead of snow there was a thunderstorm brewing, a murky underwater cast to the sky and a breathless stillness in the hot, humid air. I checked into the Cornhusker Hotel, which had not changed appreciably in the intervening half dozen years since I had last set foot in the place. An enthusiastic bellboy insisted upon carrying my overnight case up to the room for me. I had a headache from the long, monotonous drive. I went into the spotless bathroom, opened a bottle of Bufferin, and shook two aspirins into the palm of my hand. I would have liked to go out and hunt for the little Mexican joint my mother and I had eaten at, but the rain was falling now in torrents, accompanied by apocalyptic crashes of thunder and lightning. Instead, I brushed my hair—as long now as Mia Farrow's—and walked down to the bar and ordered a margarita, trying to sound blasé. I was wearing a black lacy peasant dress I'd bought in Israel. The bartender looked amused but didn't protest. "Salt or no salt?" was all he said.

"Salt," I said, remembering the crystallized rim of my mother's glass stained by her pink lipstick. I wolfed down a whole dish of peanuts while he mixed my drink. There was a newspaper lying on a small table nearby. I picked it up and opened it to the movies section.

The bartender plunked down my margarita with the flourish of a matador. "What movie you going to see?" he asked. He wasn't very old himself, probably a graduate student moonlighting to pay the rent.

"*Easy Rider*," I said, even though I had no intention of going to see a movie.

He grinned and gave me a thumbs-up sign. "I'm saving up for a Harley. Then I'm outa here."

Three businessmen in suits sat down at the other end of the bar and he hurried off to take their order. I lit a cigarette. One of the businessmen caught my eye and winked at me. More avuncular than lascivious. I looked away. My head was still pounding. I pretended to be engrossed in the story on the front page about the Arab-Israeli conflict in the Golan Heights. Then I saw the smaller headline lower down: "Woman Drowned in Car Driven by Kennedy." I read all about Mary Jo Kopechne and Chappaquiddick. There was a picture of her, blonde and pretty, a little like my sister. I gulped down the last of my margarita and paid my bill, glad, for the first time, that my mother wasn't with me. The night that Bobby Kennedy was assassinated I had rushed over to her apartment, fearing the worst, but she had sounded surprisingly calm, as if having been struck by lightning once, that was it; the rest was just history.

Back in my room I called room service and ordered a turkey sandwich and a Tab. I turned the TV on with the sound off, then changed into a loose tie-dyed T-shirt. While I waited for my supper to arrive, I read *The Chosen*, which Leo had given me for the long plane ride. Like my mother, he was not only a chain-smoker but also a chain-reader. Room service delivered my sandwich and I ate it quickly, after which I felt a little better. I looked at my watch and reached for the phone book. On the hotel pad of paper I wrote down Peggy's number and then, on impulse, the number of the Nebraska State Penitentiary. My handwriting looked identical to my mother's. We both crossed our sevens and made triangu-

lar fours. I called Peggy, who sounded delighted to hear
from me, and I made plans to drive out and visit her the
next morning. I stared at the other number for a long
time. Finally I dialed it. When the prison operator
answered, I asked if there was a Ballard Roebuck incar-
cerated there. She transferred me; someone answered and
put me on hold, then came back on the line and
informed me that he had been paroled in 1967, two years
earlier. Before I could even ask, she told me that they
weren't allowed to give out any further information, such
as where he was living or even if he was still living.
Shaken, I hung up and lit a cigarette. I wondered if my
mother knew.

After a restless night's sleep—strange room, strange
bed—I headed out for Troy. The sky was a bright,
washed blue, the fields a deep, healthy green, still glisten-
ing from last night's rain. Far different from the frozen
tundra I remembered from my mother's and my trip.
Since it was still early when I arrived in town, I drove
around until I found the cemetery. I parked and walked
through the rows of well-groomed tombstones looking
for my grandparents' graves. I found them toward the
back. Walter and Elsa Hansen. They were by no means
the only Hansens buried there, but they were the only
two who had died on the same day. I stared at the modest granite headstone, waiting to feel something.

I got back in my father's Buick and drove to my
mother's old house, just down the road from Peggy's
place. Someone had bought the property—I remember
my mother finally deciding to put it up for sale when she
moved to Israel—and knocked down what remained of

the old house and built a ranch house with pale green siding in its place. Like something you would see in some less prosperous California suburb. There was a swing set in the side yard and a hot, discouraged looking Malamute in a dog pen. It was only nine-thirty and already the dog was panting, its big tongue hanging out of its mouth. The dog perked up and wagged its tail as two little boys shrieked around the corner from the backyard, shooting each other with squirt guns. The bigger boy stopped and squirted the dog and then the smaller boy joined in. "Pow! Pow! Pow!" The dog was barking and running in circles.

"What are you doing to that dog?" A woman flung open the screen door and stood on the porch, a cigarette in one hand, a magazine in the other.

"Cooling him off." The older boy smiled innocently.

"Well, just cool it," the mother warned them, "or I'll warm your backsides!" and let the door slam shut. As soon as her back was turned, the older boy gave her the finger. He couldn't have been more than six. Not to be outdone, the younger boy stuck his tongue out. As if she had eyes in the back of her head, the mother flew out the door, grabbed them both by the arms as they tried to run away, and thwacked them each on the butt, hard, with the rolled up magazine—the way you would discipline a dog. The younger boy started to cry.

I wondered if the woman knew that a love-crazed boy had burned his girlfriend's parents alive on this very spot. I didn't see how she could very well not know. How many sensational murders could there have been in a town this size? But she didn't look or sound like the type to be spooked by ghosts. She looked, in fact, as if she might have been drawn to this spot for that very reason.

When she went back inside, I got out of my car and walked up the driveway toward the boys. The dog bristled to attention but didn't bark. The younger boy stopped crying and wiped his nose with the back of his hand.

"Who are you?" the older boy asked.

"My mother used to live here when she was a little girl," I said. "Her name was Helen."

"Mom!" he shouted. "Hey, Mo-om!"

"We aren't supposed to talk to strangers," the younger boy informed me.

"That's good." I nodded approvingly. "You can't be too careful." I turned and walked back to the car. Halfway down the driveway I heard the door squeal open and the woman's voice asking, "What did she want?"

Three days later, sitting on my sister's tiny patio in Phoenix, holding my sleeping nephew in my lap, drinking my third Carta Blanca, I found myself telling my sister about the incident. My point was how it had upset me to see those little boys treated so harshly, but my sister was more interested in the fact that I had seen my mother's old house, or at least her old yard, since the house itself no longer existed. I had never told my sister about the fire and I kept waiting for her to ask why the old house was no longer there, but it didn't seem to occur to her that it was the least bit out of the ordinary. I suppose because she was the type who would prefer a spiffy new ranch house with all the modern conveniences to a drafty old farmhouse.

"Did you take any pictures?" she said, as if I'd taken a little detour to Frontier Village.

"I don't even own a camera," I said. Although I had already shown her a stack of pictures of Israel, taken with Leo's fancy Leica, one of his few extravagances, which Bonnie had flipped through with a striking absence of curiosity, stopping to comment only on my mother's weight gain and Leo's shabby wardrobe, as well as the size of their apartment.

"It looks small." She'd frowned. "I thought Leo was supposed to be some big-deal scholar."

"The standard of living is different there," I'd said, snatching the snapshots out of her hand and stuffing them back in the envelope.

There was an awkward silence and then my sister, who still kept in close touch with her friends in Madison, proceeded to fill me in on whatever gossip there was about our former neighbors. The Crawfords' divorce and Kevin's drug bust. Denise DiNardo's surprise elopement with a rock musician. Rob Dinsmore's flight to Canada to evade the draft. She might just as well have been telling me the plot of a soap opera. Like my mother, I no longer felt any real connection to our old neighborhood.

As my sister and I made small talk, Travis sucked contentedly on his thumb, his eyelids with their long dark lashes fluttering like tiny wings. "He looks like an angel," I said. "So sweet." I pried a cold squished french fry out of his curled fist and set it in the ashtray.

"I'll put him to bed." My sister lifted him up gently and carried him into his crib in the little bedroom. I could see that she was trying to be a good mother despite her depression. The apartment was a wreck except for Travis's room, which was neat and cheerful, a bright oasis in an otherwise gloomy landscape. And although for the first time in her life my sister seemed indifferent to her appearance, she made sure that her son was bathed, his nails neatly trimmed, his clothes clean and debonair.

I still had not completely recovered from my initial shock at the way Bonnie looked. When I'd pulled up in front of the apartment building, a stucco four-plex, there was a woman sitting on the steps with a toddler. A pale woman wearing glasses and baggy shorts with her hair in a messy ponytail. It wasn't until she stood up and started walking toward me that I recognized her. The last time I'd seen her, at her wedding, she had looked like a model for *Bride's*—slim, tanned, radiant, sexy. A vision in white lace. My father teary-eyed and bursting with pride.

The first thing she'd said to me was, "I know I look like shit." The second thing was, "What happened to the fender?" I had backed into a lamppost in the parking lot of a Travel Lodge in Amarillo. She knew that my father would never have allowed a dent to remain in his car.

"I don't know." I'd shrugged, examining the dent as if I had just now seen it for the first time. Bonnie grunted suspiciously.

It was dinnertime. My sister wanted to take the Buick for a spin. She drove fast, weaving in and out past slower cars. "God, this is great!" She'd flashed me a smile, the first since I'd arrived. "The VW shakes like a blender when I go over fifty."

We swerved into a taco stand and ordered some take-home Mexican food. The loudspeaker was shaped like a giant saguaro and the guy who took our order sounded like Ricky Ricardo. As we waited for him to fill our order, Bonnie zapped the power windows up and down like a kid with a new toy. She reached over and pressed Travis's chubby index finger to the silver button. "Look!" she'd exclaimed, "Magic!" He laughed and clapped his hands.

The clerk handed her our bag of food. I whisked out my wallet and handed her a ten-dollar bill. "Compliments of Dad," I said. She accepted the money without comment. As we waited for change, I held my squirming nephew in my lap, still marveling at the fact that I had a nephew. It hardly seemed possible, even though he looked exactly like Bonnie, only with dark hair like Greg's. "Do you hear from Greg?" I'd asked.

"Greg who?" She punched in the lighter and lit a cigarette.

"Since when do you smoke?"

"Since I gained twenty-five pounds. Any more questions?" She pulled a french fry out of the bag and handed it to Travis. "French fries," she told him, "you like french fries."

Taking her at her word, he'd rammed it into his mouth.

Flicking on the radio, she'd cranked up the volume. "Bad Moon Rising" by Creedence Clearwater Revival. My sister had abandoned the guitar and folk music shortly after Greg abandoned her.

I'd noticed that she was squinting into the sun as we drove, fiddling with the visor. "I lost my prescription sunglasses," she told me. "Dad's sending me a new pair.'"

"What happened to your contact lenses?" For as long as I could remember, my sister had refused to be caught dead in glasses.

"Zero tears," she said.

"What?" We were passing rows of quaint stucco houses with tile roofs and cacti, the kind of place I had always pictured my sister living in when she announced that Greg had found a job teaching music at a private school in Phoenix. She was thrilled. She said she couldn't wait to be tanned year-round.

"I can't wear them anymore. Something to do with the dryness out here and my goddamned hormones or whatever. I went to this optometrist that Dad recommended and he did this stupid test—they stick these little strips of paper between your eyelids to measure the amount of tear production, and he said mine was zero. Zero tears. Which means my eyes are too fucking dry for contacts."

"Wow." I looked over at her. She'd looked as if she were on the verge of tears right then and there. I felt bad for her. "That's a drag."

"It really sucks," she said. "I don't even feel like myself."

I wondered if this had happened—the zero tears thing—before or after Greg left her but I didn't dare ask. To change the subject I'd told her about visiting Peggy and how she was doing all these fantastic weavings—more like paintings, really—and had even begun to sell her work at a couple of galleries in Omaha and Kansas City. I said that after a year or two at Berkley, I might consider transferring to the University of Hawaii, which, unlike Cal, had a program in weaving. My sister just nodded perfunctorily; she didn't seem particularly interested. Back at her place, we had eaten our burritos and drunk a six-pack of Carta Blanca and carried on our desultory conversation until Travis finally fell asleep.

I fidgeted impatiently, sweating in the ovenlike heat, waiting for her to return to the patio. After five or ten minutes I heard a musical mobile tinkling out a silvery lullabye in the baby's room and then the toilet flushing and Bonnie's footsteps padding down the hallway. All evening I had been waiting for this, the opportunity to really talk, to compare notes about our childhood, to exchange theories—to corroborate and contradict, like the only two eyewitnesses at the scene of an accident—but my sister walked right by me into the kitchen, grabbed the last beer from the refrigerator, collapsed onto the sofa that she'd slipcovered with bright paisley sheets, and snapped on the TV as if she'd forgotten I was there.

We watched *Hawaii Five-O.* When it ended, my sister yawned, handed me a pillow and a quilt, and announced that she was going to bed. After she got into bed I read through a couple of *Cosmopolitan*s lying on the floor next to the sofa and then went into the bathroom and brushed my teeth and washed my face, taking my time, examining all my sister's creams and cosmetics the way I had when I was younger. A nightgown and a robe were hanging on a hook on the back of the bathroom door. On an impulse I peeled off my garish T-shirt and slipped on her nightgown. It was soft white cotton with tiny yellow rosebuds. For the first time it occurred to me that I missed inheriting my sister's hand-me-downs.

I snapped off the bathroom light and groped my way down the dark, unfamiliar hallway back to the living room, where I slept on the lumpy sofa, or tried to. Passing headlights illuminated the dark room through the thin drapes, then dimmed—a disorienting strobe effect. All the things my sister and I might have talked about kept buzzing through my mind. When I finally nodded off I had a grisly, topsy-turvy nightmare about Charles Manson in which Sharon Tate was Sharon Tate but also my sister, eight months pregnant. I had read about the savage murders over a plate of *huevos rancheros* that morning in a little café in Tucumcari, New Mexico.

At dawn, I woke up stiff and tired and anxious to be gone, back on the road. Then I remembered that the whole point of the trip had been to deliver the Buick to my sister and that I was flying the rest of the way to California. My flight didn't leave until four in the afternoon. The thought of waiting around to leave was depressing. Unbearable. Suddenly, an idea occurred to me. I knew it was a bad idea, but I leapt up anyway and folded the bedclothes into a neat pile and changed into my cutoffs and tank top before I could change my mind or come to my senses.

It took me a couple of minutes to find the car keys; they were lying on the kitchen table buried under last night's burrito wrappers. For a moment I thought about leaving a note but couldn't think of what to say. Instead, I fished my airline ticket out of my shoulder bag and left it under a saltshaker on the table to speak for itself. On the way back through the living room, dim gray in the bleak dawn light, I saw my sister's white nightgown lying on top of the dark, neatly folded quilt. I stuffed it into my shoulder bag. Then, without so much as a backward glance, I snuck out of the apartment on tiptoe, while my sister was still asleep, or pretending to be.

As the desert sun rose higher in the sky behind me I drove faster than I'd ever driven before, along Interstate

10, blasting the radio, the only car in sight for miles at a stretch. The Buick's engine was powerful and quiet. I had left my watch by the sink in my sister's bathroom and I seemed to be outside time, speeding through some beautiful but inhospitable lunar landscape. I imagined my sister waking up, discovering I was gone, the Buick was gone, and calling our father in Madison. I imagined her loud outrage, his quiet bewilderment.

Sitting in my father's big car, feeling the dry desert wind blowing in my face mile after mile, I experienced a flash of déjà vu: our family vacation to the Grand Canyon. My sister and I fighting, as usual, in the backseat. Our father barking at us to cut it out. And then our mother turning around, staring us straight in the eyes and saying, "You girls don't know how lucky you are. I always wanted a sister. I hope someday, when you're older, you can appreciate each other." There was something in her expression, her tone of voice, which must have communicated itself to Bonnie and me because for hours after that we were almost nice to each other. My sister offered me a stick of Big Red gum and I thanked her. We got out a deck of cards and played gin rummy through most of Oklahoma. At one point my father was whistling away in the front seat and our mother turned around and smiled at us in the backseat. She looked so happy. I smiled back, but my sister said, "I'm hungry. How much farther?" with that sulky edge in her voice that my mother hated. My mother's smile faded. Miffed at my sister for ruining the magic of the moment, I kicked her and she kicked me back and our father yelled at us to knock it off until my mother said, "Oh, just ignore them." I leaned forward and wrapped my arms around my mother's neck and whispered in her ear, "I'm sorry." She reached up and planted a kiss in the palm of my hand and I curled my fingers into a fist, as if trying to hold onto it. As if it were something that might fly away.

That was August 1963. Or possibly July. Late summer. Early evening.

Jackie Kennedy died without warning, it seemed, a week after my one and only child was born. So swiftly it took my breath away. At the time I was in such a fog of exhaustion, stitched back together after an emergency C-section, waking every few hours to breast-feed, that when I finally got back on my feet I wondered if I had dreamed her death. I had been dreaming a lot of my own mother, dead now for two years, whose absence haunted me during my pregnancy even though I had only seen her a handful of times over the past quarter of a century. The result of geographical rather than emotional distance. My husband and I both taught art at Hilo Community College on the Big Island. Edward, my husband, had been born and bred in Hawaii. He was half haole and half Japanese. The airfare between Hawaii and Israel was astronomical. Unlike my sister, who had pulled herself together, regained her old figure and become a successful attorney married to an even more successful attorney, neither my mother nor I had money to burn.

When she died of a sudden massive heart attack, with no history of previous heart trouble, I could not even fly to Tel Aviv for the funeral because I was recovering from a miscarriage. After two years of costly and painful fertility treatments, I did not have any money or emotion left to spend on anyone else, even my own mother. So it seemed that as I lay in bed after the birth of my daughter, watching Jacqueline Kennedy's funeral on the television, drifting in and out of consciousness, it was as if I were belatedly paying my last respects to my mother. Even though my first hazy impulse when I heard that Jackie had died was to pick up the phone and call my mother to see how she was taking the news.

I have named my daughter Lily Helen and feel terribly shortchanged by the fact that I will never be able to show her off to my mother. Even though my mother never showed much grandmotherly interest in her two grandsons, Travis and Justin, even after my sister and she had finally kissed and made up, more or less, when Bonnie flew her and Leo out for her law school graduation. My sister always complained that my mother either forgot her grandsons' birthdays or sent gifts that were so inappropriate it was a joke. "What do I know about little boys?" she had protested when my sister finally told her to stop wasting her money.

My father I see at least once a year. He has retired to Phoenix with his third wife, the realtor who sold our house in Madison, to be near my sister and his grandsons where it is warm enough to play golf year-round. But every summer when the dry desert heat gets to be too much for them, they come to Hawaii for a couple of weeks of ocean breezes. "Better a sauna than an oven," he likes to joke as his wife, Roberta, wilts in the humidity. They always stay in a fancy hotel, take us out to expensive restaurants, rent a car, and are never really any trouble even if I never really look forward to the visits.

As I recuperated from the difficult labor, I felt limp and wrung out, a rag doll tossed on the waves, sinking

into sleep, then struggling up, up into consciousness—
Ah, my daughter! My beautiful baby! What a miracle!—
then sinking again, the solemn voices on the television
swimming toward me underwater. "As you go on the
voyage to Ithaca/Pray your way will be a long one/Full
of adventure, full of knowledge . . ." And the familiar
television images floating behind my closed eyelids—
Jackie in her wedding gown, Jackie on an elephant in
India, Jackie in her pink suit holding the bouquet of red
roses, Jackie in her black veil—all as familiar as pictures
from my own family albums—or yours, you know the
ones. And interspersed with those were pictures of
Bonnie and me in our new party dresses or bathrobes or
bathing suits, our new house, my father behind the wheel
of his new Bonneville, his new LeSabre, Bonnie sewing
on her new Singer zigzag, my mother with a pillbox hat
perched on her new bouffant, Bonnie and me standing
on the rim of the Grand Canyon while our father poses
us through the viewfinder of his new Kodak Instamatic.
It was as if I had grown up with two sets of families, two
sets of photograph albums, both of which were more
familiar to me than my infant daughter's face, the as yet
blank pages of her baby book. Except for the tiny,
shrunken, black footprints and the photo snapped at the
moment of birth, with her newborn eyes obediently
squeezed shut as if waiting to open them on command:
"Surprise!"

When she was born, even after the amniocentesis and
the ultrasounds, I could hardly believe that she was all
there, normal, perfect. After all, I was over forty and had
read the statistics. Too late, too late! they seemed to
scold. And even though my obstetrician was more opti-

mistic and reassuring than most, I kept thinking of Mikey Quave, dreaming about him, for the first time in over two decades, wondering what had become of him.

After we moved out of our house, Kim and I quickly drifted apart. She made new friends in her new Catholic school and went on to a small Catholic college in Illinois while, following Janet Andretti's example, I lit out for college on the West Coast. On the few occasions we got together during Christmas or summer vacation, it was clear to both of us that we no longer had much in common, except for our childhoods. And then her father's business, Everbloom, failed—in the sixties people went back to nature; the market for artificial flowers and fruit withered away—and the Quaves sold their house and moved to Florida, where Charlie went into business with his brother-in-law cleaning swimming pools. The last I heard of them, Marjorie was in West Africa—in the Peace Corps—and Kim was in nursing school in Chicago, and Mikey would have been ready to start first grade. I remembered how loving and accepting the Quaves had been toward their infant son, and I had trouble imagining my husband and myself rising to the occasion with a similar grace and fortitude.

We were both teachers. Our image of child rearing was a long row of books progressing in difficulty from *Goodnight, Moon* through *Wind in the Willows* through *Robinson Crusoe*. It seemed as if all of our friends' children were diagnosed as either "gifted" or "learning disabled." Gifted or ungifted by the gods. A normal kid seemed a thing of the past, as quaint and corny as Beaver Cleaver. For the first time, I prayed. I prayed so hard and so long that when my daughter was finally delivered unto me safe and sound, and then Jackie Kennedy died so abruptly, I felt as if I had sucked the health right out of her through some sort of voodoo. I know it sounds crazy. Half postpartum depression, half true old-fashioned grief, I supposed. What Harriet would have felt had Ozzie died.

The last time I saw my mother, on her one and only visit to the Big Island, I had driven her to a new luxury hotel that had commissioned a weaving from me. My biggest job yet. I had worked on it for six months and had just completed the installation in time for my wedding and my mother's arrival. It was hanging in the lobby, which was a tourist's dream come true—all skylights, waterfalls, and real tropical foliage that looked fake. The piece itself was the size of a billboard. Woven from feathers and handmade paper and suspended from nearly invisible wires. Hinged in the center so that both halves could flutter independently of one another with the air currents. I had called it *Paper Wings*. My mother walked over and read the small plaque with my name and the title and the date.

"It's beautiful," she declared and snapped half a dozen pictures to show to Leo, who had remained in Israel. "It's the most beautiful thing I've ever seen."

On the drive home she seemed so silent I thought maybe she was depressed. I wondered if being back in Hawaii, even if it was a different island from the one where she had lived with my father, was stirring up sad memories. Or happy memories that made her feel sad. "Does it remind you of Daddy?" I asked her hesitantly. "I mean, being in Hawaii again after all this time."

"*Oy vey*, such a romantic!" My mother laughed at her perfect imitation of Leo and lit a cigarette, shaking her head. Then she burst into a fit of hacking that brought tears to her eyes.

"When are you going to quit smoking?" I said, irked by her sarcasm. "Those things are going to kill you."

She shrugged. "Smoking's my raison d'être."

"What about Leo?"

"Leo's, too," she said. "That's why we get along so well."

It was a sunny day with the ocean stretching like smooth blue glass as far as the eye could see. We were silent for a couple of minutes. Then my mother removed her dark glasses and in a quiet, more serious tone of voice she said, "I hope you'll be very happy with Edward."

Our wedding was the next day. A small backyard affair. Neither of us was exactly young. Both of us had been married before.

"I hope so, too." I reached over and took a slow drag of her cigarette, then handed it back, the rush of smoke making me light-headed.

"You never know," she said.

"I know."

But, in fact, I didn't even know whether I meant "*I* know," as in I knew that we would be happy, or "I *know*," as in I knew that there was no way of knowing.

It felt strange to be sitting next to my mother again. For most of my adult life our relationship had been conducted primarily by letter. Flimsy air-mail envelopes addressed to me in handwriting identical to my own. In the bright, flat sunlight she looked her age. And it dawned on me suddenly that she was my age, thirty-nine, the year that Kennedy died. I remembered her sitting there on the floor in her bra, wet hair dripping, crying into a bath towel. And I remembered standing there, not knowing what to say or do. And I remembered walking over to the TV and changing the channel, and changing it again, and again, but always getting the same picture. And then I remembered sitting in my father's office as he clicked the various lenses in front of my eyes, asking me to tell him which one was clearer, "This? Or this?" Feeling his mounting impatience. "This? Or this?" And my own crushing sense of failure as it became crystal clear to me—in one of those blinding flashes of insight—that I would never see the difference between this or this. This. And this. Not even in hindsight, which they say is twenty-twenty.